WORTH DYING FOR

Book 5

KORY M. SHRUM

This book is a work of fiction. Any references to historical events, real people, or real places have been used fictitiously. Other names, characters, places, and incidents are the product of the author's imagination. Any resemblance to actual persons, living or dead, business establishments, events, or locales is entirely coincidental.

No part of this book shall be reproduced or transmitted in any form or by any means without prior written permission of the publisher. Although every precaution has been taken in preparation of the book, the publisher and the author assume no responsibility for errors or omissions. Neither is any liability assumed for damages resulting from the use of information contained in this book or its misuse.

TIMBERLANE
PRESS

WORTH DYING FOR

Connecting with my readers is the best part of my job as a writer. One way that I like to connect is by sending 2-3 newsletters a month with a subscribers-only giveaway, free stories from your favorite series, and personal updates (read: pictures of my dog).

When you first sign up for the mailing list, I send you at least three free stories right away.

If giveaways and free stories sound like something you're interested in, please look for the special offer in the back of this book.

Happy reading,

Kory M. Shrum

All this screaming is hurting my ears.

"Nine, Eight, Seven—"

Ally presses her body against mine, counting down with the crowd.

I open my coat, letting her slip her chilled arms around me. I try to protect her from the worst of the unforgiving wind cutting across our cheeks and tearing at our hair. "I never understood the countdown. Are they trying to build tension?"

Her grin stretches wider and she squeezes me again. "Four, *three*—"

"It's not like we don't know what's happening." I gesture at the swarm of bodies clustered on the balcony around us. My sides and back are protected by their mass, but leaning against the concrete railing leaves us utterly exposed in the front. If only we were more in the middle of the balcony, then Ally and I could be the queen bees of this hive, the drones vibrating to keep us warm.

"*One*—"

I gasp, pantomiming shock. "Oh look, the New Year.

What a surprise! I had no idea what was going to happen when we reached *one*!"

Ally tugs me forward by the lapels of my coat. "Shut up and kiss me."

The balcony erupts in chaos, everyone singing, cheering, and sucking on each other's faces. The ruckus is blocked out by Ally's palms covering my ears as we kiss. Her hair smells like some kind of fruity shampoo, and her lips taste like the wine she drank earlier. I kiss her deeper, my hands wrapping up in her hair. I don't care who sees us or what they think.

Tonight is all about us. Me and Ally. Gideon, Rachel, and Maisie. We're celebrating. After weeks and weeks, we finally have a plan for taking down Caldwell. And it's a *good* plan.

Ally pulls back, laughing. "I can't breathe."

"You started it." I pull her close again, kissing her.

"I *have* to breathe," she says, chest heaving.

"Right. Sorry. I forgot you have to do that."

I assault her cheeks and neck instead. She devolves into laughter, hanging heavy and drunk in my arms.

"Stop, *stop*," she begs, trying to squirm away.

"I can't. I'll die." But I do stop long enough for her to catch her breath, and because I know firsthand that if I torment a drunk girl for too long, my chances of getting vomited on increase tenfold.

Gideon and Rachel stumble forward from the crowd, arms around each other. Their dark eyes reflect the dancing lights coming from everywhere. Billboards. Lighters. The ball itself.

A boom makes us all jump. A second after the *boom* comes a *pop* and a dozen strands of red light rain down on us. Fireworks.

"We should head back," Gideon says, pushing his black frame glasses up on his nose before tightening his hold on a sagging Rachel. "Or risk being crushed by the crowd."

"Where's Maisie?" Rachel's glazed eyes slide from one face to another without really seeing anyone. She buries her chin in the neck of her jacket.

"Here." Maisie shouts over the roar. "I'm freezing. So if everyone is done making out, I'd like to go check on Winnie Pug."

Ally frowns. "We weren't making out. It's good luck to kiss on New Year's Eve."

"It is," Gideon adds with a devilish smile. He leans toward Maisie. "Do you want a little kiss for yourself?"

My nostrils flare. "I will cut you."

"I don't need your charity slobber." Maisie flips her hair over one shoulder. "I kissed that guy."

We all turn and see a kid not much older than Maisie, also sporting the double black X marks of the underaged on his hands. He's grinning, goofy but cute. His black hair hangs in his eyes. Black eyeliner encircles his eyes. Very emo and totally Maisie's type.

What does one do when they find out their little sister has been making out with some unkempt boy on a balcony? How the hell should I know? A month ago I didn't even know I had a little sister, but our father is evil so I stole her and here she is, safe—relatively, with me. So what if I don't know what to make of her on most days?

What I do know is I'm not her mother and where she puts her mouth is none of my damn business.

I shrug. "Good for you."

"Call me, Michelle!" The boy yells as the five of us start to push our way off the balcony into the club.

"Michelle?" I hold the door open for everyone.

"I couldn't give him my real name, could I?" Maisie yanks her beanie down over her red ears.

Good point. We've been on the run for a month. No one knows where we are, and we have to keep it that way.

Gideon's fancy gadgets, money, and stealth skills won't hide us from my murderous father for too long. We need to be careful until we *want* him to come to us, until we have him right where we need him to be.

I grab Ally's hand and pull her into the club after Maisie. Rachel and Gideon take up the rear. For the few minutes it takes us to squeeze past the crowd toward the street, we're warm. The collective body heat of a hundred revelers is welcome despite the sour smell of beer and sweat. And unless I'm mistaken, that *tang* is vomit. Gross.

I reach forward and grab Maisie's hand so we don't get separated. She twines her cool fingers with their chipping black nail polish in mine and pulls all of us out toward the street. We regroup on the sidewalk as people shoulder past us on all sides. The fierce wind picks up right where it left off, gnawing ruthlessly at my cheeks. I wrap my blood-red scarf tighter around my head in a feeble attempt to protect myself.

Ally slips her arms around my waist, and I tuck her icy hands into my pockets. She is so cuddly when she's drunk. I love it. I should keep her drunk all the time. She's brilliant and can spare the brain cells, but alas, I guess there's her liver to consider.

Maisie leads our little group in the direction of our hotel. Thank god, it's only about five blocks away. I don't know how much of this bitter wind I can take. I see more drunk people than I've ever seen in my life. I've only had two Shirley Temples, which left a sloshy feeling in my stomach that I tried to soak up with super greasy cheese sticks.

A *really* dumb idea.

I probably feel as nauseated as the drunk people shambling around me.

As soon as I see the neon sign of our hotel glowing overhead, I break from the group and rush into the warm lobby. I yank my scarf off my head, pulling the breath-damp fabric off of my face.

"I'm sick of being cold." I groan. "I'm so glad we're heading—"

Gideon shoots me a look that I've memorized at this point. *Don't say anything until we're in the suite.*

"—somewhere warm." I roll my eyes and pile into the elevator with them. Rachel is so drunk she mashes the buttons for floors 14 and 16 before managing to hit the correct button, number 15.

Somehow we make it to the room, a suite at the end of a beige hallway with red carpet. Gideon slides the keycard in and out of the slot and the light flickers green.

Maisie is the first one in. "Winnie Pug? Pug-Pug where are you?"

The pug in question leaps off a white Victorian chaise and runs toward her. He presents his belly for a rub in three seconds flat.

The rest of us squeeze past them into the foyer of the suite. This hotel room alone is nicer than any house I've ever slept in, but that's Gideon for you. Rachel made the suggestion that we sleep in an abandoned house one night on the road from Chicago to New York, and he snorted and arched his eyebrows at her. Then in the most self-righteous tone I'd ever heard, he said, "I have two legs not four. *I* do not sleep on the ground."

Gideon throws his keycard on the lacquered table by the door. Ally and I kick off our shoes. Rachel pulls off just about every layer of clothing she swaddled herself in except her underwear.

"Well then," Ally says, nodding at Rachel's boobs. "Good night."

Rachel stumbles into her unlit bedroom without a word of acknowledgement.

"Such a good boy," Maisie coos, scratching Winston's ears, then patting his fat belly. "You wanna go out? Let's go out."

I give Winston's ears a good scratch while Maisie finds his leash on a table by the door and slips it over his head. He prances circles around her, too excited to make the harnessing easy.

"Take Gideon's shield thingy." I point at the device on the counter.

"It's freezing out there," Ally reminds her, still hanging on to me. "Go to the little pee patch and come right back."

"Yes, Mother." Maisie's tone is annoyed, but she's smiling. I think she likes the way Ally babies her, even though Ally can't be more than nine years older than Maisie herself. But the kid is taking it well, the whole 'never-unsupervised' thing. This little two-minute jaunt with Winston is about as much space and freedom as she's had in her months with us.

Gideon disappears into the bedroom after Rachel and softly closes the door behind them. I nudge Ally toward the couch.

"So what'll it be?" I ask her. "Water? Juice? I don't think we actually have Gatorade, but I can walk down to the store."

"Water's fine." Ally falls back against cushions and grins up at me. A light pink blush spreads over her cheeks. She finger-combs her hair. "My hair is so pretty. I love my hair."

I snort. "I love your hair too."

"What else about me is cute?" she asks.

"Everything." I fluff the pillow for her and search the room for a blanket. I yank a red velvety throw off the back of a chair as Gideon slips out of the bedroom and passes me on his way to the mini fridge. He grabs one of the wrapped water glasses from the bar above.

"Grab us one too." I have zero problems assigning tasks to other people. Sometimes I wonder if it was a mistake going into death-replacing. Sure, I was a great death replacement agent, and dying for other people is cool, but I'm really good at bossing people around.

It's like a calling.

Gideon fills two water glasses with some fancy bottled water from the fridge and hands me a glass. I don't dare remind him that Ally vowed not to drink this water yesterday. She ranted about the effect of plastic on the environment for ten whole minutes. I could've reminded her that the planet is about to explode anyway, but that meant Gideon would've won the argument and I'm Team Ally all the way.

I put the glass of water in her hand. What she doesn't know won't hurt her. "Here you go. Drink up."

She waves her water around. "I just feel so *good*, you know?"

I smile. "I can tell."

She runs a hand through her hair. "It's a new year. A new beginning. And we have a great plan for kicking Caldwell's butt."

"We do."

"And you're so cute and you *kissed* me."

With arched eyebrows, Gideon closes the bedroom door behind him. Thankfully, the sound of the television comes on, affording us some privacy.

I sink down onto the sofa beside her. "I'll do it again if you want me too. I'll kiss you a *million* times."

She bites her lip and I'm about to lose it. I lean forward to kiss her but she starts talking again, so I hang there mid-smooch, lips puckered.

"Life is so good right now. No one is stabbing us, burying us alive, beating us up, or kidnapping the dog," she goes on, her voice echoing inside her water glass. Her face pinches. "That means we are probably about to die."

I press my lips together and sigh. "Don't say that. You'll jinx us."

It's difficult getting her to sit up, but I manage it. I want her to drink this water. I tilt the glass toward her lips, encouraging her.

"This is good," she says and frowns at the water. "Is this tap water?"

"Yep."

"Because I'm not drinking that $15 water Gideon bought."

"It's tap," I say again. "You're just too drunk to taste it."

Ally shrugs and finishes the glass. Then she hands me her empty glass.

"You want more?"

"No," she grins. "I want something else."

"We've got chips, but that's about it. And Rachel can't close a bag to save her life, so they're probably stale."

She shakes her head, grinning.

Then I realize what she's saying.

"*Oh*." I smile. "Okay."

She crawls over the pillow between us and pulls herself into my lap. She straddles me, wrapping her arms around my neck. She kisses me once on the cheek, probably a missed target rather than a sweet gesture, and then manages to get my mouth the second time.

She pulls back. "God, is it you or is it really hot in here?"

"We're still wearing our coats."

She laughs and looks down at herself. "Oh. Right."

I reach up behind her and pull her jacket off. "Better?"

She snuggles up to me. "You're still hot."

"Thanks for noticing."

"Let me help you take your coat off."

"Okay." I let her attempt to pull off the jacket, but it's not really going anywhere and she accidentally pulls my hair twice. So I help her get my jacket off and throw it over the arm of the sofa. One of the throw pillows falls to the floor with a *poof*.

Ally doesn't stop there. She slips her hands under my shirt, giving me a curious look. "Is this okay?"

I try to find the voice to tell her it's more than okay. She would have been naked an hour ago in the grubby bathroom of some bar if she wasn't such a germaphobe.

She is so beautiful. Her eyes are bright, reflecting the lamplight. Her face is flushed from the alcohol, her smile lazy. Her eyes half-closed. My heart pounds in my chest, thudding against my ribs so hard it hurts.

"What's wrong?" A frown creases her face and I think she can hear my heart throbbing. "Don't you think I'm pretty?"

"Don't be stupid."

I reach up and pull her down into my arms. I kiss her, even more deeply than I did on the balcony. I slip my hand under her shirt and unsnap her bra with one twist of my fingers.

She gasps in my mouth and the sound of it makes my whole body shudder.

"Lay down," I command.

She laughs, surprised, but her voice goes all deep and breathy. "Yes, *sir*."

I climb on top of her, positioning myself between her legs. I kiss her neck and she squirms, bucking her hips up against mine.

"Do you love me?" she asks.

"More than anyone."

"Are you sure?"

I cover her mouth with mine. "Please stop talking." I pull back. "Unless you want me to stop."

"No, no." She grabs the front of my hoodie, twisting it up in her fists and pulls me down on top of her.

I have the button of her jeans between my forefinger and thumb when a voice calls behind me.

"I am very sorry to interrupt, but you need to see this."

Gideon stands in the living room, his back to the bedroom he shares with Rachel.

"Great timing." I glare. "Can it wait?"

Gideon frowns. "No."

"Ugh." I pull myself off of Ally.

"You too," Gideon says to Ally. "If you're feeling all right."

"I'm fine." She fusses with her shirt, trying to make it lay right, but that's hard to do with an unclasped bra bulging through the front. Ally crosses her arms over her chest and Gideon has the decency to let his gaze slide away.

"I'm not *fine*," I grumble as I pass him.

"The news ends in a few minutes. Then you can go back to doing whatever you like, if you can stomach it." Gideon's voice is grave.

I search his face for the source of his tone. He points to the bedroom, where the blue light of the TV dances along the walls.

I creep inside, trying to be quiet, until I realize Rachel is snoring louder than a train. Gideon put her in her PJs, but the glass of water sits untouched on the nightstand beside her.

Gideon lifts the remote from the bedside table and turns up the volume. I don't need to hear to know I'm not going to like this.

Caldwell, my homicidal father, stands behind a podium, his face a mask of grief. Tears that I'm certain are fake as hell stream down his cheeks. Even in his beautifully tailored suit and nice haircut, he looks like shit. The woman beside him, Maisie's mother Georgia, doesn't look any better. Her hair is disheveled and thick black smears from her eyes to her chin.

"We want our daughter back. We want all of this to end." Caldwell panders to the sympathetic crowd. The camera sweeps the masses, and there isn't a dry cheek in the house.

"When was this?" I ask Gideon.

"It must've run earlier today. I'm surprised they didn't broadcast it in Times Square," he says, deep creases forming between his eyes.

"We want the people responsible for this to be brought to justice. We'll give a reward to anyone who provides information on our Maisie."

The camera cuts to the reporter, who also has tears in her eyes. "The following suspects are wanted for questioning in this case: Jesse Sullivan—"

My mugshot from last year flashes up on the screen. Not the most flattering picture, I must say.

"Rachel Wright—"

Rachel wearing her mental hospital gown flashes up on the screen next. At least she looks a little worse than I did. If she sees this, she's going to go ballistic. The fact she was on television without makeup and not dressed to the nines will definitely cause an uproar.

"Alice Gallagher—" Ally's driver's license photo fills the top right of the screen, making our square 3/4 complete.

"Captain Gloria Jackson—" An old photo of Gloria from her days in the military is the last to appear. She looks sharp in her uniform, her face and eyes somber.

"A fifth suspect, possibly a radical Islamic terrorist, is believed to be assisting them. They are responsible for the bombings in Chicago that took so many lives."

"What racist bullshit." I half-choke on the words. "Caldwell blew up the city himself!"

"Any information leading to the capture of these criminals or the return of Maisie Caldwell will be generously rewarded."

Gideon turns off the screen. "The first part of the program presented Maisie's disappearance as an attack against the Church. They are arguing that some have radicalized against the unification of the Church and seek retribution by harming the daughter of its leader."

I squeeze my head as if to keep the anger from splitting it in two. There are so many problems with this I don't even know where to begin. I end up shouting, "You're not a terrorist!"

"It doesn't matter." He flashes me a weak smile. "I look like a terrorist, and my devices can't hide us from the public. We are only hidden from technology. Someone will spot us on the streets."

"We aren't abandoning the plan!" No, no, *no*. We are so close to killing him once and for all. Caldwell, the evil son-of-a-bitch who murdered my handler Brinkley, abandoned me, mentally abused Maisie, and is responsible for the genocide of *hundreds* of *thousands* of people. No. I won't stop until he is cold in my grip.

"Jesse." Ally places one hand on my arm. Her eyes are big and round, and more alert than they've been in the last few hours. "If we're caught and we go to jail, we won't get our chance."

She's right. Dammit.

I look up at Gideon. "But what about our plan?"

"It can still work. With a few minor alterations, it can still work."

I accept his answer with a sense of unease. I wish I could ask Gabriel what he thought, but I've only seen him twice since we left Chicago. Until he became absolutely inaccessible, I hadn't realized how much I'd come to depend on the advice of my angel. I know he's still there. I can *feel* him so to speak, but he can't materialize as long as Rachel, Maisie, and I are together. Inconvenient.

"Just don't tell Maisie," I say at last, looking from Ally's face to Gideon's. "If she knows, she'll do something stupid and heroic."

Gideon clears his throat and cuts his eyes over my shoulder.

I turn and find Maisie standing in the doorway, her expression grim. Winston sits at her feet, his collar and leash still around his neck.

She's heard every word.

CHAPTER TWO

Jesse

"Stop, stop!" I yank the backpack out of Maisie's hand and throw it across the room.

"Hey, my laptop's in there!" She wails and rushes to the far wall, rummaging through the heap with shaking hands.

I take big breaths and try to calm myself. Freaking out on Maisie won't get me anywhere. *When you make me mad, I fixate on something benign. Like a light socket*, Ally once said. Okay, let's try that.

This room is very *luxury hotel*. Big high headboard gleaming in the soft lamplight. The walls are an agreeable cream, the carpet white—so not the best place to murder someone. Macabre aside, it doesn't look like a teenager's room. No posters or fun glittery things. No books or stereo like what I remember back at the tower where Caldwell first locked me up with Maisie. Did she miss her room? Can't it be enough that we saved her?

My anger flares. "Stop trying to leave and I won't have to keep stopping you!"

So much for anger management.

She turns her computer over and over until she's

convinced it's unharmed. Then she stands, all the fury returning to her face. "You don't need me!"

"You're wrong."

"I'll turn myself in."

"What the hell is that going to do?" Winston scuttles away from where he'd been sitting at my feet, probably afraid I'm going to make a sudden movement and accidentally step on him. He slinks out of the room, tail tucked.

"I'll tell them I ran away. I'll tell them that you had nothing to do with it. They'll call off the search."

I groan and pull at my face. I've been doing this a lot lately. "For someone so smart, you sure say stupid things."

"You're one to talk!" She throws her bag, and its unzipped mouth hemorrhages clothes, papers, and the few meager possessions Maisie has managed to acquire over the last few weeks in our care.

"Oh so you can throw your stuff around the room but I can't?" I ask.

"It's *my* bag! And my laptop!"

I can say a thousand things. Instead, I take a breath like Ally taught me before daring to speak. "My point is it doesn't matter what you say. Caldwell will get into everyone's heads and convince them otherwise. He'll say you're confused and scared. That you have to say these things because we threatened to kill you, blah, *blah*. Going back won't solve anything, and you know it."

Maisie sinks onto the bed and puts her face in her hands. I sit down beside her on the mattress.

I look around the room desperately searching for what to say.

She finally speaks, but all the fight's gone from her voice. "You can't be seen with me. If they see us together, we'll get caught in no time."

"If I'm not with you, they'll still recognize my face."

I remember the time a prostitute tried to cut off my head and my face was plastered all over the news. Nashville is a big city, but people recognized me on the street and figured out where I lived, vandalizing my house. New York is bigger, but I have doubts that will work in our favor. It's bigger, but there're more people too.

How can I comfort the kid? Take her hand? Too corny. A pat on the back? Too patronizing. A hug? Embarrassing!

So I push her off the bed.

"Hey!"

"I need you," I say. "Winston needs you. I'm not leaving Winston behind, hoping Caldwell doesn't kill him. And I can't watch him all by myself, because we've got work to do."

She picks herself up off the floor. "You only need me to watch your dog?"

"You love watching Winston. What are you mad about now?"

"You demoted me from super-powered partis to dog walk-er!" Her mouth presses into a thin line.

Right. It is hard to remember that Maisie has super-powers like me, is a chosen partis like me for two reasons. First of all, because she's a kid. She's a scrawny bag of jelly. Adorable, but defenseless. Second, her superpower isn't as flashy as mine. She can bring the dead back to life, which is no small feat, but she's only had to use the power once in the last few months. When Winston was killed in the crossfire, the last time I went head-to-head with Caldwell, she brought him back to life by blowing air into his nose. It's a hell of a trick.

I throw myself back on the bed. "You're more than a dog walker. You're an integral part of our plan. And you're my secret weapon."

Her eyes narrow suspiciously. "What do you mean?"

"I've already replaced Ally," I go on. "Once you replace

someone, it doesn't work again. If she's killed, I can't save her, but you can. If I can't save Gideon or Gloria, there's you. You *are* a super-powered partis, and we need you."

"Do you mean it?" Her tone is hopeful for the first time. "I don't want to be some loser damsel that you're dragging around."

"I want all of us to come out of this alive." I ruffle her hair. "Can you help me do that?"

"Yeah, yeah." She bats my hand away, her grin beautiful for a moment, the relief easy to read in her big, round eyes. Then her smile falters. "There can only be one partis in the end."

I turn away from her so she can't read my face. Anger. Sadness. Disgust. Hope. It's all there, I'm sure. How the hell is the kid so good at dragging all the emotions out of me at the same time? Maybe she's got other superpowers I don't know about and wrecking people's emotions is one of them.

"We're all going to die: me, you, Rachel, dad and mom—and whoever else has powers. We're all—"

I cut her off. "Hopefully not for a really long time."

I don't want to talk about the fact that killing her parents is on my to-do list. "Let's worry about that later. For now, promise you'll stick with me."

"Because you really need me?"

"I *really* do." This time I do let her search my face and I don't look away. "I really don't want you to leave, Maze."

The kid smiles, slow and genuine. "I'll stay."

"Great, now go to sleep." I stretch my arms overhead. The room is a little chilly so I cross to the thermostat on the wall and kick it up a couple of degrees. "We still have a big day ahead of us tomorrow, and that asshole Caldwell isn't going to change it."

"You should call him Dad." Maisie strips off her jeans and sweater, which reeks of beer and cigarette smoke from the bar, and steps into her PJs, not an ounce of bashfulness on her face. Of course, she doesn't have an autopsy scar to be ashamed of like I do.

"No way. Caldwell has never been a *dad* to me."

Eric Sullivan had been a great dad and I'd missed the hell out of him when he died seventeen years ago. Maisie has never met that man. She's only known the smooth talking church leader Timothy Caldwell as her father. Rough-handed, oil-slicked mechanic Eric wouldn't become Maisie's *dad* for years after he slipped out of my life.

Maisie doesn't ask any more questions or press me for any more assurances. Thank god. Instead she crawls into her bed, and I lift Winston up and put him in bed with her. He bounds up and down on the pillows before turning several circles and lying down. He tucks himself into a bagel shape of pug. A loud huffing snort sounding a lot like *finally* escapes him.

I stand there and watch until Maisie's breathing deepens to a steady rhythm. I slip out of the room, but leave the door open, even though I usually close it. I don't know why the impulse to do this is so strong. If Caldwell knew where we were, he would've already popped in and killed us all, so there's no danger he's going to pop in here and kidnap Maisie out from under me now. Still, I can't bring myself to close the door.

Ally is on the couch, her laptop open on her legs. I take a seat beside her.

"Still drunk?" I ask.

She gives me a pathetic half-smile, her brown eyes full of the low lamplight. "No, unfortunately. That newscast was quite the buzz kill."

"Tell me about it."

"Is she going to run away?"

"Who knows." I flop onto the couch beside her. "She says she won't, but she does whatever the hell she wants anyway."

Ally grins.

I scowl. "What?"

Her smile doubles. "I might know someone like that."

I know exactly what she's saying. I give her a look. Then I gesture at her laptop. "What are you doing?"

"Reading the news." She presses her fingers into her forehead as if her skull is bulging out and she hopes to push it back into place. "I think it's moving me right into the hangover phase."

"Take some aspirin."

"I already took three trying to head it off," she says.

"Head, ha!" I snort. "*Head* it off...get it?"

She sighs, unamused.

I gesture at the laptop. "Anything else about us?"

"Not much more than what was in the news report. It's too soon, I think." She continues to rub her forehead with the tips of her fingers. "But I'm actually not looking for those stories."

"What are you looking for?"

"The partis," she says. "I want to find Number 7."

I throw myself back against the couch. Right. Caldwell has done a fine job of ferreting out all of the partis—me, Maisie, Rachel, Cindy, Georgia, Monroe and Minli—those of us with superpowers. Caldwell's mission is to kill each of us and absorb our gifts. If a partis is killed and the gift isn't absorbed, then it's passed on to some other Necronite—a person with NRD, who can die but come back to life because of their brain disorder—assuming their brain wasn't destroyed in the death, of course.

That was exactly what happened. Minli was killed, but her power wasn't absorbed. So now anyone can have it—any of the one million people on the planet who have the NRD condition. Someone will be *called* up.

"I don't like not knowing who it is." Ally echoes my concern. "I don't want another Jason on our hands."

"Yeah, that would blow." Jason nearly killed us a couple of times, chasing us out of the 34th floor of a high-rise building. It was either jump and hope I live, or let him tear me apart. Some of these partis—*cough, cough, Caldwell*—are crazy drunk on their power. They want more of it and are absolutely ruthless about ripping each other's heads off. Of course, a few are absolutely sweet too. Gloria seems to think Monroe is one of the kind ones, and god knows what she is doing with him down in Louisiana. And I think Maisie and Rachel are some of the best people on the planet.

Of course, I'm absolutely biased. Maisie is my kid sister and Rachel is my best friend after Ally.

But Ally is right. The next partis could be a lunatic with a bloodthirsty desire to gurgle our entrails.

I come out of my thoughts, realizing Ally is talking again. "I've been looking for anything weird. Unexplained phenomenon, shooting or blinding lights, anything that sounds like Minli's power."

"Nada?"

Ally frowns. "No. Sorry."

"It's not your fault." I cuddle closer to her. I nudge the laptop on her lap and close it, shoving it between the cushion and couch arm. "You didn't start any of this bullshit."

Ally snuggles into my arms and I like the warmth of her.

We could fall asleep like this, but before sleep can grab ahold of me and pull me down into the thick darkness, a sharp memory surfaces. Caldwell in my grip, engulfed in blue flames and burning. Me hissing all my hatred into his face as his flesh blackened, peeling away from the skull.

You want to burn, let's burn.

I'd engulfed us both in fire, trying to boil his eyes in his sockets until Ally stopped me.

"Why did you stop me?" I whisper, my eyes fluttering open. The low-lit living room is perfectly still and quiet around us.

She doesn't answer, her arms still wrapped around me.

"We could be that much closer to ending all this insanity if he were already dead. Don't you want it to be over?" I ask, trying to turn her so I can look into her face.

She's asleep.

With her head on my chest and arms around me, she draws slow deep breaths against the hollow of my throat.

"You can't stop me next time," I whisper into her hair. Our plan gives us only one shot.

One and no room for mistakes.

CHAPTER THREE

Jesse

"Oh my god, what is that *sound?*" Rachel screams from the bedroom.

That sound is Gideon in the kitchen shoving apple slices and kale leaves into a juicer. He insists on making this racket every morning, saying some crap about his body is a temple and it's to be worshiped on a bed of kale leaves or some shit. Every time I get a whiff of that green mush the machine spits out, my stomach churns and I get an intense craving for French fries.

"Here we go," I grumble to Ally who casts me a weary look over her cup of black coffee. She isn't looking that great this morning either. She sits on the sofa with her legs crossed under her. Her eyes are puffy and her hair unbrushed. Thick smears of leftover makeup give her a racoonish appearance, but she's the cutest raccoon I've ever seen.

"I'm going to stab someone." Rachel throws the door to the bedroom open. It bounces off the wall behind it.

Rachel looks like death baked crusty on a highway. Road-kill walking. Her hair is knotted into a thick nest on one side of her head. Makeup is smeared in all directions, giving the impression that she made out with a clown last night. Her magenta pajamas are decent enough, but wrinkly and riding up in places. Her entire left calf is exposed up to the knee.

"I told you to hydrate her," I say to Gideon, who has paused in his masticating, a kale leaf in each hand. "You'll wish you'd poured that water down her throat."

Gideon smiles, unaware of the horror that's about to unfold. "I'm making you a juice, my love. It'll make you feel better."

"You didn't offer me any juice," Ally mutters over her black coffee.

Rachel's eyes narrow to slits. "You want to make me feel better?"

Her voice can be mistaken for sweet as she crosses the living room and comes to the other side of the bar, opposite Gideon and his juicer. "Is that your goal, *love*? You want to make me feel *better*?"

"Of course." A shadow of doubt crosses his face. He bends down to look at her over the black rim of his glasses.

Without warning, Rachel waves her hand and the juicer flies off the counter. The cord anchoring it to the wall gives with a snap and a spark, and the whole machine flies across the room, passing through the breakfast nook and over the cherry wood table. It bursts through the window, shattering it. Gravity takes over once the juicer clears the window and it begins to plummet toward the street below.

Maisie snorts.

Ally runs toward the window and shouts. "Look out below!"

"Not running that goddamn machine at six in the morning would make me feel better!" Rachel screams, her voice shrill. She marches to the bathroom and slams the door closed behind her.

"It's almost eleven," Maisie says from the chair where she reads some lovey-dovey book about emo-vampire boyfriends.

Gideon sighs and looks up at the ceiling. "That's a $400 juicer."

He says this as if he isn't possibly one of the wealthiest men on the planet.

"You could've killed someone." Ally shakes spilled coffee off her hand. "That could have hit someone in the head."

Gideon looks at the kale leaves in his hands and frowns as if unsure what to do with them now that his juicer is gone. With a noticeable pout, he puts the leaves on the counter and throws back the half glass of green juice. Then he sticks out his tongue and grimaces. "Delicious. You ladies should try juicing."

"Yes, your face is really selling it," I say with an arched eyebrow. "Anyhoo, while she's—uh, getting ready—I want to look at the schematics one more time."

"Right." Gideon comes around the island to where I kneel by the coffee table. He reaches under the table and grabs a folder.

Ally comes to kneel on the opposite side of the table as Gideon spreads the schematics along the top. I grab one of the sheets.

"So here is the utility building," I say, pointing to a square which is supposed to represent a building. "We'll turn the power on first."

"Yes," Gideon nods. "Jackson will turn on the power to building 206 first. That's where the chamber is."

I give him a look and we both flick our gaze to Maisie who watches us over the rim of her book.

"Yes, go on," she says. "Talk about how you're going to lock my mom in a torture chamber as a way to bait my dad into getting murdered."

"Maze—" I begin, but she's already slamming her book closed and marching out of the room.

"Come on Winnie Pug," she says and Winston hops down off the chaise and trots after her.

Gideon gives me a cold look.

"Don't," I warn him.

"She shouldn't be here," he says.

"You're right," I snort. "She should be with her homicidal cult parents. That's so much better."

"She could sabotage the plan or interfere."

"Maisie understands what has to be done."

"Does she?" Ally asks, tapping the side of her coffee mug.

I scowl at her. "Whose side are you on?"

"I'm only saying that this is a lot for a sixteen-year-old to deal with."

"I can hear you!" Maisie calls from her bedroom, her voice muffled by the closed door.

Ally lowers her voice. "I'm saying we need to figure out where she will be when *it* happens."

It. The murder of her parents. Not only have her mother and father tried to kill me right in front of Maisie before, but Caldwell is responsible for most of the heartache, grief, and torture I've experienced in my adult life. Worse, he's responsible for the genocide of thousands. *Hundreds* of thousands of innocent people. I know his kill count is that high, because Ally likes to remind me every time I suggest that we should ditch this ridiculous hero thing and go live on some island in the Bahamas. Hell, Gideon could buy us an island far, far away from all this partis, superhero bullshit.

Yet they've made it clear that my superpowers have to be used for good. *Boo.*

"We can probably find a way to lure Georgia and Caldwell into A8673 without using Maisie as bait. Then it will be a matter of incapacitating them long enough to get Georgia's body sealed in the chamber." Gideon slides the building plans to one side and pulls up what is essentially the instruction manual for a chamber than can easily be mistaken for a medieval torture device.

"And you think he'll be willing to bargain with her locked up?" Ally asks, turning the coffee cup in her hands.

"Or he'll murder us all in a rage," I say. "If someone took Ally and locked her up, I'd destroy the place. I wouldn't be thinking clearly at all."

"Exactly," Gideon says with a sly grin. "Jackson insists that the chamber will bring back a great many horrible memories for Caldwell. This move is equal parts logistical and psychological warfare."

I look at the drawing of the chamber. It looks like a steel coffin but with rounded edges, suggesting the outline of a person. "Are you sure you know how to work this?"

Gideon puffs out his chest. "I've read this manual no less than twenty times. I could turn this machine on with my eyes closed. Now." Gideon turns toward us, but frowns when he sees the hole in the window again. He speaks to us without taking his eyes off of it. "We will have to act rather quickly today. Caldwell's hunt will limit our movements, but we should still reach New Orleans on schedule. Fortunately, we are in a cold, windy city. As much as you hate it Jess, the cold might actually work to our advantage this time. Rachel and I will pick up extra hats and scarves, and maybe sunglasses for good measure. We'll hide our faces well as we leave this afternoon."

Gideon crosses to the window and yanks the curtain closed, blocking most of the horrible wind whistling through the broken panes. "So pack up, clean up, and be ready by three this afternoon."

"Plan B?" Ally asks before throwing back the last of her coffee.

"If we aren't back by four, you should leave the hotel. Hide your face as best as you can and leave out the side exit by the pool rather than the front, in case there is trouble. Walk ten blocks east to the subway and take it five stops to the bus station. Buy three tickets for Albuquerque, but get off in Oklahoma City. Travel to New Orleans from there."

I need to remember to pack Winston's super fake service dog vest if it comes to that. How Gideon managed to find a vest in the first place that fit the obese pug is beyond me. But already it has proven helpful in getting the pug into all the places we would have otherwise been denied. Hotels, stores, buses, and so on. I keep expecting Gideon or Rachel or anyone to say *enough is enough! Leave the damn dog!* But everyone has been really good about it. It makes me love them a little more.

"I suppose Gloria will see us coming," Ally says, crossing to the sink. She turns on the tap to rinse her mug. "And we're to assume you're dead?"

"Exactly." He leans against the kitchen door frame. "Or captured."

"And while we wait, what should we do? Our nails?" I snort.

"Eat and pack. You can order room service, but don't answer the door. Tell them you're not dressed if they insist. Also, I would use this time wisely to check in with friends."

My laugh is real this time. "What friends do I have that aren't here?"

Gideon gives me a pointed look and I blink at him. "Your fine feathered friend?"

"Gabriel?" I snort with surprise. "I haven't seen Gabriel since...well, since Rachel and Maisie have been here."

"Rachel will be with me and you can send Maisie out for a walk."

Maisie's bedroom door flies open. "Finally! Let's get out of here Winnie." I give the girl a suspicious stare. How much of our conversation did she overhear?

"I'll go with her." Ally stands and stretches. "I'll bundle up too."

"Great." Gideon claps his hands. "Keep it short. No more than 15-20 minutes outside."

Maisie gives Gideon her usual *do-I-look-like-a-moron* glare. She is very fond of giving him that look.

The bathroom door swings open and Rachel steps out, looking better than she did when she went in. Her hair is wet and her eyes are a little puffy, but otherwise, she looks like a presentable young woman. Lucky for her, her darker skin is better at hiding dark circles than mine would be.

"Breakfast," she says to Gideon. "Now."

"Your hair is wet."

She takes one of Gideon's scarves and wraps it around her face twice, it's so long. As if in reply to his wet hair comment, she tugs a hat down over her head and yanks on each boot. When she finishes, she gives him a glare, not very intimidating since two tiny slits is really all we can see of her.

Gideon grabs his leather coat off the hook. "All right, off we go. Remember what I said ladies. Only fifteen minutes out. Don't open the door for anyone."

Rachel gives us one stiff wave, which could have easily been a middle finger in that bulky mitten of hers, and disappears. The door clicks shut behind them.

"Why does he get to boss us around?" Maisie sulks. "Just because he's a dude doesn't make him the boss."

"No," Ally agrees. "But he does have the money and the technology."

"Who cares about money? He doesn't have superpowers."

"Shall we get that walk out of the way?" Ally places her empty coffee mug on the table and crosses to the remaining pile of coats.

Maisie slips on her coat and then slaps her thighs to encourage the sluggish pug. "Come on Winnie Pug. Wanna go for a walk?"

Winston flops over onto all fours rather ungracefully and his cinnamon bun tail trembles.

Ally wraps the scarf around her head and hides the rest of her blond hair under her hat. She mumbles words that I can't understand as Maisie slips Winston's collar and leash on.

I tug the scarf down, uncovering her mouth. "What was that?"

"I said, 'can you tell it's me?'"

I put the scarf back in place and take a step back. No. I can't. I doubt anyone else could recognize her from the slit between her hood and scarf either. Maisie bundles up too, but she doesn't have a long scarf. I grab mine one off the back of a chair and wrap it around her head until she's only a pair of eyes too.

"Okay. You guys can go."

I get two bundled waves and the pair shuffles from the room.

I watch the door click closed for a second time, a growing sense of unease settling over me. When I can no longer hear feet shuffling down the hall and the clank of Winston's collar against the chain, I close my eyes.

"Gabriel?" I ask the empty room.

Silence.

I take a breath and try to still my pounding heart.

"Gabriel, are you still there?"

CHAPTER FOUR

Rachel

"I'm freezing!" I yank at the bottom of my dress. The stiff fabric doesn't give. We hang a right at the next street corner and the wind is even worse on this avenue. "Where's this goddamn subway tunnel?"

"Love, perhaps you'd be warmer if you wore pants." Gideon's eyes fall on the bare skin between my knee-high boots and the lace of the petticoat protruding from beneath my dress. He grins, the look in his eyes devilish.

"Why would I hide my legs when I garner such a strong reaction from you, Cariño?" I purr, rolling the word between my teeth.

"I'm not complaining." A smile tucks into one corner of his mouth. "*You* are."

I dip my chin into the scarf around my head. Only my eyes are exposed to the bitter air. It's enough to pull tears from their corners.

"Will you be all right? We need you focused for the day ahead."

"Don't insinuate that I'm weak." I glare at him. "I know what has to be done."

"Perhaps you've changed your mind about murdering the girl. It wouldn't be weakness. I would understand."

I push Gideon. He trips, stumbling on the pavement, but doesn't fall.

"Stop questioning me, Gid. Brinkley trusted me with this."

Brinkley. I see him in my mind: the leather jacket, the scars, the gruff voice. So rough around the edges, a very fuck-you-I'm-Johnny-Cash kind of man. My hero. He pulled me from a hell worse than I could've imagined and returned me to the world of the living. When he liberated me from that merciless drug lord's tyranny, Brinkley could've asked me for anything. *Anything* and I would've given it to him.

"I don't question your loyalty to the cause," Gideon says, righting himself. His smile is tight. "I know what he did for you."

"He gave me my revenge." I unclench my jaw before I crack my teeth. "He made sure there was nothing left of Chaplain."

"Almost nothing," Gideon corrects.

I stop walking. "What?"

"If you think about it, Chaplain still lives on in Caldwell. Caldwell has his gift, his partis power. I suppose as long as that exists, a part of Chaplain will also exist."

"No."

"Regardless, we'll get the documents, pick up some scarves, and then kill the girl. Then we will be that much closer to saving the world. Are you coming?"

I can't draw enough breath into my nose. The idea that even the smallest part of Chaplain still exists—Chaplain the rapist. Chaplain the snuff filmmaker. Chaplain with the burning eyes that haunt my dreams. Oh, how I play the day we met over and over in my head—Chaplain with his long and easy stride, his black turtleneck and leather pants. His curls. The way he reached out and tucked the hair behind my ear as if he didn't need permission to touch me. And the stupid way I'd liked it. What a fool I was. What had he said?

"You're beautiful enough to be an actress. Come with me. I want to show you something."

God, I'd lapped it up. I followed him back to the run-down white house. As soon as I saw it, my insides screamed. *Run away. Get away from this place.* On the pavement outside, I turned to Chaplain, ready to make my excuses, but he trailed a soft hand down my arm. His smile made me go hot all over.

"You'll understand why I'm renting such a shithole, when you see the set up," Chaplain said, his voice amused. It was enough to coax me inside. Why? Because I was raised to be polite. To be a good, accommodating girl. And look where the hell it got me. See if I'm ever polite again.

The moment the front door closed behind us, the second my eyes focused on the bed in the spotlight, he jabbed a needle in my arm. He dosed me with enough heroin to sink a moose.

My legs gave instantly.

"My beautiful girl. *Mi perra.* You're going to make me so much money." His breath was moist on my ear. My body sagged in his arms as he ripped away my clothes and the cold air licked my skin.

Blind terror. Panic pulsed from my heart. Do you know what it means to be a prisoner in your own body? My arms and legs were made of wet sand. I couldn't push him away. I couldn't get my tongue to form articulate words. Fighting wasn't an option. I had only one choice: go inside myself. Endure this. Or be broken by it.

And no one is going to break me. Not Chaplain. Not Caldwell.

"Are you all right?" Gideon asks. There's an edge to his words. I know that tone from Brinkley. *Are you still here with me? Are you in control of yourself? Are you about to completely lose your fucking mind?* This tone is always my cue to pretend.

But a lump of coal is stuck in my throat and it's burning.

"Maybe we should head back to the hotel." Gideon turns, surveying the street around us.

"Caldwell has to die," I say.

"Oh, he will." Gideon slips his hands into his pockets. "Either you or Jesse—"

"*I'll* kill him," I say and hear the tremor of mania in my voice. I release a slow exhale. "It's what Brinkley wanted."

Back in the St. Louis asylum, Brinkley told me what he wanted. Protect Jessup. Do what Jessup can't. Kill the monster. And I will because the fact remains that Jessup can't kill him. She doesn't have it in her. I have it in me. Chaplain saw to that.

Gideon takes my gloved hand in his and pulls me down the stairs leading into the underbelly of the city. I can hear the subway squealing somewhere down the tracks.

This place is filthy. Soda cans and wrappers cluster in the corners of steps, kicked by rushing feet. The air is sour. The steps are smeared with mud from countless shoes.

"It smells like a dumpster down here."

Gideon shrugs. "Welcome to New York."

I use the scarf to hide the vehement emotions puppeteering my face.

You are so beautiful. You could be an actress.

I am an actress. Every day. The more I think of Chaplain as somehow alive, the more the urge to plunge my thumbs into Caldwell's eye sockets intensifies.

How will it feel? Wet? Resistant until the eyeballs pop? Then perhaps warm as I slide in deeper. I imagine if I close my eyes at that very moment, I could pretend it's Chaplain I'm murdering. And when his power transfers from his body to mine, will I feel Chaplain? That last piece of him absorbed by my body, becoming a slave to my will as I was once a slave to his.

I would own the last piece of him. That's exactly how I want it.

Put Chaplain from your mind for now, my angel Uriel commands. He's little more than a dim shape in the corner of my eye, but his presence is unmistakable. The flare of heat. The weight of him. *You are frightening your companion.*

Gideon is tense beside me. I push through the turnstile, our tickets disappearing in the machines only to reappear on the other side. The lace brushes my thighs as I jog to keep pace with the pushing crowd. The train is about to close its doors when we descend the final steps onto the concrete platform. We dart through, into the warm car. Warm from bodies. Warm from artificial heat pouring through unseen vents. There's only one seat.

Gideon motions for me to sit but I shake my head.

"I'm better with a pole." I grin and this acting feels a little less forced.

Good. Uriel encourages my deceit. *There is plenty of time for revenge.*

I grab the silver pole running from floor to ceiling in the center of the subway car. From his seat, Gideon's gaze slides up my thigh. I twirl around the pole once at arm's length. *Caldwell will die. I will be his murderess.* I repeat this to myself over and over until my joy surges.

"Behave," Gideon warns me with an arched brow.

"Why?" I pout my lip but realize he can't see it. Unfortunate. "I feel so much better."

Lies, and more lies. How many times can a person lie in a day?

He cocks his head. "The Vicodin must be working."

"Yes." True, the little elves that set up a workshop in my head this morning, with all their banging and raucous, have grown quiet. The urge to snap necks with the flick of a wrist has subsided. Mostly. Yet I believe the long list of ways to murder Caldwell is cheering me most. I can kill him slowly. Painfully. Perhaps a snuff film could be made with his body. Something nice and gory. He's spent time in the camps. He can take the pain.

I rub my bare thigh against Gideon's leg. "Do you *want* me to behave?"

I press my back to the pole and finger the edge of my petticoat. I yank down my scarf so he can see my smile. He's on his feet kissing me before I can draw a proper breath. Hot chills roll through me and I think I could do it. Have sex right here on the train with everyone watching. Who cares? I'm not just another rat in the sewers. I'm so much more.

Gideon breaks the kiss, breathless and tugs my scarf into place. He coos into my ear. "Reckless, wench. There are authorities on this train."

"So?" I don't yank the scarf down again. I'm tempted to do it. Defy him for fun. He's so cute when I frustrate him.

He laughs, a true, robust voice that turns the heads of several women on the train. A blond in red lipstick smiles at him.

With the smallest of finger twitches, I loosen the top of her coffee cup. Then with a more forceful two-finger twitch, her cup jerks upward, spitting coffee into her face. Her hair is soaked and her makeup ruined.

I giggle. Oh yes, I'm feeling *much* better. I twirl once around the pole until the overhead voice announces the stop and Gideon pulls me toward the door, unsmiling.

The train screeches to a stop and we step out onto the platform.

"I can't take you anywhere."

I barely register Gideon's disgruntled tone because the *whoosh* of wings catches my ears and I see a shadow in the corner of my eyes. The shadow can easily be the outline of an angel, majestic with his wings outstretched.

On guard, Uriel's voice commands, slithering across my mind like a snake, the muscular underbelly of his words palpable. Three men step off the subway behind us. Men in navy blue suits and long coats, their gazes fixed on us.

I squeeze Gideon's hand but he keeps pulling me forward toward the lighted street above. I tug again, hard.

"I *know*," he says.

"And?" We aren't running, are we? That might work in the movies but this is life. Furthermore, if these fools think I'll let them stop me from wiping the last piece of Chaplain off the face of this planet, they are *so* wrong.

"And—" he begins, letting go of my hand so he can reach into his coat pocket and grab—anything. It could be anything. A gun. A Taser. A grenade. A tube of lipstick. One thing I love about Gideon, he's always a surprise. He smiles as his fist closes on something. "Get ready."

CHAPTER FIVE

Jesse

*N*othing.

"What the hell?" I murmur to the quiet room. "Come on, Gabriel! Get out here!"

A strange sensation washes over me, like I'm being watched. The hair on the back of my neck pricks up and muscles in my abdomen clench. I whirl around half-expecting Caldwell to be standing there, ready to pluck my eyes out of my head.

"Gabriel." I sigh his name in relief. I didn't realize how much I missed him until now, seeing him standing in the soft lamplight of the hotel room. And I forgot how damn *pretty* he is.

He hasn't changed at all. His cat-like green eyes, unnaturally brilliant, dim to a more human shade. Black wings stretch wide on either side of him, the tips of his feathers brush against an impressionistic painting of peonies hanging from the wall, making a scratching sound.

"You've grown accustomed to the power you possess. You are more—" his voice trails off as he searches my face, like he's going to find the word he wants written on my forehead or something. "—stable than when I left you last."

"Yeah, I have it together." Kind of. "Don't sound so surprised."

I climb off the couch and go around the black lacquer coffee table with its marble top. I stop short of him, unsure what I intend to do now that I'm so close.

"I've heard you in my head, whispering all creepy and shit. You make me feel like I need an exorcism. Doesn't the connection work both ways?"

"No," he says. "When you are with each other, there is interference. The connection is weak."

"Um-okay." I shrug. "That means nothing to me."

Gabriel often tries to explain our connection, our special bond or the reason he is here trying to usher me through this secret mission to save the world. I've yet to understand.

"You must kill them, Jesse. Rachel and Maisie."

"No fucking way!" I shove his chest. I'm knocked back rather than him. It's more like I pushed a wall than a man. "I don't know if you're really an angel, or if you're an alien like Rachel believes, or just some massive acid trip we're all having, but whatever the hell you are, you're not going to command me to kill my friends. Or my *sister*. It's bad enough you've set me up to murder my father. Okay, so he totally deserves it, but my *friends? No.*"

"There can only be one partis. The girl understands that." He reaches a pale hand out of his pocket and stretches those fingers toward my face. I don't know if he intends to brush my bangs out of my eyes or what, but I slap his hand away.

"I don't care if there can only be one partis. You can't force me to murder my friends."

"If you do not absorb the powers and become the apex, the Earth will perish. Is that what you want?"

I stamp my foot. "Kill my friends or kill my friends *and* everyone? Who says that?"

"This is your choice. I cannot make it for you."

"Why can't life just be totally beyond my control like it is for everyone else?" I pace away from him. Whose idea was it to talk to Gabriel? "Okay, you know what? I thought I was missing your wise counsel, but nope. I'm not. You can go away now."

Gabriel doesn't budge. Though I think I see his wings twitch in irritation. "Would you have Caldwell be the apex? He will kill Rachel, Maisie, Georgia, and you."

"Is there a box that says 'we all live happily ever after'? I'll check that one."

He blinks lazily like a mildly irritated cat.

I pull at my face and flop back on the couch. "Listen, don't you have any good news? Anything helpful? I was hoping you would approve our plan or give me tips or tell me that I'm going to win. You know, something useful."

"You will win," he says with an air of unshaken confidence.

I smile. "That's better. Thank you."

"I chose you—"

"Yeah, that's your mistake, not mine."

"—I have never been wrong before."

"There's always a first. Tell me that we are all going to be okay. I'm warming up to the idea that I will have to sacrifice myself for everyone. I might be okay with that, in a few more weeks or decades. But I want Maisie, and Rachel, and Ally to survive. Can't I have that? Is there a way for Maisie and Rachel to give me their powers without being hurt?"

A look that could be mistaken for sympathy crosses Gabriel's face. "That will not be possible."

"You're the least helpful angel ever." I lean forward, elbows on my knees. "Can you even tell me what's Caldwell doing now?"

"Searching for you."

My tongue suddenly feels super heavy. "Is he close?"

"Yes."

"Wow. Just tell it like it is."

"He must wait for an opening." He closes his wings and steps toward me. "I've hidden you from his sight. In a way that Gideon cannot hide you."

"Thanks?" I'm not sure what else to say.

"Each angel advocates for their own apex." He pulls me into his arms. "I want you, Jesse."

"I'm sure this is being lost in translation, but I'm pretty sure you mean I want you *to win*."

His tie and eyes deepen to a midnight blue and I make the mistake of looking into them. Instantly, it's as if I'm falling. My stomach drops, my body leaning forward, off balance. I wrench myself from his arms.

"Okay, enough of that." I cross the room and snatch the room service menu off the table. "If you don't have anything nice to say, you can go now."

"If you will not kill them, distance yourself. I cannot help you when the three of you are together."

He's right. And I hate it when people who aren't me are right. He's saved our ass numerous times when Caldwell was trying to get the drop on us, and going into our showdown with a blind eye makes me nervous. I want him with us when we confront Caldwell, but I also want Maisie and Rachel close.

Gabriel preys on my anxiety. "There may come a time when you will need me."

He disappears.

"Oh come on, don't be a drama queen! Get back here!"

He doesn't come back. I strain to hear his whispers in my head, but the only thing I hear are the pounding footsteps in the hall, charging my way. More than one pair.

And a strange jingle sound.

My power rolls up from my navel, encircling my spine and flowing down my arms as my palms open. If someone bad bursts through that door, I'm going to firebomb their asses.

"Open up!" Maisie shouts. "Jess, open up!"

"Shit." I suppress my firepower and rush to the door. I yank it open and Maisie rushes in, crushing the pug to her chest. Ally is right on her heels, shoving the door closed behind them.

She's limping. Winston is panting. And Maisie fights to control her breath.

"What the hell happened?"

"Grab everything," Ally says, chest heaving. "No, not everything. Whatever is important."

Maisie drops Winston on the couch and flies into her room.

"Why?" I search Ally's face, trying to get a sense of how much trouble we're in.

"There's a SWAT van positioning themselves outside the hotel."

"Shit. What are the chances there's a drug lord holed up in this hotel and they're coming after that guy and not us?"

Ally's nostrils flare.

"Okay, dumb question. Did you see Caldwell?" I ask as Maisie comes back into the living room, her backpack stuffed to the brim. She starts gathering up Winston's things without being asked, shoving them into a canvas sack labeled Dmitri's Whole Foods, in navy blue letters.

"No." Ally fingers her ankle with a grimacing face.

"Can you go through Rachel and Gideon's room and gather up their stuff? We don't want to leave anything important."

Maisie goes into the room obediently.

"How bad?" I ask her, bending down to look at her ankle.

"My ankle is okay. It's really sore. I sort of whirled around, thinking they'd seen my face, and slipped off the curb. It was stupid."

"Okay, let's get together what we can carry. I'll burn the rest. Then we're gone."

Maisie came and dumped a leather satchel on the floor. "This is the only thing that looks important. The rest is just clothes and stuff."

"Leave them. We can't carry Rachel's wardrobe across the city. In fact, Maze, go through your pack again and dump what you don't absolutely need, okay?"

"I'll get our stuff together," Ally says.

"I'll do it." I run to the kitchenette and throw some ice in a plastic shopping bag. Then I unzip one of the fancy pillow cases and pull out the stuffing, using the pillowcase as a cover for the makeshift ice pack. I kiss her. "I won't let anything happen to you. You'll be okay."

She reaches up and touches my cheek. "Oh Jess, I'm not worried about me. Only one thing in this world scares me."

I find the aspirin bottle on the table, twist off the cap and plop two aspirin into Ally's hand and toss the bottle to Maisie. She catches it and tucks it into the front pocket of her bright yellow bag.

"What's the one thing that scares you?" I ask, hefting the bags onto my shoulders, giving the room one last look before abandoning it.

She takes my hand. "Losing you."

CHAPTER SIX

Jesse

We are packed and ready but there's still no sign of Rachel and Gideon. "We better go."

Ally bites her lip, casting a last glance around the hotel room. "Maisie?"

Maisie jingles Winston's leash and then shifts the pack on her back. "Ready."

It's not difficult to leave given how frigid the room has grown over the last few hours. Honestly, I'm surprised that someone hasn't come to ask about the broken window yet. Lucky us.

I slide open the door to the room and peer out into the hallway. Nada. To the left, the red carpet stretches endlessly away from us. The vintage fan-shaped lamps mounted about ten feet apart cast shadows on the cream walls.

"Meet me in the stairwell," I tell Ally. "I'm going to clean up."

I watch the girls slink down the hall and through the door at the end. I don't duck back inside until Ally's face appears in the little window, watching.

I slip back into the room, and before the door even closes

all the way behind me, I ignite. Flames lick up the carpet, latch onto the chaise, and incinerate the furniture. I go into Maisie's room next, still burning and watch the flames spread over the floor and furnishings as quickly as if I'd doused this place in gasoline first. I do Rachel and Gideon's room next, and it has the most stuff left behind. As Rachel's clothes begin to curl and blacken I can imagine how furious she'd be if she saw this.

Then I step into our room. It is the smallest of the three rooms, but I didn't mind. Neither Ally nor I have much stuff and though the bed is only a full, it left us with more than enough room to snuggle and—oh come on, Jesse. Stop daydreaming and get the hell out of here!

As I step out into the hallway, the elevator dings. I run toward the stairwell, shoving open the door and hear Winston's collar jingle, probably as he lurches back from the swinging door. I swear and stoop to pinch his tags together, silencing them. I give him a few reassuring pats on the head before I hand Winston over to Maisie, jabbing a finger at the tags. She gets it. Her fingers pinch the tags as she shifts the pug in her arms. Then I ease the hallway door back in place to hide my tracks. I wave for them to go on without me.

Ally's brow furrows. She mouths, "What about you?"

I hold up a finger, asking her to give me a minute. Positioning myself behind the door leading toward the hallway, I peer through the little window. The ice machine makes a *crack*-dump sound and I half jump out of my skin.

I'm not leaving until I see who got off the elevator. Maybe it's another hotel guest returning to their room. Fine, but what if it's Rachel and Gideon? I can't let them walk into a burning room.

A swarm of men in black explode around the corner like a small army of locusts, their bodies fast, guns up as they pool outside the room we just escaped.

I don't wait for them to bust down the door to the suite before I'm running. I take the stairs two at a time, catching up to Ally and Maisie in no time. As soon as they see me running, they move faster. Maisie stumbles a lot with Winston in her arms, and Ally manages by keeping one hand on the wall to steady herself as she rushes from landing to landing as quickly as her ankle will allow.

The red EXIT sign hangs over the door and Maisie bursts through before I can stop her.

"Wait!" Ally and I shout in unison.

We run after her, stepping out into full blown chaos.

A compressed alley behind the hotel connects two major streets. I've only been through the alley once before. Gideon insisted we do a dry run of our escape route before we made this hotel our home base. The alley had seemed creepy and cramped then, reeking of garbage and piss. Now it was even worse.

Both ends of the alley are blocked by a clot of cars and vans. Dispersed in front of the cars are men with guns.

"Fuck!" I throw my shield up around Ally without think-ing. Maisie shrieks and I realize my timing was shit. I drop the shield, let Ally grab ahold of Maisie and then erect it again so at least the three of them are safe inside the barrier even if I can't shield myself too.

True, my shield has gotten bigger in the last month or so. Gabriel once told me, when we were still chatting on a regular basis, that it was because I'd acquired a second partis power, in addition to the firebomb and shield stuff.

"Jessica Sullivan, drop your weapons and give us the girl."

I hold up my hands. "What weapons, idiot?"

Men from the other end of the alley rush toward Maisie and Ally. Two men collide with the shield and bounce off as if they'd run right into a brick wall. They tumble to the pavement holding themselves and swearing. They can't see the shield apparently.

My flames ignite. Blue fire courses up my limbs and torso, twisting in an arc. It pulses erratically. Both rows of officers, agents, whatever the hell they call themselves, leap back, giving us room.

"Drop your weapons—" someone says over the loud-speaker again.

"You want to see a weapon?" I purr as my blast powers up. It feels so good. Drunken. Giddy. I'm trying not to twirl or fall into a fit of laughter.

"Don't," Ally begs. "There are too many people."

"You're safe." I remind her.

"I'm not worried about us," she begs. "They can see you."

She thrusts a hand up toward the sky as a helicopter blots out the clouds. An aerial news crew flying at an angle above two tall buildings cuts left and out of my view. I can hear the whirling blades long after it slips from sight, the *whomp-whomp-whomp-whomp* hurting my ears.

Shit.

Caldwell must know where we are now. Perfect. No scarf. No tech device. It's only my face on prime time television.

I open and close my fist, delighting in the intoxicating warmth of the electricity rippling over me. *Please give me a reason,* I beg them. *Make one little move.*

"No," Ally says again. "No!"

If I drop my guard they'll take Maisie, hurt Ally, and kill me. No way.

And hesitating will cost me. The girls and Winston are safe in the shield, but I'm vulnerable. If any of them get the bright idea to put a bullet in my head, it's over. I'm hoping the erratic fire is making it hard to see me clearly, a sort of armor in its own right. But if I cut the flame entirely, they'll see me perfectly. Or they could rush forward and try to take me by force. Then what will happen?

I meet Ally's desperate wide eyes. "I'm sorry."

The fire around me brightens, growing, expanding and whipping wildly. The men fall back, ducking behind cars and vans, shielding their bodies while their eyes remain trained on me.

I blast one side of the alley, hopefully pushing the men and the vehicles back enough that we can squeeze through with minimal casualties. The fire flares forward and shots ring out. A solid hit like a punch in the gut strikes me an inch below my left breast. The force of the bullet knocks me back and I cry out.

My flames sputter out.

"Gee-*zus*." I lift my shirt to inspect the bullet wound. The men around me stand breathless, waiting.

Before the pain even stops radiating through my guts, the wound begins to itch. Then an icy feeling slides over my skin as the wound puckers and spits a bullet out onto the pavement. The blood that spilled down my stomach, staining the top of my jeans a dark burgundy, stops flowing and the flesh stitches itself together in front of my eyes.

"Fuck," someone says, one of the men in the first row of defense. His jaw unhinges and the barrel of his gun dips. Three more shots ring out, catching my chest and shoulder, each bullet a little higher than the last. If they shoot me in the head—

I wouldn't let them finish you off. That pleasure will be all mine.

My head snaps up at the sound of that serpentine voice, cruel and perfectly articulate despite the commotion on all sides. Only one person can pull off that trick.

Caldwell stands to the right. Positioned between the men and the hotel building. Of course he's issuing orders from the sidelines. With a gift like his, why dirty his own hands?

You've been sloppy, Jesse. You won't lose me again.

I fire bomb the alley.

The pain of being shot *four* freaking times paired with Caldwell's taunts amplifies my anger. The blue flame pulses out from me in all directions. The first row of cars lifts off the ground, blown back like umbrellas caught in the wind. I see a lot of feet, the bottom of rubber shoes floating away. The crunch of metal and the shriek of brakes resounds from the adjacent street. Cars slam into one another as those blocking the alley collide with those passing through a stoplight. No sooner than the brakes stop squealing do the shouts begin.

So ungrateful. Is that the thanks I get after saving your precious little life?

Pretty sure they shot me on your command, I reply, using the same mind speak that Caldwell prefers.

Yes, but not in the head.

"Caldwell," I shout. I don't think Maisie and Ally can hear me. I can barely speak, my voice breathless against the pain crippling me.

My heart sputters and my vision blackens, splotchy at the edges. I taste salt on my lips and copper, probably blood.

Hands yank me up to my full height, shoving me against the wall.

"Jess, no. Come on. Don't pass out." It's Ally pleading with me. "Stay awake, baby. We can't carry you."

Oh no. If she can touch me then I dropped the shield. No, no, no. I try to erect it again. Does it work? I can't tell. My vision is spotting.

"Caldwell," I say again. Or at least I think I do. Ally gives no indication that she's heard me.

"It's her heart," Maisie says, and I feel trembling fingers gingerly poking at my chest. "She got shot in the heart. She's dying."

The world comes into focus and a black van bursts

through the flaming wreckage of my firebomb. The doors fly open and two or three people in tactical gear, guns held across their chests step out.

No, no. I think, trying to summon my strength and focus. *Ally—look—look behind you.*

Surely she can see the van. She's smart enough to run. *Leave me. Take Maisie and go.* I hope I'm saying all of this aloud, but I fear my voice is being drowned out by the blaring sirens and thick smoke filling my nose and burning my eyes.

Rough hands grab me and shove me into the van, my cheek scratching against the rough carpet of the floorboard.

That's the last thing I feel before my heart fails me.

CHAPTER SEVEN

Rachel

The first man places a hand on Gideon's elbow and turns him around.

"Hey!" Gideon speaks in perfect American English. His British accent drops away without a trace and he adopts a half dumb, half bewildered look. His posture slumps, his lips pouting out in petulance. "What the hell, man?"

The transformation is shocking, but not unexpected. I've seen Gideon act before. He's quite the chameleon which is probably why he's still alive.

The train car pulls away taking most of the commuters with it. Gideon and I are overlooked by the others rushing up the stairs toward the exit, briefcases swinging at their sides, patent leather shoes unscuffed. A woman with long beautiful legs marches past us wearing leopard print heels.

I tug on Gideon's arm. "Let's go shopping."

"Now?" Gideon's face pinches.

One of the suits snorts.

"Do you think we can find them in Midtown?" Fresh air swoops down from the street above, blowing the hair back off my face.

"Not today," the suit clutching Gideon says. "You're coming with us."

This gets my attention. "No."

"This isn't a negotiation," the man says.

"Okay." I twitch my left hand and Gideon's elbow is yanked free. Then I shove both of my hands out in front of me like a push. The three men sail back away from us. They fall into the chasm between the parallel platforms. Someone's skull connects with the tracks in a sickening *crack*. Another wails as if he's busted several bones on the rails. I hope so.

Gideon balks at me.

"What?" I throw up my hands. "They said it wasn't a negotiation!"

"Excellent acting," Gideon says, relief washing over his features. "When confronted with authorities like that, feigning indifference and boredom is an excellent approach."

"I wasn't acting. I *want* to go shopping."

"Of course you do," he says with a disappointed sigh. "You're easily distracted today."

The insult stings. "And you're disappointing! I thought you were going to pull something exciting out of your pocket."

He opens his palm to reveal a lock pick, presumably for the cuffs we would've worn had I not taken care of business. "You were going to let them *take* you?"

Gideon places a hand on his hip. "You used to love my ideas. Is our relationship getting stale?"

"Ask me again...after you buy me something pretty."

"You know it isn't very feminist, allowing a man to buy you everything."

"I want to walk into the store, murder all the associates and simply take what I want. But since you disapprove of that, you can *buy* them. It's a perfect compromise and very feminist—men and women working together as equals to achieve a goal."

"I don't think—" he begins, but stops at the sound of heels pounding the steps. Police descend the stairs, their badges catching the winter light. Their walkie-talkies buzz on their shoulders. I throw my hands up again and shove the air away from me. The officers fall back, toppling like a wall. Several cry out as their elbows and tailbones connect with the steps.

"Stop that!" Gideon grabs my hands, cupping them together. Without letting go of me, he looks around the subway tunnel before catching sight of a promising door beside a turnstile exit at the end. He yanks me forward. "Run."

Gabriel. His black wings are draped over each shoulder like a fashion statement, looking as proud and petulant as any runway model. His green feline eyes regard me with a certain irritation. If he was a cat, I'm certain his ears would be laid back, ever so slightly.

"Oh god, he has us again." I push myself up on my elbows and notice that the ache in my chest is gone. "Caldwell took Maisie. Killed Ally. I fucking died and—"

"You did not die." Gabriel uncrosses his ankles and crosses the room. "You passed out while your heart healed."

I take a minute to process this. I didn't die? I was shot in the heart at least once, but I didn't die? Wow. Jason's healing powers are more awesome than I thought. No, not Jason's powers. Jason's gift. The power I took that allows me to heal any wound instantly. Unless of course that wound is fatal. Apparently, I can't heal a wounded heart in a heartbeat. Heh. It's a useful thing to know. If I'm in a situation where I don't want to black out, I probably shouldn't get seriously wounded.

"Ally?"

It's as if saying her name has made her magically appear. Still wearing her red, fur-lined coat, Ally bursts into the room, taking my cheeks in her hands. Her fingers are freezing and make the hair on the back of my neck rise.

"Oh thank god. That was even quicker than I hoped."

She plants kisses on my ear, neck and cheek. She finishes by brushing her lips against mine. I wrap my arms around her.

"How long was I out?" I squeeze her hard until she lets out an audible gasp. "Sorry."

"About ten minutes?" Ally pulls back, taking a breath. "I can't be sure. We've only been here for about five minutes, and the ride was a few minutes."

"Where is *here*?" My eyes take in the bland room. The walls are the color of oatmeal and the carpet a soft rose. It looks like a break room. There's a mini-fridge, a navy blue leather sofa on which I've just taken my power nap, and an unimpressive side table with a fake plant on it.

As my eyes return to their original corner where I first regarded Gabriel, the angel flickers and fades.

"Jeremiah's New York station."

"So another big commercial building in another big city. Original. That guy should really diversify his investments. Where're Maisie and Winston?"

"Upstairs. Did you say you saw Caldwell?"

"He was there. I thought he was the one taking us."

"We didn't see him," a cold voice says from the doorway. Nikki leans against the door frame, decked out head to toe in her body armor. She looks like a comic book hero with overly defined muscles and a gun on each hip. She isn't as bulky as the body armor makes her look, thank god. Her blond ponytail is sleek and pulled up high.

"Why are you leaning in the doorway?" I ask. "All that armor too heavy for you?" Is it too much to hope Nikki was shot? Possibly wounded?

Ally sighs.

"I liked the purple streak better than this orange one," I say, talking about a strip of dyed hair curling behind Nikki's right ear.

Ally's face scrunches with anger. "Don't be rude. They saved us back there."

"Stalked us, you mean. How did you know where we were?"

"I could find you in a bar full of Jesse Sullivan lookalikes all wearing sombreros and eye patches. You're far from subtle."

"I'm pretty sure what you said is racist and misrepresents Mexican culture. I'm telling Rachel."

Nikki's mouth falls open.

"Stop it." Ally rubs the center of her forehead with two fingers. "I don't care if she was following us. I'm glad she showed up. After you went and killed eight people, there was no escaping without her help."

My next insult sticks in my throat. I swallow it down before I manage to say, "Eight people?"

"Your firebomb was reckless. Of course, reckless is what you do best," Nikki says, one hand gripping her hip.

The heat rises in my chest, and I can feel the static electricity crackle between my palms. God, what I wouldn't give to set her hair on fire. If she wants orange hair, I'll give her orange hair. Just one strand would take care of the rest, wouldn't it?

"Jess," Ally says, watching my face. "Tell Nick thank you."

"Thanks for letting me know you're still stalking my girlfriend, Sasquatch. I'll have to keep a closer eye on you." I turn to Ally and find her blushing furiously. "Get Maisie. We aren't staying here."

"We can't leave yet," Ally says. "What happened in the alley is all over the news. They're twisting the story."

I look around the little room. The small, stiff sofa where I sit. The fake tree in a corner, the mini fridge. There's no TV to confirm what she's saying, but I guess I don't need one. I'm not surprised that the authorities would twist what really happened into a tale that makes us look like the bad guys, especially with Caldwell's help. "Of course they are, but that doesn't mean we can stay here. We need to get to Gloria and find out if Rachel and Gideon are okay."

"We're searching for Gideon and Rachel now," Nikki says, but she isn't talking to me. Her voice goes all low and sweet for Ally. "I'll notify you immediately if we learn anything."

Ally smiles at her. "Thanks. I don't know what we'd do without you."

"Have sex?" I guess. "Play Jenga? I'm sure there's lots of things we can do without her, babe."

Nikki's head angles slightly as her blue earpiece blinks to life. "I have to go. Try to act like a guest."

Nikki glowers at me from her glorified height. I hate that she is like eight inches taller than me. Of course, it makes it easier to sucker punch her in the gut. I consider doing just that, but with her fancy body armor it'll probably hurt my hand. If I cry about my broken hand that wouldn't look very cool. Of course, my healing powers would fix it pretty quick, which *would* look cool. Ah, decisions, decisions.

"If I'm your guest then can I get a sandwich? I'd love a PB and J," I say.

Nikki slinks from the room with her teeth clenched.

I sigh, daring to meet Ally's eyes, knowing I'm in big trouble. "Can we go now?"

"No." Ally's face is flushed red and her shoulders are scrunched up toward her ears. "No, we can't go. You know why?"

I open my mouth before I realize answering that question would be a death sentence.

"We can't go because Rachel and Gideon are missing, you've murdered eight people on live television, and I need to get ahold of Gloria!"

You murdered eight people on live television. It's like I've been shot in the chest again. Her words wind me. "You think I *murdered* them? Like on purpose? Like some heartless—"

"I didn't mean it like that. I know why you did it, but you shouldn't have used your firebomb. It's too dangerous." Ally frowns and pulls at her face.

"If 100 people or 1000 people point guns at you, I'll do it again," I tell her. I take both her hands in mine, trying to warm them. "You understand that, right? I don't care how many people I have to kill to keep you safe."

Ally pulls away from me and takes a deep breath before rubbing her forehead. "I know. I know, and that's a problem."

I'm sure as hell not going to apologize for protecting her. Even if that's what she wants me to do. Suddenly the room feels too warm, heat itching at my collar. The shirt is scratchy where the blood dried into the fabric, making it stiff.

"I'm going to try Gloria," Ally says at last, turning away from me without a kiss, a hug, nothing. "Maybe she saw this, or if she didn't, maybe she has insight. If I can't get ahold of her, we'll stick to the original plan."

I'm trying to remember the plan.

Buy three tickets for Albuquerque, but get off in Oklahoma City. Travel to New Orleans from there.

Ally sighs, her train of thought catching up to mine. "Maybe we can get Nikki to escort us to New Orleans."

I cock my head and give her a warning look.

Ally mirrors me, mocking me. "Refusing help is what idiots do."

I snap my mouth shut and suck in a deep breath before speaking. My self-control lasts for about three seconds. "If *you* want to get back together with your ex-girlfriend, *fine*. But let's not pretend that we didn't leave them for a reason, and that now they've conveniently shown up. Nikki and Jeremiah are supposed to be in Chicago. It's no coincidence that she's here, following us around."

Ally stamps her foot. "I do not want to get back together with her!"

Nikki appears in the doorway, stopping midstride. Both Ally and I turn toward the sound of her boots squeaking to a halt.

"Don't stop on my account." Nikki's face is blank and her voice suspiciously flat.

"I'm sorry. I didn't mean for that to sound so—" Ally's face flushes a deeper red.

I fold my arms over my chest. "Nikki is a big girl. She can take it."

Nikki extends the wrapped sub sandwiches with a hint of regret. "You don't owe me any explanations. Here. Eat something."

This magnanimous declaration seems to warm Ally even more. Jesus Christ. It's a sandwich. Not the queen's jewels.

"Hey, there's ham on this!" I squeal.

"Pick it off," Nikki says with a glare. Her face softens when she turns to Ally. "The secure line is clear if you want to make that call."

Ally watches her go. Gee-*zus. Really?* Do I really have to worry about this right now? I look down at the pale, slimy flesh on my Kaiser roll.

Ally hands me her sandwich and then hops up to leave the room. "I'm going to call Gloria. Hopefully she can tell us something useful."

Ally follows Nikki out of the room, leaving me with the sandwiches. I pinch the meat between my fingers, and try not to think about how much the marbled flesh looks like my thigh muscle the time it got split open by a collapsing construction beam. A clean, vulnerable deli slice before the blood started pouring out.

I gag and drop the ham on the floor. The splat is punctuated by the whoosh of wings and a breeze blowing my bangs back from my eyes.

"Did Nikki scare you off?" I ask him.

"Maisie was at the door listening to your plan."

"Well, she must have snuck away when she heard Nikki leaving."

Gabriel doesn't humor me with a reply.

"So is Rachel dead?" I take a bite of my cheese and mayo sandwich. Wow. I'm really slumming it.

"No."

"Are you omniscient?"

"No." Gabriel's wings puff indignantly. "I must turn my gaze as you do."

"O-kay," I say, pretending to know what that means. "Then how do you know Rachel isn't dead?"

"Her power is still present. I can sense it the way you can sense your own gifts."

And he's right of course. I can feel them: the electricity coursing over my skin, making my little hairs stand up and shift with my agitation, like a million little feelers. And my cells too. Ever since Jason's healing power kicked into full force, it's like I can feel my systems on guard. My little sentinels constantly searching every inch of my body for the slightest hint of damage. It's a constant, jittery feeling very similar to the need to pee.

"That's a relief."

Gabriel flickers again. "I never said Rachel was okay."

Maisie bursts into the room and Gabriel vanishes completely. "God, is the blonde always so bossy? 'Don't let that pug on the couch. Get your feet off the coffee table. Tell me about your father.'"

I groan. "Go away."

Maisie huffs. "What's your problem? None of this is *my* fault."

I unclench my teeth and take a breath. "I was talking to Gabriel, and he said Rachel was in trouble. You came in and he disappeared, so I'm freaking out to be interrupted at such a crucial moment. Got it?"

Her mouth parts in surprise. "Oh. Yeah. Okay. Can I get some change for the soda machine?"

I fish some coins out of my pocket and hand them over. I call after her before she disappears. Her head pops back in.

"Yeah?"

"Don't talk to Nikki about Caldwell."

Maisie smirks. "Duh. I don't know these people."

"They have a history of pitting Caldwell and me against each other. Let's not give them anything to work with."

"As if you guys need a reason to kill each other," Maisie says and disappears again. The sound of her rubber soles shrieking against the floor grows faint. I barely even hear the swoosh of a door when Gabriel appears again.

"Tell me everything you know about Rachel."

"I cannot see her clearly."

"What?" I scream. "What the hell do you mean? Turn your gaze or whatever you were talking about."

"Her angel protects her."

My mouth opens and closes as my brain and mouth fail to coordinate with each other. I consider throwing the fake plant at him, but it'll make a mess on the floor, and that'll be something else that's my fault.

Finally, I settle upon, "Protects her *from*?"

"You."

"Me! Why in the world does Rachel need protection from me?"

CHAPTER NINE

Rachel

I'm skipping and singing through Central Park. It feels so good! Until Gideon grabs me by the elbow and whirls me around to face him.

"This is not a game!"

I wrench my arm free. "You don't own me."

His face crumples. "I'm sorry. You frightened me back there." He jabs a finger over his shoulder in the direction of the station we left behind several blocks ago. "You utilized your power in the open without any regard for the consequences."

"You've got your device. Unless it's stopped working, we're fine."

He puts his hands on his hip. "Sure, it may be a matter of the officers convincing others of what they saw—"

"If they saw anything at all—" I interrupt.

"Even if there is no digital evidence, that's not the point," he says, running one hand through his hair. "We want to appear weak."

"I'm not weak."

He removes his glasses and pinches the bridge of his nose.

"The idea is to not let anyone know what you can do unless you have no choice."

"We had no choice," I say, crossing my arms over my chest.

"We did. We could have waited until we learned who they were and what they wanted. It's good to have a sense of what someone doesn't know before you show them your cards, love."

I scowl at him and his utter cluelessness. "I don't know if your mother covered this. Maybe you only have snakes and jackals in Afghanistan, but in America, we don't go willingly with the first strange man who asks."

"You do if that man has a big toy that you want. Or enough money."

"You'd crawl into a crocodile's mouth to see if he has a gold tooth!" I snort. "And *I'm* the reckless one!"

Gideon looks away from me, surveying the park. I know he's trying to regain his composure as well as evaluate our situation.

The park is full of people despite being the middle of the day and winter. Women jog with large dogs at their sides. A couple of men walk arm in arm. A hobo sleeps beneath a tree with a puffy black trash bag under his head as a pillow, three bare toes protruding from the end of a worn boot.

Gideon stops a gaggle of kids under an oak tree beside a row of benches.

"Can I interest you three in a magnificent business proposition?" he asks them in crisp, accented English.

The youngest girl with thick eyeliner and a skateboard under one hand grins at him. Though she is at least as tall as I am, I don't feel the same murderous rage I did for the woman on the subway with the coffee.

"I like to party," she says, stepping forward from her friends. "What've you got? X? Speed?"

"I made a bet with my friend here that you wouldn't trade clothes with us. I bet her four thousand dollars that you wouldn't trade!"

The three kids frown and step back.

"Told you," I say, playing along. "Pay up!"

"No, no," Gideon begs in false desperation. "She hasn't even properly refused me yet."

One of the girls frowns at us. "What kind of scam is this? Screw this. Let's go."

I force a laugh. "Pay up sucker."

"Wait!" Gideon cries out as they turn away. "I'll give you and your boyfriend each a thousand dollars if you trade clothes with us."

Gideon pulls out a large money clip and the kids' eyes double in size. The friend who was offered no money at all, given that neither Gideon nor I could fit into extra small garments, swore.

"$1500," the girl says, looking up from the clip into Gideon's eyes.

"A business woman," Gideon says, stiffening. "Of course you are. $1250, and that's my final offer."

She shakes her head. "$1500 firm. You'll save $1000 than if you lost the wager, and you'll have the satisfaction of being right." The girl turns her eyes on me then. "Besides I wouldn't be caught dead in *that* for anything less than $1500." She gestures at my beautiful magenta dress and petticoat.

I scoff. "This is Versace."

"It's hideous."

"You're one to talk!" I wave my hand up and down her body. "What do you call this? Dumpster diving chic?"

They turn to leave and Gideon blocks the path that would lead them into the tunnel.

"$1750 each. Compensation for my lady's poor manners."

"Sold!" the girl exclaims, her face lighting up. "But I keep the board and my underwear."

"Of course," Gideon says and begins to count out the money into their outstretched palms. He stops halfway through the promised amount and motions for them to strip. "Half now. Half after."

I assume that there is a good reason for all of this, so I strip down to my underwear, leaving the scarf wrapped around my head. Both Gideon and the kids stare at me for several heartbeats.

"This is the opposite of leopard print heels," I moan. I should be getting nice new things, not giving my nice things away. I wiggle my fingers at the girl. "I'm not getting any warmer here!"

She looks around the park wildly and then rolls her eyes. "Fuck it, whatever."

She thrusts her clothes at me and then steps into my dress. She scowls. "God, there's so much air up *there*. How can you stand it?"

Her friend giggles. "I'd pay $1500 to see you in a dress!"

"Why do you keep your face covered with that scarf?" She casts a look at Gideon. "You're not one of those Arab women, are you?"

"Don't be stupid," the lanky boy says. He trades his shirt and hoodie for Gideon's sweater and button up shirt. They seem to prefer going piece by piece in their exchange. "She wouldn't have torn all her clothes off in the middle of Central Park. And that's like a *scarf* scarf, not a hijab or whatever."

"Give us the scarf," Gideon says, waving his fingers at the friend.

"You didn't give me $1500!" she protests.

"$200 then."

"$500."

"Oh come off it, Bev. Your stupid scarf isn't worth $20."

"My grandmother made this scarf!"

"Who cares? Get her to make you another."

"She's dead. And the yarn in my scarf is worth more than your Goodwill resale which you just got $1750 for!"

"Fine," Gideon huffs. "$500 for the dead grandmother's artwork."

The girl tosses the scarf to Gideon with so much enthusiasm that I'm fairly certain she never even loved this grandmother or her collection of expensive yarn.

"I'm freezing," the girl tugs at the bottom of my dress—her dress—still clutching the petticoat in one hand as if she's unsure what to do with it. "Can we go now?"

Gideon counts out the rest of the money, and they scamper off hooting and hollering.

"Just how much money are you carrying on you?" I ask.

"About ten thousand. I have a few cards under aliases, but I wanted to change our clothing quickly to make us less recognizable."

When they are out of sight, I switch the girl's rainbow scarf for the one I've been carrying. Gideon wraps the boy's scarf around his head.

"Are we going to rob a bank now? That would be fun."

"I'm sure," he says, his voice muffled by the yarn. "But we should get our papers and get back. Can you suppress your chaotic nature until then, little nymph?"

I huff despite his compliment. "Anything is possible. What if her parents ask her why she came home in a dress?"

He makes an acknowledging sound. "Yes, they might report the suspicious activity, but I don't suspect they'll go straight home with $3500 between them, and if they do, they'll likely not mention it. Most parents would insist they give it back. Therefore, I conclude we have a little time. At least enough to get back to the hotel, and then out of town."

I shrug and we begin walking again.

We walk forever. Thank goodness I kept my own shoes, but even those are beginning to rub blisters on my heels. It's an hour before we stumble into Little Italy. Gideon points at a sign.

"That's Luca's place," he says. "We won't be but a few minutes, then we'll head back to the hotel."

The smell of bread and spices ignites my hunger. But it must be coming from somewhere else because this restaurant is unlit and a *sorry we're closed* sign hangs crookedly in the door's window.

"Are you sure this is the place?" I press my face against the glass. The chairs are upturned, seats resting on the table top. "It looks like someone swept up last night and never came back."

"I have a feeling I know why he didn't answer my calls." Gideon's tone is low. "Come on."

We creep down the dim and narrow space between two buildings. At the back of the trattoria, we find a dented screen door slightly ajar. A single black slit of darkness lines the entrance, ominous and uninviting. A black cat with white paws jumps up onto a barren window box and begins scratching at the frozen earth there.

"Be careful," Gideon says, and I don't know who he is talking to. Me? I'm not the one with my hand on the door, pushing it open.

"Are you sure he's here?" I'm having doubts that some random Italian with the ability to acquire travel documents for total strangers is here.

"Shall we see?" He glances over his shoulder, taking in the small alcove between buildings with its overflowing dumpster to one side and the crooked walkway leading to another street. Whatever he's looking for, he doesn't see it before he ducks into the restaurant.

We creep through the dim hallway, past two empty bathrooms and a door labeled "employees only." This command holds no sanctity for Gideon, so he twists the handle. His face crumples.

"What?" I whisper, unable to see around his body.

"It's unlocked." He lets go of the handle. "We should go."

"What if the papers are in there? You said we needed them."

His shoulders slump and he pushes open the door. The little room is especially warm and crowded with filing cabinets and a large desk. Luca sits behind it, a bullet hole in his head and a stream of thick, sticky blood on the side of his face, soaking the upper collar of his crisp linen shirt. His black eyes are dull and unfocused.

Gideon sighs. "Check the drawers. Perhaps we can still find our papers."

A large pile slips precariously to the edge, threatening to tumble into the floor.

Gideon yanks open the nearest drawer and begins ruffling through its contents. "We can still get to Arizona if we don't have the papers to fly. We will simply have to drive instead. It will take longer, but it will be safer."

On guard.

I stiffen at the sound of Uriel's voice. "We've got trouble."

A small sound draws my ear and I whirl, expecting to see police or whomever must have been called in response to the sound of a bullet blasting out Luca's brains. But it isn't the police blocking our exit, trapping us in the small office. It's five men in dark suits and opaque glasses, guns drawn. They aren't the men I threw onto the tracks earlier, yet they have a similar look to them like perhaps they all fell off the same assembly line.

"Hello Gideon," the one with a blond crew cut says. His neck is thicker than his head, giving it a squished look. As if someone had mounted his skull in a hurry, pressing it down into the nape with too much force. "Ms. Wright."

I don't hesitate. I throw my arms out in front of me and shove the men back. Their bodies slam into the wall and then through it, ripping holes in the plaster.

We run, spilling out into the nook cradling the back exit. The cat screeches, leaping out of the window box and over the fence. We squeeze down the walkway to the street. As soon as we're immersed in the crowd, we slow our pace. We walk like perfectly calm and rational people. It's fun pretending.

"Damn," Gideon swears. "We shouldn't have gone there. When he didn't answer my call this morning, we should have moved right on to plan B."

"You mean our $3500 wardrobe was all for naught? $6000 if you count the loss of my dress."

He doesn't even smile at my humor. I don't know if it's because he saw a dead body, if Luca was a friend, or because he's frustrated by our lack of progress this morning.

"Who are they?" I ask, my breath still hitching in my throat.

"I can wager a guess or two." He runs a hand through his hair and flashes me a lopsided grin.

There's something different about his face. It takes me a minute to realize it's bare. "Your scarf!"

"Keep yours." He stops me from removing it by placing his hand over mine. "Your face is more recognizable than mine."

"I'll take that as a compliment."

"The absolute best." He glances over his shoulder. "I think we are in the clear."

I look back too, but see only power walkers with their paper cups of coffee marching in all directions. Most on cell phones. "They knew who I was. Why should I even wear this thing?"

Gideon points at a woman in a black mink coat walking a Pomeranian. "She doesn't know who you are. And she might have watched the news last night or this morning. Leave it on."

"Fine. But what's up with the MIB?" I'm pleased he isn't yelling at me for using my power this time.

"They had American accents, so let's cross off the long list of international agencies who are hunting me. That leaves us with CIA, FBI, the Secret Service, Caldwell's lackeys, or perhaps the underling of some minor lord or another that I've offended. Perhaps even a businessman I've swindled or a drug boss with a particularly beautiful daughter."

I glare.

"I see those brown eyes smoldering in their sockets." Gideon flashes a tight smile. "I never claimed to be a saint, my love. In fact, I've often protested the notion."

"Your point?"

"I have no idea who they were and what they want. They could want only me, or they could be after all of us. They knew your name and that is my only clue."

We round another corner, and I realize we are only a few blocks from the hotel.

I place a hand on his arm. "We can't go straight to the hotel."

"You're right," he says and casts a look around.

A sharp pinch hits me in the middle of my back. "Ow!"

I stumble forward and Gideon grabs one of my arms. "Are you all right?"

"I got bit by a really big bee." I try to turn and see what got me.

"Hold still." Gideon's fingers smooth over my coat. "Fuck."

The drug hits me. My limbs thicken and mind slows. "Gideon—"

I stagger.

Gideon hoists me up and ducks into the nearest building. "Fight it, Rachel."

"I'm trying," I slur. "I really am trying." Gideon tries to carry me somewhere, but he doesn't get far.

More men in black—at least seven or eight—rush us. Gideon is forced to lay me down on the frosty ground and raise his hands over his head as they order. All I can make out are the dark shapes swelling and swallowing him whole. He's being arrested, carted away, and I'm just laying here like an absolute twat.

"No," I murmur. I try to flick my wrist, to break Gideon free, but nothing happens. "No."

Someone bends down, peering into my face but I don't recognize him. The room grows darker, falls quiet and I am helpless to resist.

"Sweet dreams, Ms. Wright," a pitiless voice says. "Sweet dreams."

CHAPTER TEN

Jesse

"Anything?" I ask Ally as she comes into the lounge, her laptop under her arm.

I've been laying on the stiff sofa contemplating my life since she left me to make the phone call. I'm doing my best to examine my options but I'm not getting very far.

"Gideon is in custody, but Gloria doesn't seem worried about that. She thinks he'll be free soon. Rachel is M.I.A. Caldwell is busy."

"Busy with what?"

"I don't know. She only said he was busy and that we need to come to Louisiana now while we have the opportunity, and get there as fast as we can. Nikki said she'll fly us."

"Can't we drive?"

Sure we don't have a car, but there are cars everywhere. We can borrow one. Okay, I have no intention of bringing it back, but someone would find it. Eventually.

"It's a twenty-hour drive. Do you really want to be in the car with Winston for that long?"

"How long does it take to fly?"

"Just under three hours."

Shit. "Fine. She can fly us as long as she leaves us the hell alone after that."

Ally bites her lip.

"Oh god, what? You married her? I turn my back for five minutes and—"

Her face pinches with anger. "Don't be insane."

"Too late."

"I don't think she's simply going to go away."

"She will if I burn all that pretty blond hair off her head."

"She can't. Jeremiah has ordered her to track us and offer assistance if needed. She won't go against his orders."

Convenient. I bet she begged Jeremiah for these orders. Follow my ex around like a lovesick puppy? Yes, please! "She will if her life depends on it."

"Jess, come on. I know it's not ideal, but I could use the help. I'm still trying to find the seventh partis."

"I help!"

"I'm not saying—"

I leap up from the stiff couch and slap the fake plant's leaves. Dust billows into the air. I whirl away trying to breathe fresh air. I guess no one has time around here for dusting. "How the hell did Nikki track us? Gideon's fancy gadgets were supposed to make us invisible."

Sasquatch appears in the doorway. "Rachel was going out alone."

I rub my irritated nose. "Bullshit."

I'm about to lay into Nikki for lying, for trying to stir up grief and chaos at the worst possible time. I flash Ally an angry look but stop. Her face is crumpled with concern. "You *believe* her?"

Ally licks her lips. "I saw Rachel leave the apartment one night, alone. I'd gotten up to get a drink of water. I was standing in the kitchen nook, in the dark, because I didn't want to turn on the lights and wake everyone. She crept right past me and slipped out of the suite. I didn't think too much about it. I confronted her later telling her that I realize she's probably sick of all of us, but she can't go out alone. It's not safe." Ally shrugs. "She promised not to do it again."

"That doesn't prove anything. Even I can understand wanting to get away from someone for five minutes." I shoot a pointed look at Nikki.

"She's going to kill you," Nikki says, leaning against the frame.

"You'd like that wouldn't you?"

"No."

"Because you want to do it yourself?"

Nikki says nothing.

"She has a point," Ally says. She lays her laptop on the sofa and stands.

"Which is what?"

"Rachel's angel could be telling her to kill you. You told me once that Gabriel—"

"Al!" I exclaim. "Are we really going to do that here?" I jab a hand at Nikki. "In front of *her*?"

Ally presses her lips together. "Regardless of why she's been doing it, the fact remains that Rachel has been sneaking around, and because of that, we've been detected. It's careless."

Careless. Reckless. I've noticed the uptick in these two words lately. Why does everyone think Rachel and I are acting so unhinged? I think I'm holding it together pretty well, actually.

Why did she sneak out? My mind races with the possibilities. Maybe she did want to talk to her angel. I get a little antsy when I feel like I should talk to Gabriel, but can't. Or maybe this has to do with Brinkley, our dead handler. Before he died, he asked Rachel to escape the asylum and team up with me against Caldwell. Maybe that isn't the only thing he asked her to do. Maybe she's on some secret mission he tasked her with. Who knows! I'm not going to let this soldier Barbie come in here and try to convince me that one of my oldest and closest friends is secretly plotting to cut my head off.

Ally steps closer to me and takes my hand. She lowers her voice. "Jess, you told me once that Gabriel wants you to kill Rachel, right? These angels—whoever or whatever they are—they seem pretty determined that only one of you will survive. Coupled with the fact that Rachel lost her mind once already—"

"You can't hold that against her." I swallow, trying to check my anger. I don't want to lash out at Ally, especially not in front of Nikki. But I also don't want to listen to either of them questioning Rachel's loyalty. She wouldn't betray me. She *wouldn't*. "If anyone is a murderer it's me. As far as I know, Rachel has never killed anyone. What about me? How much blood is on my hands?"

Ally's eyes fall to the floor. She gives my hands a gentle squeeze and then she lets go.

Probably because what I'm saying is absolutely true. More people have died at my hands than Rachel's. I killed Eddie, my stepfather. Granted, that bastard deserved it. I killed three of Jeremiah's men in a firebomb. Okay, that was accidental but still my fault, and the alley firebomb brings my total to twelve people.

Thirteen if we count Eve's little girl who got killed by Caldwell's goons because I escaped. Fourteen if we count the boy who raised his gun at me in the old abandoned house the night Brinkley died. He was about to blow my brains out but Gabriel whipped out my firebomb power and saved the day. And Brinkley...

My heart feels like someone is squeezing it.

A flash of Rachel, naked and bloody in the living room, floods my memory. She stood there, looking like a creature who'd crawled out of hell, clutching a knife. Bloody finger-prints smeared across her dark cheek, drying like the circle crusted into the carpet at her feet. That was when she charged me. Brinkley came to the rescue that time.

No.

That was different. I understand why Rachel lost it so long ago. The whole angel power thing, it's overwhelming and we didn't know what the hell it was. She can't be blamed for that.

"I'm the monster, not her," I insist. "I even got you killed."

Ally wraps her arms around me and Nikki's gaze slides away. She looks suddenly very interested in the recently abused houseplant.

She looks me in the eyes. "You're not a monster."

Gabriel appears in the corner of the room, surveying us. I look at him, but say nothing. Both Nikki and Ally follow my gaze, but if they want to ask the question I never get tired of hearing—*are you seeing him now?*—at least they don't.

Is she betraying me? I ask him without saying it aloud.

He doesn't answer.

Is she going to show up and stab me in the back? She couldn't manage it the first time.

"She isn't as strong as you." He doesn't have to speak directly into my mind since no one can hear him.

"She's strong," I hiss.

"Which is why you should consider her a threat," Nikki says. Ally says nothing because unlike Nikki, she noticed that I'm yelling at the corner like a big weirdo and not actually talking to anyone in the room.

"Rachel wouldn't hurt me." And I really believe this to be true. Not Rachel. Not my sassy mentor who was so good to me those first years after I learned what I was. She taught me all about my condition, about death-replacing, but more importantly, about how to stomach a shitty past.

Something fucked up happened to you, she's said one night. We were sitting in the floor of our apartment, crossed legged and shoveling takeout into our mouths.

I'd shrugged. *Fucked up things happen to everyone.*

She'd arched an eyebrow at that and had given a little nod of her head. "True enough, but you're still carrying it around."

"No I'm not."

She looked me up and down. "Oh, it's written all over you. It's like you've got this suitcase, blood seeping from its seams, and you're dragging it around everywhere. Leaking all over the place."

"No comprendo," I said, dodging her insinuations, though I understood exactly what she meant. Killing Eddie was too fresh in my mind.

"Listen carefully Jessup."

God how I'd loved that nickname. Not at first. It sounded too much like ketchup and therefore was vaguely insulting, but after about a month, it'd grown on me.

"A shitty past is like a leech. It'll follow you around. It'll suck all the life out of you unless you cut that thing off. Cut it off or you'll never get the chance to be happy again."

"What would you know about shitty pasts?" I'd asked her. I was reeling from the shame and anger at the impossible task she'd given me. How the hell was I going to forget that I'd killed someone? How the hell was I going to "cut off" all the horrible things that Eddie had done to me?

It was her face that'd given me hope. She'd put her take out box down and looked out the window. The St. Louis skyline stretched before us. The river glimmering and copper-colored in the sunset.

"I know," she said. And it was the look in her face that struck me. I didn't dare ask another question. Because I had a clear feeling that whatever horrible thing had happened to her was maybe even worse than the horrible things that had happened to me. "You can get past it, Jessup."

And I was able to put mine behind me. My father's abandonment. Eddie's pervert bullshit. My mother's rejection. Rachel helped me push through it all. For the most part anyway.

Cut it off, Jessup. Or it'll kill you.

"She wouldn't betray me." The present moment comes into sharp focus around me. Ally, still holding on to me, searches my face. "You don't know her like I do."

Nikki meets my gaze at last, eyebrow arched. "You better hope you're right about that."

CHAPTER ELEVEN

Rachel

I wake up on a park bench. Still wearing these god awful potato sacks for clothes, I look like I should be here. My head throbs and my fingertips are frozen. It hurts even to bend them. I open and close my fists hoping to improve circulation.

Several crows walk along the pale dead grass a few feet away from my bench, searching for food. Every few steps, one pecks the ground half-heartedly. A man in a long tan coat, one arm wrapped around himself, smokes a cigarette like it might be his last, blowing his smoke straight up into the sky. I haven't seen anyone relish anything so whole-heartedly since Jessup went to town on an éclair from a delicatessen a couple of weeks ago.

I reach up and feel the scarf around my face. Why would they take Gideon but leave me bundled on a park bench? They must not be with Caldwell—and yet, they knew about my power and they used the tranquilizer dart on me. Caldwell used similar darts on Jesse before. Or perhaps that's a ridiculous conjecture. Maybe every jerk gets a box of sedation darts in their Asshole-of-the-Day starter kit.

My head is clouded. It's like my hangover came back with a vengeance. My whole body aches as I push myself up off of the bench and onto my feet. I start walking, my head clearing with every step.

At first I wander toward the hotel. The bench where I was dumped is surprisingly close to the giant Art Deco building. I guess they couldn't be bothered moving me far.

As I stand in the adjacent park, trying to decide if I should return to the hotel, or proceed with the plan, my decision is made for me.

The hotel is swarming with uniformed officers filing in and out of the lobby like honeybee drones. The alleyways on both sides of the building are completely taped off and cars are turned at an angle, working as barricades.

There is no way I'm going in.

I don't see Jessup, Alz, or the kid. If they were taken into custody, I don't know where they'd hold them. If they got away, they'll be on their way to Gloria.

And that is bad for a whole other reason. What has she seen about me so far? Of my schemes and intentions? It's probably best to move quickly and execute the plan. Jessup is a big girl. She can take care of herself.

I turn and creep away from the hotel. I walk for a long time before I recognize Centre Street. I'm careful to match the frantic pace around me. Another New Yorker here, rushing off to do some important errand, eat a slice of pizza, or sleep with someone's husband. You know. New York things.

I rehearse my murder plan. I imagine being attacked, my possible defense moves. I wish I had Jesse's fancy shield. It compliments my telekinesis perfectly.

Kill her and you'll have her shield and so much more, a sweet voice says. It slides down my neck like a caress. The small hairs covering my body stand on end.

Shut up, Uriel. I cut my eyes to the angel beside me. It's the first time he's chosen to fully materialize today. He's about twice my size, at least, with his chest puffed up and hair flowing around his head like a lion's mane. A gold belt cinches his waist as he takes one monstrous step after another beside me. I tell him all the time that he looks like Lion-O from the Saturday morning Thundercats cartoon I loved as a child. He never appreciates this.

"You're wasting too much time."

"You're not the boss of me." My voice is muffled by the scarf. "You're *my* bitch."

A Chinese man carrying a brown sack of vegetables stops at the sound of my voice and then gives me the finger.

"Smite him," Uriel says.

"No. No smiting. This one doesn't concern us." I use Uriel's proud tone in jest. I'm still looking at the Chinese man who shakes his head and scurries away from me.

"You need to kill the girl soon. You're wasting too much time."

"Sorry I got sedated and wasted the morning. How pathetic of me."

I know better than to argue with Uriel Lion-O. He's been relentless ever since I caught up to Jesse. Kill her, take her power. Confront Caldwell. Kill him. It's like he's a Dalek or something. *Exterminate! Exterminate!* If only he could be more like The Doctor. Charming. Lovable. Resourceful. My mission would be much more pleasant. But this isn't a television show I watched reruns of in the asylum while eating copious amounts of banana pudding.

Uriel scowls at me again. That's the problem with telepathy. A bitch can't have a few hateful thoughts for herself.

"Do you know where they took Gideon or not?"

"He told you to go on without him."

He did say that, standing inside the hallway outside the apartment door on 72nd street. *Now whatever happens, don't fret your pretty head over me.*

Then who will save you? I'd asked.

There won't be a need to save me. Besides, haven't you got your own schemes?

That's certainly true. I have plans. But the run-in with the men in the suits has me questioning my next move. If they let me go then they must not want me. But that doesn't eliminate Caldwell as a threat. Or another partis for that matter. It might be best to enact my plans with Gideon's help, but what to do about Gloria? If Gloria sees my schemes beforehand, she'll most certainly warn Jesse.

"You do not need his help to kill her," Uriel says.

"Thank you for your vote of confidence." I burrow deeper into my coat to escape the biting chill. The farther I walk, the less groggy I feel. Hopefully the dart will wear off entirely soon.

Stepping off of Centre Street and hooking a left onto Grand, I hurry past the open shop windows with the smell of pancakes and fried foods hanging in the air. A television flashing the news catches my eye, causing me to stop in front of an electronics store window. The newscast from the night before plays again: Caldwell's wet cheeks, Georgia desolated, and then the four faces I know so well flashing up on the screen one after another.

I search Jesse's flat eyes. Face twice removed—once by a photograph, again by the television—

doesn't look anything like the funny but broken girl I met so long ago. They've taken the representation of such a lively girl and simplified, dehumanized her. It isn't a person they are hunting, but an idea. A concept. Simply another monster. And that is what I have to do if I hope to succeed in my plan.

She's not a person, I think. *It's not murder. It's only a task that has to be done.*

"Yes. There's no time to waste," Uriel says.

"I can do what needs to be done," I murmur to the glass, my breath warm behind the scarf and one finger on Jesse Sullivan's cheek.

CHAPTER TWELVE

Jesse

"*T*ry not to jump out of this plane." Nikki's gaze is cold.

I'm a grown ass woman! I'll jump out of whatever I want! A car. A plane. A cake—ah, so much smartassery to choose from and so little time.

Instead, I watch Maisie climb the metal steps and suck in a breath. "It was a helicopter actually." One withering look from Ally and I tone it down even more. "No one likes a hater, Sasquatch."

Now that she mentions it, it's hard not to recall the last time I was airborne. We were in Chicago, and the city was in absolute chaos from the bombs Caldwell had set off. Smoke rose through the sky while we stood helpless on the Lake Michigan beach watching the panic swell around us. Then Gideon showed up with a helicopter and got us off the ground.

"Actually," I turn back toward Nikki. "We jumped out of that helicopter because Gloria wouldn't land and Al insisted that we go down and check on you. She saw your collapsed building and thought you might be dead."

As if I could get so lucky.

Nikki's face softens and Ally blushes.

"Not just you," I'm quick to add. "All your people."

"I don't want you to endanger yourself," Nikki says to her. "Not even for my sake."

"I'll make sure she won't," I grumble.

I'm about to vomit on myself. To quell the nausea, I march up metal stairs extending from the plane. The airfield is quiet. A white, snowy gloom coats the sky despite the high noon. It looks so peaceful even if it is freezing. I glance back to see Nikki helping Ally over the especially high first step onto the stairs. Their hands brush and they flash awkward smiles.

That's it. I'm going to have to murder her. She's not leaving me with much of a choice here. I should set her hair on fire and be done with it. But with my luck, Ally will be all like oh no, poor baby! Your head was on fire. Let me kiss it better.

I suck in deep breaths trying to pull myself together. I need to take my own advice and keep my hate-feels under control. Flames plus a metal fuel-filled death trap is a stupid combination, even to me.

The wobbly metal stairs terminate at the entrance to the plane's small cabin. Once I duck inside, I see four armed guards are sitting in the back of the plane, their face shields down and guns across their chests. This must be what the president feels like when he flies.

Ally places a hand on my shoulder. "Everything okay?"

"I'm not sure all this is necessary." I gesture at the soldiers. I don't know if they're men or women. Their postures are exactly the same, their bodies taunt and unmoving.

"It's a precaution," Nikki says.

"They can't do anything with those little guns that I can't

do with these." I flex both my arms. I waggle my eyebrows at Ally. "Get it. Guns?"

She humors me with a weak smile. "Yes, baby. Now put those away."

"Actually, it's for our protection against you."

I frown at Nick. "I am well aware that I haven't ever hurt you. *Super* aware." As in, I've counted every time that I wanted to but didn't because you know, reasons. Forty-three, including the most recent episode on the steps.

Nikki turns her back on me and marches toward the cockpit One of the soldiers moves and it's like seeing a statue come to life. He waits for the stairs to be pulled away from the plane before he snaps the door into place. He flips the handle up, sealing the door. The cabin warms instantly, cut off from the winter raging outside.

Nikki comes back from the cockpit. "He says we'll arrive in three hours."

"Cool." Maisie shoves her bags into the overhead bin and plops into a seat near the front. She pats the seat beside her and Winston jumps up. "Let's take naps, Winnie Pug. Do you love naps?"

Winston wags his cinnamon bun tail. She rewards his adoring stare with a scratch behind the ears.

"Yeah me too. I'm beat." Ally plops into one of four seats facing each other.

I take the seat beside her and Nikki takes the one opposite, against the window. Everyone buckles their seat belt but me, until I'm forced to or endure Ally's relentless stare. I sigh and snap the metal buckle into place with a *click*. The plane begins its taxi, the airfield narrow beyond the slender windows. I glimpse muddy patches of earth here, white sky there. Otherwise, not much. I give up on the view and settle back into my seat. I try to remain calm, breathing slowly in and out of my nose while the plane rattles and shakes on the runway. We'll probably be fine, right? Caldwell seems to have lost track of us. I take zero comfort from the idea that he can't materialize on a moving plane. He materialized on a moving helicopter just fine. Lovely prospect. Forty thousand feet high and in a firefight with Caldwell? Nah. Nothing could possibly go wrong there.

"You're breathing hard," Nikki says, her face stoic.

"Just thinking about flaming fiery deaths. Got any gum?"

Her brow furrows.

"For my ears. They're popping like crazy."

"Sorry."

It takes no time at all for all three of them to pass out. Maisie sleeps with her mouth open slightly, head propped back against her seat. Winston snores with the ferocity of a dragon. Ally is the only one who looks angelic. Her cheek is smooshed against the back of her hands, which are pressed palm to palm as if in prayer against the window. She looks so sweet when she sleeps. Blond strands of hair cling to her cheek. Her lashes are long and dark.

And I'm not the only one staring.

Nikki and I exchange a glance.

"Do you always watch people sleep?" I ask.

She doesn't say anything. She doesn't even manage an apologetic shrug, but to be fair, maybe that's not possible in all her body armor. She looks ridiculous sitting there in all that. Like a big black beetle on its back.

"It's pretty creepy." I fidget in my seat. My shoulder has been a little tender since I woke up. Despite my awesome healing abilities, apparently it doesn't make me impervious to pain. Bummer. Jason acted like he didn't feel a thing all the times we tried to kill him. Maybe he was that crazy.

"I miss her." Nikki's face is unreadable, perfectly smooth, but her voice is tender.

I open my mouth and she tenses. Wow. I must have a

strong track record of dickery then, if just by opening my mouth, someone expects the worst.

I close my mouth and huff.

"That's it? No smart ass retort?"

I shrug. "It's no fun kicking someone who's already down."

Nikki scowls. "I don't need your pity."

"You don't have it. Don't worry."

Nikki's brow furrows. She searches my face as if looking for the trick.

I shrug again. "I didn't like it when she was with you. I'm sure you don't like it that she's with me."

Wow. I feel so magnanimous! Of course, it feels delicious to say she's with me, but the other parts are actually meant to be nice. Where's my cookie?

Nikki turns toward the window. "She's with you."

I swallow the *duh* that comes to mind, a replica of the one that Maisie loves to throw around. I also don't say *she's always been mine, really*.

"I hope she's happy." Nikki's eyes are vicious. It's a taunt. Like if she isn't happy it's my fault and she's going to rip off my arm for it.

"It's not like I go around deliberately making her *un*happy. For your information, I didn't force her to be my girlfriend. In fact, I never even told her to be my girlfriend. We—" my voice trails off. We *what* exactly? I wasn't even sure how to finish that sentence. We get hot and heavy? We pushed the beds together and—

"You—" Nikki stops herself. "Don't answer that. I don't want to know."

"We—"

"Seriously, shut your mouth."

"Can you please not talk about *that* while I'm sitting right here?" Ally's voice is dry with her anger.

I start. "I thought you were asleep."

God, what a dumb thing for me to say.

"How can I sleep with all of your yammering?" Ally stands up and storms off toward the bathroom at the back of the plane.

"She started it!" I cry but it's too late. She gives me the most annoyed look before slamming the bathroom door shut.

Nikki looks out the window.

I fold my arms and slump against my seat. "That's what I get for being nice to you."

"You don't have to be nice to me," Nikki says.

I force an exaggerated sigh. "Really? Whew! Thank god. What a relief. I'll have so much more energy now."

Nikki grins and I'm not stupid enough to think it's because of my charming humor. "Do you know why you shouldn't bother being nice to me, Sullivan?"

"Because you can't be bothered to say people's whole names?"

"Because she'll be mine eventually."

"Like hell!" I feel the air thicken around me, powering up with my electric charge.

"Think about it," Nikki says leaning forward in her seat. "As I understand it, one of two things are going to happen. You're going to be murdered by one of the partis or you'll survive long enough to be the apex, only to die saving the world. Do I have the story straight?"

My face burns. "What's your point?"

Nikki leans back in her seat and laces her fingers over her lap. "Who do you think is going to be here to pick up the pieces when you're gone?"

CHAPTER THIRTEEN

Rachel

The New York Public Library stands like a Grecian temple on the right side of the street, its washed out columns held aloft by six coquettish women draped in sheets. The building is beautiful. Old European Style. Like it's been here for centuries. And maybe it has.

Outside the building a surprisingly large cluster of people populates the steps, despite the frigid temperature. Some sit at black tables with their books open before them. One man in fingerless gloves tosses breadcrumbs from a plastic baggie. The pigeons flock at his feet, covering the stone walk with their shuffling gray bodies. Two majestic stone lions survey Fifth Ave with an air of superior indifference.

It's open and free of charge. That's a plus. Along with the obvious chance to get warm. Also, if I leave the scarf on, it won't seem weird right away. Onlookers might think I'm simply popping in to grab a book before rushing out to catch the subway again.

Even better, the library has the internet. I can try to contact Gideon and let him know I'm still in the city, and that I intend to execute my plan within the hour.

I'll say something short and sweet: *She's coming. We're meeting in the study rooms.*

He might not be able to respond right away, if he's tied up —literally or figuratively—but I don't believe anyone can hold that boy for long.

I trot up the stairs toward the gilded door, passing two advertisement banners for cultural events happening later this month and a temporary exhibit at the art museum across town. I manage not to look directly at the cameras, mounted clearly on the poles. I could use my power, twist the dilated electronic eyes away from me, but Gideon warned against that indulgence if it isn't absolutely necessary.

You are in the big leagues now, poppet. Anyone with an ounce of brains will look for consistent abnormalities. Oddities. Signals that you're in the city. Consider using your power like signing your name. The less you sign, the less likely they'll trace you. Be smart, love.

God, sometimes he could be an awful lot like Brinkley. His pedantic tendency to instruct, the caring under his orders. It makes my chest hurt to think about it. B's influence on the boy is plain. If I squeeze my eyes tight and forget the British accent, it's like Brinkley is still here, looking out for me.

I never left you, kid.

My chest compresses tighter. Brinkley couldn't do what needed to be done, and look where it got him. I won't be making the same mistake. I'll do the hard work and I'll have my revenge. The sensation of Chaplain's fingers brushing my cheek makes me cringe.

It's only a memory, and memories can't hurt you. Oh, if only that were true.

I slip inside the library behind a trio of teenage girls. At the information desk, I fork left, past desks offering maps of the place and tour times. I slip into the nearest room and then slide down a row of stacks. I pretend to peruse the spines with great interest until my fingers tingle back to life.

This gallery is far from empty. People amble in and out of the stacks. Others sit at tables with piles of books so high they threaten to topple over at the smallest bump.

I grab a book at random. Then another and another, until I have three in my arms. Once I've skimmed this gallery, I slip into another massive room, searching for the study nooks where I agreed to meet her.

An empty research room beckons. I slip inside and close the door. So small. So warm. So quiet. Heaven. I pull off my scarf and coat, and beg the heat to soak into my body. I want my bones to soften like warm butter. I plop down into the chair. Relief washes over me the second my feet are off the floor. So much walking! How do New Yorkers stand it? I place all but one of the books in a tidy pile. Then I open the last, the spine so broken it lays flat on the desk without resistance. Now the scene is set for any nosey passersby.

Uriel, in all his Lion-O glory, appears beside me. The small space of the study room barely enough to accommodate him. He towers over me, his flaming hair aglow.

"She is coming. Don't waste this opportunity."

"I'm sorry," I say, biting down on my irritation. "But I'm not in the mood to be slicing and dicing a girl in a study room today. Wouldn't you rather I pick somewhere safer? I will die, you know. And when I do, I'll need a safe place to recoup. I'm hoping I can get her to take me back to her place. Without Gideon, it should be easier to do."

Uriel makes no protests to this.

My wait in the New York Public Library stretches into a small eternity, and I begin to feel restless. I consider shoving things around the room with my mind, but I have doubts that even that will satiate my boredom. No, not boredom. Anticipation. She's on her way and I'm *nervous*.

A soft knock resounds at the door. I look to Uriel, but he is gone.

"Rach?" A soft voice murmurs. "Are you in there?"

I stand and push open the study room door. Nivedha gives me a weak smile of relief.

She's as petite as I remember, even tinier than Jessup. I could wrap my entire hand around her wrist and my fingers would overlap. Her skin is the color of cinnamon bark and her hair black. Her hazel eyes look brighter because of her coloring. She's bustier than I remember, but not from implants. Our NRD+ bodies would reject those. Perhaps she is one of those women who benefit from gaining a bit of weight. She is healthier than she was when I saw her last. Her face and hips are rounder. There's a light in her eyes now that I never saw in Chaplain's basement.

I remember the first night Chaplain took her. Each evening we were fed from a metal dish on the floor like dogs. Then we were taken one by one, doused in hot water, scrubbed, and given a thin shift to wear. You would think they'd rape us at every step, but they didn't. Chaplain said he wanted the terror to be real each time. Real for the camera. No desensitization.

She was terrified out of her mind, sitting on the floor, having been freshly scrubbed and re-shackled like the rest of us. A bar ran along the four walls and the girls waited in the pitch black room. As uncomfortable as it was to sit on the concrete floor with a thin nightgown on, it was preferable to the alternative. An aching, bloodless arm was unmeasurably better than being chosen for Chaplain's nightly film.

The door opened and a triangle of light fell on us. It was a mixed blessing. In the light, the quiet crying stopped. In the light, the consuming, obsessive, repetitive thoughts would cease if only for a moment. Of course, the light also meant the monsters had come.

Instinctively, each one of us shrank away from the light. Even I tried to tuck myself deeper into the corner as far away as the wall would allow. The girl beside me convulsed horribly. I didn't know if it was from fear, or if the drugs had worn off. She'd caused a scene earlier and Chaplain had one protocol for that. Act a fool and you were dosed into submission. Behave and you'd stay clean.

I preferred the latter.

That night when the guard and Chaplain entered the room, they took Niv. She'd thrashed, screamed, begged.

"This is no way to behave. You're a professional, Nivedha," Chaplain purred. He used the sultry voice that lured us into the trap to begin with.

"Let me go. Please. I won't tell anyone what you're doing here. I swear. I won't say a word to anyone. Just let me go."

"You can't think only of yourself," he purred, trailing his fingers over her wet cheeks. "We have half a million subscribers to satisfy."

They'd grabbed her by the hair and drug her kicking and screaming from the room. No drugs. That was always a very, very bad sign. It meant a particularly gruesome film where full-blown hysterics were not only welcome but expected.

I blink back the past and try to focus on the creature in front of me. She's speaking.

"—already apologized to two strangers," she says. She looks me up and down. "What are you wearing?"

"Whatever the hell I want," I snap. My $2300 Versace dress would've been a significant confidence booster for the task ahead. No one told me I'd have to murder someone wearing a potato sack! But I'm not sure it can be helped. I must remain steadfast in my aim.

"I'm in disguise, Niv. I told you."

Niv's stricken face softens, but not entirely. I've lost some ground. "At least it's not white. I can't ever wear white."

That made two of us. Anything in the white or cream family reminded me too much of the *uniforms* Chaplain gave us.

"I'm hoping we can go somewhere safe where we can talk?" I prompt her.

Nivedha nods. "Sure. If you think it is safe to walk on the streets. Your face is all over the news."

"We won't be seen," I tell her, wrapping the scarf around my head. "Don't worry about that."

Bundled up, I follow Nivedha out of the library and into the street. Thankfully, she'd chosen a meetup near her apartment, and we wouldn't have to get on the subway again. We walk seven city blocks in relative silence. Nivedha keeps looking around, probably half-expecting someone to leap out and start attacking us as they would in an action movie. I know better. They never kill you in the open. They kill you the moment you're behind doors.

At least that's what I intend to do.

"This is me," Niv says to me before turning to greet the doorman. We cross the lobby of a very nice apartment building. Her red-bottom heels click across the marble floors toward a man who holds the elevator open for her. The elevator man gives me a disgusted look after a once-over at my current attire. I resist the urge to pick him up and hurl him across the room. But my eyes never leave his face as he leans in and presses the number eight button on the panel inside the elevator.

"Have a good day, Miss Nivedha."

"You too Duncan," Nivedha flirts.

I don't speak until the elevator doors close. "Sorry I'm underdressed."

She smiles. "It's nice actually. To see you a little less beautiful than usual."

"Chaplain had good taste in women."

Her face blanches and she says nothing.

When we step off the elevator we are greeted by a miniature foyer. More marble and an ornate door serve as the centerpiece. Two large plants stand erect on either side of a door marked "8".

Nivedha twists a key in a lock, and I hear a television for the first time. My heart lurches. It didn't occur to me that anyone else would be here.

But when we cross the threshold into the living quarters and slip down a hallway past a mahogany desk and a gilded mirror, I see that the large living space complete with New York view is empty. The television is playing for no one.

"Where's your man?" I ask casually.

"Oh he isn't here," she says, stopping between the rectangular glass coffee table and the long white sofa with rolled arms. On the coffee table rests a stone Buddha holding a remote. "He won't be home until late. We won't be disturbed."

"Good," I say with a wicked smile. "It's easier if we aren't disturbed. But first things first: do you have a dress I can borrow?"

Nivedha frowns, looking me up and down. "I don't think I have anything in your size."

The urge to snap my fingers and twist her head is overwhelming. I take a deep breath. "You're right. Who has time to talk about dresses? We should get right to business." Because I'm going to kill you and take that damn dress off your dead body if I have to.

"Yeah, okay." Nivedha's face darkens with her misery. She plops down on the couch as if all her strength has left her. Pulling a mauve throw pillow into her lap, she cradles it against her body.

She turns her brown eyes up to meet mine and again I see the girl from long ago, curled into a ball beside me, sobbing uncontrollably. I had reached out and placed one hand on her hair. It was crusted with her blood and would remain so until we were taken one by one, scrubbed, and dressed again.

She prayed in a language I didn't understand, but I knew prayers when I heard them. It's begging all the same.

"Shhh," I said and ran a hand down her back, my knuckles trailing over her spine. "Shhhhh."

My consolations were pathetic.

"My name's Rachel." It was the first time I'd spoken to anyone in eighteen days. "What's your name?"

"Nivedha Parvarti. Or I was, but I've died and woken up and this is hell. Surely this is hell!"

Boy, had she been right about that.

Niv opens her palms. Light swirls in the center of each, growing brighter until her entire hands are eclipsed by it. Her wrists and forearms making a torch for the strange luminescence. She holds them up for me to see, gazing into my face with such despair. Then she says the exact same words she said to me so long ago.

"Rachel, what's happening to me?"

CHAPTER FOURTEEN

Jesse

When you're gone...when you're gone...when...

Every time I replay Nikki's words in my head, it's accompanied by a slew of violent urges. I want to slap the spit out of her mouth for starters. Then I want to burn her hair off. Her hair and eyebrows, and then maybe break her fingers one at a time until—I'm *gone*.

The hate abates and what I'm left with is...what? Shock? I can't wrap my head around the idea of *gone*. Dead. Like *dead* dead. What does that even mean?

Is it because I've died and resurrected over a hundred times that I just can't comprehend what dead means? Brinkley died. And now he's *gone*. I can't call him. I can't talk to him. I can't see his face. And when I'm *gone,* what? Where will I go? What the hell will I be doing with my sudden abundance of free time?

When I die now, I'm with Gabriel. It's like dreaming. We talk. He shows me things like ethereal landscapes. Scenarios. Before Gabriel came around I saw nothing. I died. Then I woke up to find myself somewhere else. Like a child who has fallen asleep in the car, ignorant of the ongoing journey, only to wake up in a familiar bed later, cocooned by pillows and sheets and covers with a familiar smell to them.

Or maybe I will cease to exist at all. I'll be nothing. Nowhere. Or worse, utterly alone.

Never alone. I will never leave you. Gabriel's whispered words blow like a breeze through my mind.

I suck in a breath and keep walking.

At the bottom of the steps, Gloria waits for us. I flash her a weak smile, letting her know I'm happy to see her again after so many months apart, but mostly I'm still lost in my own thoughts. She hugs each of us in turn: me, Ally, and the Maisie-Winston combo. It's nice that she met us at the airport and I'm relieved that she doesn't look stressed or exhausted. She's prone to overworking after all. And without Ally around to harass her into taking a break, I'm sure she worked around the clock and lived off of Coca-Cola and fast food.

Gloria leads us off the airfield, away from the plane and toward a beat up station wagon with wooden siding at the edge of the lot.

"Are you okay?" Ally asks, placing a hand on my arm. The urge to jerk away from her is strong but I squash that down. *You'll just run back to her* that vicious little voice in my head says. *She's so right about that. You won't even mourn me at all.*

"I'm fine. Just hungry."

I see the beach house in my mind. The sable sand. The warm breeze. The gentle gray waves lapping at the shore. Ally standing on the back deck, shielding her eyes from the sun.

It was a dream or a vision. Gabriel presented this paradise as one of my choices—*as apex you create the world. What is your heart's desire?*

And while I did see paradise there once—me and Ally together and happy—I also saw an alternative future. Ally and Nikki with kids. Happy. Sure, she'd named her firstborn after me. But it remained that in this version of the future I was dead and Nikki had won. Why show me a world where Nikki and Ally were happy together? Does Gabriel think I'm capable of some magnanimous decision where I do what is best for Ally? If that was his goal, he doesn't know me at all.

And yet, I can't help but assume that "taking Ally to the beach house" is code for killing her. Maybe not with my own hands, but there's only one way that I know of where Ally and I end up in the same place and I happen to be dead. Unless I'm dead and it's only her memory that I take with me, while Ally really is alive and happy.

A crushing wave of sadness overcomes me. Hell, no I won't let Ally die. Even if she ends up with the twat with the orange hair and has a thousand babies. I would never—could never.

"Seriously, Jess, are you okay?" Ally stops me in the middle of the parking lot, a few feet from Gloria's car. She lowers her voice. "You look like you're about to cry."

"I'm just so hungry," I lie and tears start to flow down my cheeks. "I would kill someone for a pizza right now."

Ally frowns, tilts her head slightly to one side but says nothing to contradict me.

"Come on. All I've had today is a cheese and mayonnaise sandwich," I insist and give Sasquatch the side eye. "Haven't you been so hungry you could kill someone?"

"Totally," Maisie says without missing a beat. "I could've chased a pig down, tackled it and chewed on its bacon-y butt."

Despite Maisie's help, I don't think Ally believes my pathetic lie for a second, but thank god she doesn't demand I share my thoughts here in front of Sasquatch and everyone. Especially since now everyone is staring at me—Gloria, Nikki, and the other partis named Monroe included. At least

Monroe has the decency to let his gaze slide away, climbing into the passenger seat without so much as a lingering smile.

"Come on then," Ally says, yanking open the door to the backseat. "Let's get you something to eat."

The only consolation is that Sasquatch and her team have to ride separately. Despite the boat size car Gloria is driving, it barely holds the six of us: Gloria, Monroe, Maisie, Ally, Winston, and me. The seats are leather, but battered. My seat in particular has a huge strip of duct tape over a puncture where something sliced through the material. And the car has a faint odor of cigarettes. I realize why when Monroe rolls down the window and pulls a hand-rolled cigarette from his pocket.

He catches me staring and raises the wrapped tobacco in salute. "Them store-bought kind is too damn expensive these days. I've got to roll my own."

"You're going to get cancer," Maisie says.

Monroe laughs, a languid sound. "Oh I wish. I wish, Miss Maisie. But I ain't been able to find the thing that'll kill me yet."

Suicidal. *They chose us because we wanted to die.* Caldwell's words echo through my memory. It might be true that all the partis wanted to die at one time or another, but now I don't want to die at all. Now I want to save the world and keep the girl.

As Gloria drives us out of airfield and into the Louisiana bayou, the trees thicken and the Spanish moss spreads over everything like cobwebs in an old abandoned house.

"We've made a lot of progress," Gloria says, flicking her eyes up to meet mine in the rearview. "And we will still make it to Arizona in time."

"In time to murder my father," Maisie quips, her gaze turning away from us toward the window. I know she's pretending to search the thick foliage for animals or anything of interest. Winston nudges her hand for an ear scratch and she sluggishly returns his attention. Offended, he gives up on her and hops into my lap. I'm extra generous with the love.

"That's wonderful that you've made progress," Ally says to Gloria from her place sandwiched between me and Maisie. Her gaze goes from my face to Maisie's to Monroe's. "We need some good news around here. Something to raise our spirits."

Monroe gives another bemused, languid laugh. "Only the Lord can help us now."

"Everyone needs to calm down," I say, frowning at one grumpy face after another. "We are way too happy in here."

The rest of the ride into the city is quiet. The dense bayou gives way to a freeway, which gives way to cramped city streets. The outskirts of town are still derelict from the hurricane, but the closer we move toward the city center, towards tourism, the sights improve. I'm sure that's no accident. Gloria maneuvers her boat car around a horse and buggy carrying a bride and groom and into a parking garage.

From here, we are out and walking again. On the street, the cobblestones feel uneven underfoot. We march beneath iron banisters and balconies. A woman on a balcony drinks a glass of wine and blows me a kiss.

I blush. "The people here seem very friendly."

"Welcome to N'awlins," Monroe says, his slow and steady walk matching his laugh. "The Big Easy. Southern hospitality."

Whatever he was about to say next is drowned out by a girl with a violin. She sways on the street outside the door of a restaurant, her case open at her feet. She looks like some kind of rag-ma-tag gypsy in layers of cotton, her hair half hidden under a bandana. She's whiter than me, so I know she's probably not Romany or anything, but she's working the look. Maisie throws a crumpled up dollar into her case.

"Our place is just up here," Monroe says.

"Our place?" I ask Gloria with a smile. Has she been shacking up with this dude? I'm about to verbalize my approval of her living la vida loca when Gloria shoots me the most menacing look. I'm pretty sure that smoke puffs from her nostrils and her eyes burn red.

I snap my mouth shut.

Ally makes a small sound of surprise.

"What?" I turn away from Gloria and the bustle of the French Quarter, past little cramped shops lining the walkway and partiers stumbling about with drinks in hand. I check the time on my pug wristwatch and see that it's only about four. So the party starts early in New Orleans.

"Oh," Ally says, her eyebrows shooting up. She continues to scroll down her screen. "*Oh*."

"*What?*"

Ally's lips flatten into a thin line as she slips her hands into her pocket. "I got an interesting email. That's all."

I blink at her, waving for her to go on.

"I think I know why we were in New York," she says, glancing around the street. Her eyes pause on a tarot reader encased in a glass shop window, flipping cards over for two young girls who giggle.

"Which is—"

"Tell her later," Gloria says and they share a look between them.

"Yes," Ally nods as if she's read Gloria's mind. "It's probably best to wait."

Monroe stops in front of the gate. He leans over the top of the wrought iron and undoes the latch from in the inside. The gate creaks open, revealing a thin garden path, overrun by plants on each side. "After you ladies."

I marvel at Gloria again, so surprised that she's willing to accept this chivalry from another person, let alone a man! She starts up the garden path without an ounce of complaint. Hell, she wouldn't even let Brinkley clean her gun for her, let alone treat her like a lady.

Leaves brush my face as we walk single-file down the path. Even in the dead of winter, I catch a sweet scent blooming in the misty air.

"Are we in a jungle or a city?" I ask. "I can't tell anymore."

"That'd be the Magnolia and the Camellia japonica, Miss Jesse," Monroe says as the foliage falls away revealing a miniature courtyard and covered porch. "They sure do smell nice, don't they?"

Gloria produces a key and opens this door herself, Monroe not catching up until the last minute. He holds the screen door open for her as she struggles with the lock.

Then we are inside. From the porch, I can only see the stairs leading up and a doorway to the left. Dim light and awkward angles makes it harder to see deeper into the house.

"These apartments used to be slave quarters," Monroe says, in a tone far too chipper for the subject. "These houses were set just behind the main houses back in them days. But now, they is all apartments."

"Does that bother you?" Ally asks, coming into the house and unbuttoning her coat. It is too warm in here for our winter coats. Too warm in all of New Orleans probably. "To be living in a place with such a history."

"No, Miss Alice," Monroe says, lifting his hat to scratch the balding, gray-haired scalp beneath. "This way I know this place was made by good hands. Strong hands. And if I was to be upset by such a thing, I need not live anywhere in the state. There are but a few houses we didn't build in this city."

We, I assume, means black people.

I turn to Gloria, expecting her to continue my education of the city. She says nothing of the sort. "There's a room upstairs for you." She nods toward the stairs. "First door on the right. You can nap if you want, clean up, then we'll have lunch. After that, we need to get to work."

Gloria disappears around a corner, leaving Ally, Maisie and I standing somewhat dazed in the company of Monroe, who is busy twisting another handmade cigarette between his fingers. Monroe looks at the three of us and then laughs to himself. I wish I knew what's so funny about our faces.

"Best do what she says," Monroe advises. "I sure do."

Laughing, he shuffles out of the room as if in pursuit of Gloria.

Winston squirms in Maisie's arms. "I think he needs to potty."

"Yeah, okay." I point at a patch of grass out the window. "Go right there. Where we can see you. Without Gideon's device we can't wander far from each other."

"Oh, poop bags!" Ally says, fishing two green plastic bags from her pocket. "Pick up after him, okay?"

Maisie's shoulders slump. "Where am I supposed to put it?"

"Just tie off the bag and leave it by the bottom step. I'll find the trash."

I can't help but laugh as Maisie slips out with the pug, leaving us alone.

Ally frowns at me. "What's so funny?"

"You, worrying about dog poop when the world is literally coming to an end."

She puts her hands on her hips, her scowl deepening. "We can't stop being considerate of other people just because the world is going to end."

"I'm pretty sure that's exactly what we can do," I say.

Ally does not like this answer and I'm not in a mood to fight with her. "Tell me about the email."

"I got an email from Gideon," Ally says, her face lighting up.

"What? How?"

"Who knows. But he used the safe word I gave him, so I would know any such communication was from him."

"How do we know Caldwell doesn't have him, didn't snatch the safe word from his mind and use it to write you an email?"

Ally takes a deep breath. "Possible, but for the sake of argument, let's pretend it's Gideon and get to the point."

"Fine, fine." I wave her on. "Why were we in New York?"

"Remember when I said Rachel was going out at night alone?"

"Yes."

"She was meeting a friend."

"What friend? We're her only friends."

A strange look crosses over Ally's face. "Do you remember the snuff films Henry Chaplain was making?"

I did. In the months while we planned our retaliation against Caldwell, I read Brinkley's journals. Part memoir, part final instructions, it was sad for a lot of reasons. Mostly because it sounded so much like him, every word like his voice in my mind. And when I'd learned about how Rachel had come into his life, how a crime boss with mind powers was using her to make these horrible films, I was devastated. And when it was Rachel's turn to read the journals and she realized that we all knew what she had been through, I think it changed our relationship. Would I have wanted anyone to read a journal about the fucked up things Eddie had done to me? No.

"There's a girl in New York that Rachel knew from Chaplain's sex ring, or whatever you want to call it." Ally tucks her hair behind her ears. "She was another Necronite that they were killing on camera for the films."

"So they are meeting up to what, remember the good old days?" I ask. "Oh hey, remember when we were raped

and stabbed to death on camera. Fun times, yeah?"
Doubt it.

"It's more than that," Ally says with an arched eyebrow. "Do you remember what Caldwell said about how the partis are chosen? They gravitate toward one another. They tend to be people we know for whatever reason."

It was Liza who'd said that actually, but I don't correct her.

"So this friend is partis? She's the one who got Minli's power?"

"That's what Gideon says," Ally goes on.

"So what? Is Rachel going to invite her to come along for the ride? Join up with us against Caldwell?"

Ally's smile falters. "Not exactly. It seems like they had another plan altogether."

CHAPTER FIFTEEN

Rachel

"I'm partis," Nivedha repeats, her brown eyes searching mine. "But I don't have an angel."

Nivedha stands from the leather sofa and begins to pace in front of the great windows. She wraps both arms around body. She squeezes tight as if trying to hold herself together. The day is dying behind her, the horizon orange, fading to red.

"Because she was not chosen," Uriel says. "No one serves her."

Then why does she even have the power? I ask him.

"So what does it mean?" Nivedha asks again. She stands in front of the big windows. "If I don't have an angel, am I damned?"

"No." I comfort her on reflex. The surge of compassion muddles my mind. *Focus. You have one job here. You've spent weeks reconnecting with this girl, cultivating your connection through shared horrors. Don't get confused now. Remember the mission.*

None of my self-talk is helping. All I can see is Nivedha. Small, shaking with fear as she sits huddled in the floor with a dozen other girls. I can still see the bruises on her throat, the slow healing that came after every death, every attack. The way we would have to lean on one other as we hovered over the toilet, teeth clenched. When they finished with us, everything hurt. Even taking a piss.

"We'll die here," Nivedha had said to me, her hand on my shoulder to steady herself. Her legs trembled violently.

"No," I'd told her, though I didn't believe it.

And here I am lying again.

"No, you're not damned. We're unlucky."

"What am I supposed to do? You're saying this man Caldwell has Chaplain's power. That he wants to kill every one of us. I've seen him on television, and if he's the new Henry, I'd rather die than see what he has in store for me."

Big wet tears fill her eyes. She stops clutching herself and comes to stand in front of me. She's searching my face for answers I don't have.

"Tell me this is different," Nivedha begs. She places her hand on my shoulder, echoing again those long nights in Chaplain's harem. As we would wait in the dark to see who would be taken upstairs, each one praying it wasn't their turn.

"Please," Nivedha says, squeezing my shoulder until it hurts. "Tell me he won't hurt me."

I swallow the thick lump blocking my throat. "I'm so sorry."

"Why me?" she asks and her voice breaks. She steps back from the window. "Why me *again*?"

"I don't know." My voice fails me, cracking around the edges. I need a drink of water, but asking her for one would send her from the room and I need her here. Right here. For what I'm about to do.

"Eliot won't understand," Nivedha says, referring to the owner of the loafers I'd seen by the door, the long suit jacket in the front closet. "He knows I have NRD, but this is different. I'm scaring him. If he throws me out on the street, I don't know where I'll go."

I swallow half a dozen empty promises: *you'll come with me. You'll be safe with us. We won't hurt you. We aren't Caldwell.* Lies. Because the truth is more apparent to me than ever.

I need to be stronger. And I know of only one way to do that.

I take a step toward Nivedha, then another until I'm face to face with her, only inches between us.

"I know you're scared," I say, but it's my voice that's shaking. "But you don't have to worry."

She reaches up and wipes at her eyes with her sleeve, smearing her makeup. "Really? Do you promise?"

I try to breathe around the thunderous pounding in my chest and head. I feel like I'm going to faint. I'm going to stop breathing and fall over.

"You must do this," Uriel says, breaking into my thoughts. "You need the strength. She doesn't want this power."

"You don't want the power," I echo, whispering it, or at least it seems so over the monstrous roar of my thrashing heart.

"No," Nivedha croaks. "I never asked for any of this."

"Do it," Uriel commands.

But I see Nivedha in the white gown crying.

Do it.

Nivedha clinging to my side in the dark.

Do it.

Nivedha's eyes when she first wakes to the pain of living again. Her first words devolving into sobs.

Now!

My hand shoots from my pocket into Nivedha's chest. Her thin gossamer clothes give easily, providing no barrier to speak of. Nivedha's eyes go wide with surprise. She stumbles back with a little "Oh" slipping from her lips between a gasp and a cry. She looks down at the knife protruding from her chest then up into my eyes again.

"You—?"

Sobs erupt from my throat. I fall on her, tearing the knife from her chest. I take her into my arms.

"You—?" she says again.

"I'm here," I say, rocking her. Crying into her hair. "I'm right here."

I can't catch my breath as Nivedha pushes against me, trying to squirm away. I crush her to me tighter, cooing into her hair, kissing the top of her head. She struggles in my arms, but each push is a little weaker than the last until she isn't moving at all.

"Shhh," I say. "You don't have to worry about any of this. Any of it. I'm here. I'm here."

I let go of her only long enough to toss away the remote and lift the stone Buddha from the coffee table. I slam it into Niv's skull. I can't look at what I've done. I feel for the head wound with my fingers inching over her breasts, chin, cheekbones, all while keeping my eyes closed. Inches above her eye I feel the warm, wet wound. The skull feels like the cracked shell of an egg. I push my fingers in deeper until a burst of bright blue fire explodes and consumes me whole.

CHAPTER SIXTEEN

Jesse

Gloria may not have been getting sexy with Monroe after all. It's somewhat implied by the sheer volume of sketches crowding the walls of not one but *two* back rooms of the little house. Who would have the time with all of this drawing going on? I could be wrong, but I'm pretty sure people can't have sex and draw at the same time. I feel like the lines would be jagged at least and the drawings would lack a certain *finesse*.

Also, it seems that Monroe has been sleeping in the upstairs apartment and Gloria has been sleeping down here in the cramped room by the kitchen. Maybe it feels cramped because there are four of us trying to fit into this tiny space. Add the sofa with a pillow and sheet thrown over it. On the pillow lays a battered paperback with the title barely legible on the cover. *The Things They Carried.*

My chest aches as I imagine a scene described in Brinkley's journal. Gloria healing from a gunshot wound in the hospital and Brinkley at her bedside reading to her from this book. I want to pick up the book and ask if this is the same one from so long ago. Ask her if she's really carried it around for twelve years, but Gloria's look stops me. She's braced for my question.

I turn away without touching the book, focusing on the pictures taped to the walls.

"Gloria." I hope my voice is casual as I circle the room. My eyes search one picture then another. "I gave you the sketchbook so you wouldn't do the creepy drawings all over the wall thing."

"Next we'll find a body in a meat locker," Maisie adds. She's in one corner of the room, lifting a page when Gloria slaps the page down.

Maisie makes a sound of surprise. "I was kidding. I know you're way too smart to use anything as obvious as a meat locker. You'd probably dissolve them in acid."

"Don't look at the drawings underneath," Gloria says, without an inch of forgiveness in her voice.

"*Sorry*." Maisie gives me a look and I shrug. How the hell am I supposed to know what Gloria is thinking?

"Gloria is this—accurate?" Ally calls from the other room.

I'm the first to file into the attached sunroom. It's a little cooler in here even with the bright sunshine filtered through the windows. Well, through the few windows not covered by her drawings. Ally is frowning at a sketch on the opposite wall, her hands in her pockets.

I come to stand beside her and gasp. In the drawing, Rachel is mid thrust, a knife about to plunge into the chest of a girl who doesn't look any older than we do.

Maisie leans over my shoulder and I throw my palms over her eyes.

"Hey!" she cries out. "Why is everyone censoring me? I'm practically 17!"

But we only half hear her. In the next image, Rachel is rocking the girl to sleep, or at least cradling her against her body while blood pools around them on the carpet.

"So she did it?" Ally asks, sighing out the words. "This is what Gideon said would happen." Ally turns to Gloria. "Do you think the influx of power will change her?"

Gloria steps into the room with an eyebrow. "We'll find out soon."

"You're kidding," I say. "You think Rachel murdered some innocent girl for her power? Is this what you were going on about in the hallway earlier?"

I look from Gloria to Ally, recalling all that Ally said about Nivedha, the girl who was apparently in Henry Chaplain's snuff film harem. "She's not Caldwell, guys. She wouldn't do that."

"I wouldn't be so quick to say that if I were you." Maisie makes her way around the room to find some pictures we wouldn't slap out of her hands. She gestures for me to look at the drawing between her fingers.

I lean over her shoulder. In the black and white sketch, we're fighting. Rachel's face is twisted in rage, her arms extending out in front of her. The objects in the room swirl around me while I stand in my shield. But I'm not holding my ground very well. I'm bent forward as if resisting a great wind, my shield bending around me.

"It's out of context." I give Gloria a hopeful look. "Caldwell could be behind me or—"

"She attacks you." Gloria measures my expression. "As I saw it, she intends to kill you."

The world falls out from under me. The room spins as if on tilt, growing hot. I want to pull off my hoodie and maybe even the shirt underneath.

"Jess," Ally says. "Jess the floor."

Her words don't make any sense until I look down and see the floorboards of the little room smoking under my feet. I suck in a breath and step back to see a charred circle where I stood. A strange smell like a campfire fills the air.

I meet each of their eyes in turn. "Rachel wouldn't betray me."

"I saw—" Gloria begins.

"I don't care!" I scream. "You saw it wrong!"

Everyone goes silent and I'm more than a little embarrassed by how stupid I sound. Monroe appears in the doorway. I look away from Gloria, grateful for the distraction.

"There is another way." Monroe lifts his hat to scratch his scalp again. He pulls his tobacco pouch from the front pocket of his shirt and pinches a wad of it between two fingers. He holds it there, patting his jeans' front pockets, searching for the rolling papers.

"Another way to what?" Ally asks.

"To exchange powers." Monroe pulls a thin rolling paper from its case.

"You're kidding," Maisie says, her voice rising the way it might if we told her we'd gotten her a pony. "You mean we don't have to kill each other? That's freaking awesome!"

Monroe tucks the tobacco into the paper. "It was Samael who told me."

"Samuel?" Maisie asks.

"Sam-*ael*," he corrects, rolling the tobacco between two fingers and twisting off the ends. "My angel. You've got one of them, don't you?"

Maisie's face flushes.

"Well he told me we did it all wrong before. And we still be doing it wrong."

I turn to Gloria. "Translate please."

Gloria is about to answer me, her mouth open in response, when Nikki appears in the doorway.

"Caldwell's MIA," she says. Her nose wrinkles at the cigarette that Monroe slips between his lips. She takes a step around him into the room as he pulls a lighter from the pocket.

"What do you mean?" Ally asks.

"We have an eye on him at all times," Nikki says. Her voice goes all stupid soft any time she talks to Ally. "When he's MIA, it means we can't see him. I thought you should know—"

"He's here." Gloria whips her gun from its holster in one fluid movement.

Ally reaches up and covers her ears as if they ache. She grimaces. "Ow, yeah."

Maisie whirls on me wide-eyed, Winston in her arms. "Jesse!"

Several things happen at once.

A hand clamps down on my shoulder and instinctually I shield Ally. It flares to life, bright purple around her. This knocks Maisie to the floor. Oops. Both she and Winston cry out as they hit the ground. Nikki raises her gun, fires a shot, but the shield blocks it and it ricochets through the window. The glass shatters on impact.

Monroe removes the cigarette from his mouth, purses his lips, and whistles. A fierce wind comes out of nowhere. Some of Gloria's drawings are torn from the wall whirling like a paper cyclone. Caldwell is lifted and hurled through a window, only he won't let go of me, so my ass goes out the window with him. Glass slices across my right cheek and I squeeze my eyes shut and cover my face at the last moment, terrified of losing an eye.

We hit the ground, Caldwell breaking my fall. He makes an *oomph* sound when my elbow connects with his solar plexus on impact.

At last I feel like I can speak again, and of course, I say the dumbest thing. "Let go of me!"

This is especially stupid when I realize Caldwell has already let go of me, his arms apparently going out on either side of him to break his own fall.

Ally is screaming and so is Maisie.

"Shut up," Gloria snaps and Monroe is laughing again, that low bemused chuckle that seems more natural to him than conversation.

I fire up whirling around with the intention of blowing Caldwell to kingdom come, but he's gone. I stand alone in the little garden. I do a full circle but he's truly gone. I walk up to the broken window and see that Gloria and Nikki still stand with guns drawn. Ally and Maisie are slack jawed and waiting.

"You okay?" I ask them, looking from one face to another.

Maisie runs her hands down the length of her body. "I'm okay. Winnie?"

She stoops, disappearing beneath the window's frame. She reappears with a fat pug in her arms.

"He's okay too," she says.

"What the hell was that?" I demand. I look from Gloria to Ally, since they seem to have some magical way to tell if he's here.

"Reconnaissance," Gloria says, at long last, lowering her gun. She looks to Monroe. "It's working."

Monroe laughs.

"Someone tell me what's going on."

Ally covers her ears, uncovers her ears and then does it again. "That pressure in my head is gone."

"Answer me!"

"We've made him blind," Monroe says with a great belly laugh. "His angel can't see us. His people can't see us. He can only see us one way."

Monroe looks at Ally. "Through your eyes."

Ally turns on Monroe. "I'm so sorry. I'm so, so sorry."

"What the hell are you apologizing for?" I'm shaking.

"We led him right to you. He probably waited until we got here so he'd know where you were."

Monroe nods as if he already knew this.

I glare at Gloria. "You should've seen that coming."

"We knew, we knew," Monroe says, with that low chuckle. "But you can't be sure the fox is blind 'til you let him in the hen house."

I don't get any of these analogies.

Ally's face scrunches. "Why would you bring us here if you knew it'd make you a target?"

"Being dead is what I've been hoping for." Monroe relights his cigarette and takes a long, slow drag. "But I needed to be sure he was blind first."

"Why?" I'm getting tired of asking this. "What does he need to be blind for?"

Monroe gives us all a wicked grin, baring his yellow teeth. "So he don't see what we is about to do."

CHAPTER SEVENTEEN

Rachel

I wake on the floor of Nivedha's apartment. It's dark now, the lights of the city dancing in my eyes. I sit up and touch the side of my head. I feel sick, shaky with adrenaline. I pull myself up to standing by clutching onto the nearby coffee table. It creaks under my weight.

My legs shake, threatening to buckle beneath me.

Uriel appears in all his Lion-O glory.

"What's happening to me?" I fall forward into his arms and he pulls me up.

"You're acclimating to the power. Look," he says with a malicious grin. His eyes slide over the shadowed furniture in the unlit room.

I follow his gaze but see nothing. A slow realization blossoms. Everything in the room is vibrating. The coffee table, a handful of loose coins in a dish beside two remotes. It's subtle, certainly not an earthquake, if those are possible in New York, but a tremor nonetheless. I note the growing darkness of the room, and the lamps come on simply because I want them to. I don't even move my fingers this time. Not the slightest twitch.

"I'm going to bring this building down," I say.

Uriel laughs, a robust exhalation. "If you so desire."

I look down at myself. I'm trembling. Worse, I'm covered in Nivedha's blood and ashy soot. It's under my nails, and all over my arms and body. By the gritty feeling of my cheeks, I'd say it was on my face too.

A key turns in the lock. My head snaps up.

Uriel doesn't move from his place in the middle of the room, halfway between the coffee table and the ridiculously large television.

"Nivvy," a man with a deep voice calls. "I'm home."

He sets his briefcase down and looks up. His face goes from hopeful to terrified in seconds.

"Who the hell are you?"

No sooner does he ask this question then he decides he doesn't care. His slender fingers slip into the smooth pocket of his suit and grab his cell phone. He's about to dial 911 when the phone is ripped from his hand and sails across the room. It hits the big windows and shatters into a million pieces. The window, remarkably, remains unmarred, being the stronger of the two objects.

The man's mouth hangs open, his eyes darting around the room as if to anticipate what might happen next. I must admit that at first, I don't know what will happen either. What to do with this man? In his nice suit jacket and winter scarf. One gloved hand, one bare. The other removed to make the call. His slick hair parted to one side.

He will alert the authorities. You need more time. Uriel's voice has a new quality to it. A giddy excitement.

And then I know exactly what to do with him.

Yes, Uriel purrs. His red hair flaming as if on fire. *Smite him.*

The man collapses to his knees, a choked sound clucking in the back of his throat. By the time his elbows connect with the carpet, he makes no sound at all. I cross the room and kneel down to look into his lifeless eyes. He wears—wore—contacts, the irises the color of dog shit.

"Did I—?" I ask Uriel.

"Crushed his heart," Uriel says aloud, beaming like a proud papa. "Well done."

I reach up and scratch a nail along the side of his jaw. It's oily. Nivedha's ashes leave a trail along the bone.

"I need a shower." I step away from the body propped against the back of the front door, still wearing his coat and one leather glove.

The bathroom is like a spa. Huge skylights give the creamy tiles a soft glow. The backlighting of the mirrors makes my face foreign.

I open the shower door and step into a large stall, white marble tiles surrounding me. I turn the water all the way to the right, letting steam fill up the space before adjusting the knob back to a temperature my skin can tolerate.

Under the waterfall shower head, I come alive. It seemed like a dream before, standing in Nivedha's apartment, killing a strange man, a potential threat. But with the potato sack clothes off and most of her blood and ashes washed down the drain, I feel more like myself.

I think of Gideon.

I see his beautiful face for the first time.

"Hello, gorgeous," he'd said, rolling down the window of the Ferrari. It was two in the morning, and I was a mile from the asylum I'd just escaped.

"If you're some kind of rich axe murderer, you're not very subtle," I said. The trees lining the road connecting the asylum and the interstate swayed menacingly. I kept expecting Caldwell to step out at any time. I kept waiting for him to wrap his hands around my neck and choke me to death without further ado.

"Get in the car, Rachel," he'd said, the British accent sexier than any sound I'd heard in years. Of course, insane asylums are notoriously devoid of sexy.

"I don't get into strange cars with strange men who happen to know my name." I told him this through the open window. Uriel had appeared then, and Gideon's brow had furrowed as I turned to look the angel up and down.

"This isn't a strange car, it's a Ferrari," Gideon said and leaned over to open the door for me.

"He isn't Caldwell's," Uriel had said, vouching for the handsome foreigner.

Gideon had a thin beard, neat and trimmed close to his face. He was even darker than I was, probably because sunshine isn't exactly abundant in insane asylums. But the car, watch, clothes, and even his eyeglasses were expensive.

"Brinkley sent me to help you escape, darling. You and I are on the same mission to save the world and a damsel. Jesse Sullivan."

"He speaks the truth," Uriel vouched at about the same time I decided that my feet hurt and I was cold.

I slipped into the leather seat and pulled the door closed.

"So you *do* get into Ferraris with strange men," Gideon smiled, easing back onto the road, kicking it up to 60, then 80, then 100 in a matter of seconds.

I frowned at the speedometer. "You're going to kill us before we save anyone."

"What have you to worry about? How many times have you died?"

"216," I said.

He snorted. "What's one more—?"

It was his easy smile. The mischief in his eyes. I relaxed against my seat and let him drive me far away from the asylum and my life for the last few years.

I reach out and turn off the hot water. I grab a plush

towel off the rack and began to dry myself. With one hand, I wipe the mirror to reveal my face in the foggy glass. I search for any trace of blood or ash. How many times had Nivedha stood here looking at herself, thinking of Henry Chaplain? Of the lights and camera and a man stepping into a room?

I use Nivedha's deodorant, toothbrush, even her makeup, though she was a little fairer than me. Then I raid her closet. Her closet is bigger than the room I had back at the asylum, and I had had to share that with someone.

"I could spend days in here," I tell Uriel as he leans against the door frame. "Smell that?"

I give an exaggerated sniff.

"*Shoes.*"

Not only does—did—Nivedha have—had—whole racks of unworn clothes, the price tags dangling from silky sleeves, but shelves and shelves of shoe boxes line the top of the closet.

I pull them down one at a time, letting the boxes hit the floor without ceremony. Heels, boots, flats, of all colors, pile on top of each other. Some fall completely from the box; others remain partially swaddled in their tissue wrappings.

Leopard print heels. I run a finger down the side of the shoe, feeling the soft fur bristle at my touch. They are identical to the beauties I saw earlier, down to the square tip at the heel.

I slip them on and stand, naked except for the heels, and turn in the full-length mirror to admire my body. They pinch a little in the toes but I don't care. They make my calves flex and lengthen my legs in the mirror.

Gideon loves my body. I can tell by the way he looks at me. His gaze isn't quite as carnivorous as most of the men I've encountered, but hunger is recognizable on any face. The fact that he delights in my body isn't what I enjoy most. Sure, it feels good to be attractive, to know someone wants you desperately. But that isn't what I crave.

I want his respect. His admiration. I died but was reborn from the ashes. Not only in body but also in mind and spirit. I want someone who can appreciate that. Gideon can. And he does. In my mind as well as his, I'm not the victim anymore. I'm the predator, not the prey. You don't take your eyes off me, not because I'm beautiful, but because it would be a very foolish thing to do.

I find black panties and bras also with the tags still on. The bras don't fit, Nivedha's chest being smaller than mine, so I go for a supportive camisole instead. Then I slip on the panties and stockings. I run garters from the top of the stockings to my hips. Add a short, tight black dress, and because I'm being practical, a full length mink coat.

I look *amazing*.

You're more than a gorgeous face. Gideon said once.

"Is he alive?" I ask Uriel. Uriel still leans in the doorframe, his expression drunken with satisfaction. Not for my body of course. I don't think he has that kind of inclination. Only one thing seems to excite the angel, *smiting* people.

"Yes," Uriel says. "He is not in danger. You are. You are wasting too much time."

I give myself one more look in the full mirror and wink. The gorgeous vixen with coal-lined eyes winks back.

"Fine," I say with a huff. "Off we go."

I march out of the closet, reveling in the feel of the sleek clothes on my body. There's nothing like expensive clothes to make you feel like a million dollars.

I stoop down and search the man's pockets for money. He's got a money clip in the front breast pocket and another one in the briefcase.

"Do you intend to cover your face?" Uriel asks.

"I pity the fool stupid enough to challenge me."

And I do. The power coursing through me is hurricane-force. Tsunamis. Unstoppable and unparalleled. Why would I fear anything as pathetic as humans with their silly guns?

With cash and a nice coat, I slip from the room and take the elevator to the lobby.

The doorman smiles at me and asks about Nivedha. I smile, wink and drop my tone. "She's busy."

Being dead.

The man grins and lets me go on my way. Good for him, disappointing for me. I'd love to discover how many hearts I can stop in one day.

"Will you kill her now?" Uriel asks, his tone hopeful.

I step up to the curb and throw up my hand for a taxi. One weaves out of traffic, cutting toward me sharply across three lanes.

"Not yet," I tell him. "We have one more stop."

CHAPTER EIGHTEEN

Jesse

Gloria assures us that Caldwell will not be back tonight.

Lounging in Maisie's temporary bedroom, we poke and prod Gloria for answers, but all we get is *he will have his hands too full this evening.*

But Maisie is pretty shaken up by the encounter, despite Gloria's attempts to console her.

"He told me to kill Jesse." She runs one hand down Winston's back. Winston snoozes on the coverlet of the twin-sized bed, his head on Maisie's knee. "I could never kill you. I don't think I can kill anyone. Not even him."

"I know." I'm at the end of her bed with the soles of her feet pressed against my thigh. I pat her unicorn-socked feet in sympathy.

"But I felt him in my head you know. I felt him trying to confuse me."

"You're too smart," I say again, but a horrible feeling settles in my chest. I've been mindfucked by Caldwell myself. I know what he can do to a person. He's not as effective with us as he is with people who don't have NRD, but he's still pretty good. The magnetite in our brain, what gives us the condition, also runs interference.

"Try not to think about it," I insist. "We've got an awesome plan. Tomorrow or the day after we'll go to Arizona and then it'll all be over. Hang in there."

Gloria gives me a hard look. I shrug. Okay, so the next 48 hours of our lives might be the worst thing ever, but she didn't expect me to say *that*, did she?

Maisie looks anything but convinced. "I'm going to take a nap with Winnie."

"Good idea." I leap up, perhaps too enthusiastic to get off of big sister duty. I give Gloria a half-pleading, half-hesitant look which could be translated to *you've got this right?*

Gloria nods.

I slip from the room as Gloria stands to tuck Maisie and the pug in. A sound stops me at the top of the stairs. They're a faded old wood, mostly covered by a dusty carpet runner. Overlooking the banister, I can see Nikki and Ally talking, keeping their voices low. I can't see Ally's face, only half of Nikki's. Her features are full of sweet concern.

God, she's good. Damn it.

She reaches out to touch Ally's arm and then pulls her into a hug. I scoff.

They both turn and look up at me.

"Oh please, don't stop. It's starting to get good," I say, my face hot and chest tight. I can feel the power rising, warmth flooding my limbs. *Breathe, Jesse.* Gabriel's voice comes from somewhere deep in my mind. *Breathe.*

"Jess—" Ally begins, one foot on the bottom of the step.

I wave my hand. "Save it."

I storm off to the bedroom I'm supposed to share with her and shut myself in the room. I lock the door so that everyone will leave me alone.

Jesse, Gabriel says as I fall onto the stiff bed. The brass frame slaps against the bare wall. *Jesse, speak to me.*

I sit up on my elbows and see Gabriel. At the end of the bed, he flickers in and out of focus, forcing me to blink several times. It's because Maisie is at the end of the hallway. Too close.

Why are you crying? His words are clear enough in my mind, but his mouth doesn't move. Is it too hard to make a voice, a human voice, when he can't even form the rest of himself? Maybe.

"I'm not crying," I say, wiping at my face.

He doesn't humor me with a rebuttal. He watches me wipe at my face, coming closer to the bed.

I wish you were real, I think suddenly. *I could really use a hug.*

I'm more than a little horrified by how pathetic I sound, even to myself. But it's true. The image of Nikki holding Ally. Nikki saying *who do you think will pick up the pieces?* It's—it's all just—

I'm so confused, I tell him, in my mind. *I don't want Ally to die. I don't. Please don't think anything else no matter what I might think or feel out of anger, got it?*

Gabriel kneels by the bed, his face at my level. *I know what you want.*

But I hate the idea of her being with someone else. I don't want to think about me dead and her alive, popping out babies with Sasquatch.

The soft caress of feathers grazes my cheek, tucking under my chin. The scent of a summer rain overtakes the room.

"Why did you show me the beach house?" I recall the beach house perfectly in my mind.

Because I'm not talking about the first vision—me and Ally cozied up with Winston. The pale sand-smoothed wood, the lighthouse décor, the breathtaking view of blue-grey waters lapping at the sable shore. I'm talking about the second vision. The one with Nikki and Ally in the same house, with two daughters.

"Why show me that?" I ask. "If you want to give me my so-called heart's desire, why show me that?"

The smell of rain intensifies. And for the first time I feel Gabriel's hands on me. He lifts me from the bed—or at least, he lifts some part of me from the bed. Feathers brush my cheeks as he unfurls them wide, far too wide for the little bedroom we are in, except I understand somehow that Gabriel was never in the bedroom. Not really.

The world shifts and the black wings envelop me. Then they open, revealing sunshine and the beach. The blue-gray waves lap at the shore as gulls quietly glide overhead. In the middle sits an A-frame beach house, complete with rickety, sand-smoothed steps and giant windows.

"Oh no, no, no," I say, looking at the beach house. "I'm not going in there. This time they'll have four kids. Or a sex sling in the living room beside a clown playing Beyoncé on a violin. No, thank you."

Gabriel blinks his cat-eyes at me. "Someone is waiting for you on the back porch."

A strange fear crawls over my flesh and the very last thing I want to do is to go around the house and see who is sitting on the porch.

Yet my feet start moving one after the other. My sneakers sink into the sand with each step I take toward the shoreline. I give the house a wide berth, coming around the corner with the expectation that maybe someone—or some*thing*—is about to jump out at me.

But as soon as I get around the corner I stop.

There is someone waiting. He's sitting on a beach chair on the porch, overlooking the water. He's got a slight grin on his face that can easily be mistaken for peace. It's as if he likes what he sees and he's got all day to enjoy it. The can of beer in his hand certainly suggests so.

"Brinkley?" I choke on the name.

He turns and the lazy grin widens. "Hey kid."

He stands, his leather jacket falling open to reveal an AC/DC shirt. He's a 40-year-old James Dean with a touch more rock 'n roll.

"Brinkley?" I say it again. I whirl on Gabriel to see if he's still there. He is, watching me with those unreadable eyes.

"We don't have a lot of time, kid." Brinkley puts his beer down and jumps off the porch, coming toward me. "Or I should say you don't have a lot of time."

"Yeah, I know. I'm going to blow up apparently. Did you know that when you recruited me? That I'd either save the world or destroy it?"

"No," Brinkley says with a grin. "Can't say I saw that one coming. But I don't think you'll blow up the world. I don't think he would have picked you if he thought you'd destroy it. He seems to be in the business of keeping the rock spinning."

Brinkley looks over my shoulder at Gabriel. They lock eyes but neither speaks.

"Do you know what they are?" I ask. "Are they really angels? Rachel has this theory—"

Brinkley holds up a hand to stop my rant. "We'll talk metaphysics later."

My hopes fall. "Yeah, I guess we'll have all the time in the world to chat when I'm dead. What's that like? Being dead?"

Brinkley gives me a sad smile.

"Is it boring? I bet it's boring. So is this heaven?"

"For you maybe," he says. "But not in the way you mean. It's more like a place between heaven and earth. Closer to earth than heaven actually."

"Why would you need a place between? And why does

Gabriel keep bringing me here?"

"Too many questions kid, and you should be doing the listening. Me the talking."

"Right, sorry."

Brinkley smiles. He's got more patience now, but maybe being dead will do that to you. After all, what pressing appointment could he possibly have now?

"Rachel needs you."

My brow furrows. "Oh god, no. You're not going to start talking about how she's betraying me too are you?"

"She doesn't see it as betrayal. She's doing what she believes is right. I gave her a mission and I asked too much. Forgive her. Forgive me." Brinkley says.

"Forgive you?" I'm shocked. "That's the message?"

"That's it for now," Brinkley says, breaking into another brilliant smile. "I'll see you around, kid."

"Wait, what?" I shout at his back as he turns to go. "That's it? That's really it? Brinkley, wait!"

Brinkley stoops down to pick up his can of beer before turning back to face me.

"If Rachel's losing it again, I can't save her. I don't know how!"

Brinkley gives me a lopsided grin. "You're capable of so much more than you think you are. I knew it when I first met you, and I believe it now more than ever."

A crushing sense of grief washes over me. Tears choke my eyes, my throat constricts and I'm running across the beach at full speed.

I slam into Brinkley and throw my arms around him. He's real. Completely, blessedly real. God, I don't know what I would do if he turned out to be immaterial.

I squeeze him harder. "God, don't go. I can't do this shit by myself. I need you to tell me what to do. Every second of every day I feel like I'm fucking it up. I feel like—"

"You won't, as they say, screw the pooch."

His praise hurts me more than a slap across the face or a punch in the gut.

"I'm sorry. Brinkley, I'm so sorry. I should've—if I'd killed Caldwell, you might've—"

Brinkley yanks me out of his arms then, roughly. But he's still smiling.

"I used to think it was my fault for bringing you into this, but I see it differently now. We aren't as in control as we think we are, kid. I didn't put you in danger any more than you got me killed. You'll see that someday."

"But how am I supposed to help Rachel?"

"Remember what I did for her last time. You've forgotten, but you'll remember."

He clasps a hand on my shoulder as the wind kicks up. He tosses his head back to finish off his beer.

Gabriel places a hand on my back. "We're out of time."

The smell of rain overtakes the beach. I look up to see dark clouds forming on the horizon.

I want to say goodbye to Brinkley one more time. One more apology for being such an ungrateful little dick when he was alive. But Brinkley isn't on the porch anymore. He's farther down the beach at the edge where the shore meets a copse of trees. He stands at the mouth of the path and waves.

His voice comes one more time. *Remember how I brought her back.*

Then he ducks beneath a branch and is gone.

A fat rain droplet hits my cheek.

Furious lightning shatters the sky in the distance. The wind blowing in off the water pushes me back into Gabriel's arms.

With his hands around my waist, he takes off. His two black wings thrust us up into the darkening sky.

CHAPTER NINETEEN

Rachel

I use my mind to blow back the colossal wooden doors of the church. Though tremendously large, the panels swing and hit the stone interior with enough force that they crack.

I step onto the burgundy runner that leads me through the vestibule and narthex into the sanctuary. Overhead, a martyr with her barbed heart holds a hand out in blessing. Candles burn in their candelabras on both sides of the room as polished pews stretch from one end to the altar ahead.

A priest in white and gold robes of the Unified Church rushes down the aisle toward me. He's walking faster than those grannies in the mall with their fanny packs and visors, yet too dignified to break into a run.

"Miss." His voice strains against its own volume. He wants to yell at me, I'm sure, but holds himself back. "Miss, the church is closed. You must leave."

"No." I slip off the mink coat and lay it over the back of a pew. I don't want it to get dirty. Then I lift all the prayer books from their little holders behind the seats. They rise, floating in place about a foot above the polished pews.

He stops in the center aisle, his hands coming up in front of him.

I throw one book after another at him. They pelt his body and he gives out a little cry. I can't help but laugh at his cowering form. Once the books have been thrown and none hang in the air, I make the suspended candelabras swing furiously.

It all feels so *so* good. Is this what it's like every time we power up? I should've been knocking off those partis sooner.

"It's pathetic how blindly you follow him," I say, twirling. The priest stumbles back out of the pile of prayer books surrounding him. "He isn't a god. He has no real power. He uses and abuses every one of you."

I see Chaplain in head-to-toe black, speaking his false promises to lure stupid girls into a trap.

"He is the one true Lord," the priest cries out. He begins chanting furiously and I start to laugh. I can't help myself. I don't speak Latin, but I know the word *daemon* well enough.

I lift the priest off his feet. I shove him across the room and skip after him as he sails toward the vestibule.

I pin him to the man-sized cross, white and gleaming in the center of the room. I stretch his arms out to a T, while the man cries to himself, continuing his useless prayers.

"Wh-what are you going to do?" he asks at last.

"Play telephone." I grin up from my place at his feet. "And you're the telephone."

"I don't—"

"Understand? I know. Do as I tell you and you won't die. Today. Well, I guess I can't promise that, can I? You could step off those steps outside and break your neck or get hit by a bus. I should know how easy it is to die. I've done it over 200 times!"

"What do you want?"

"Right," I say stretching my arms overhead. "I want you

to make a call to Caldwell. You know who Timothy Caldwell is right?"

"Yes, b—"

"Good. Call him. Pretty, pretty please with a cherry on top?"

"I don't have a phone."

"Oh, silly, you don't need one. Call him up here." I tap the side of my head. "Think pitiful thoughts about how I'm tormenting you. About where we are. Show him my face. Picture my face."

I stare up at the slack-jawed priest, this ancient balding man trembling on the cross.

"Are you calling him, Telephone?" I ask, putting my hands on my hips.

"He is doing as you say," Uriel says beside me.

"Good, good!" I say and clap my hands.

The priest looks down at me.

"I'm not talking to you! Keep praying as if your life depends on it."

His eyes go unfocused again, sweat forming on the top of his fat upper lip.

"How long do you think it'll take for Caldwell to get the message?" I ask Uriel, succumbing to the sudden urge to do a cartwheel. The priest makes a disgusted cluck with his tongue and pinches his eyes closed until I pull my dress back down over my head.

"Oh, relax Father," I say with a giggle. "They're just black panties. You see them in commercials all the time, don't you? Victoria's Secret ads."

"Ms. Wright," a sultry voice calls from the end of the walkway. At least two dozen rows of pews stand between us, but I'd recognize that voice and face anywhere. "Causing trouble are we?"

I hang onto one end of the pew and lean over, stretching

out into the aisle. "Don't act like you don't enjoy causing trouble yourself, Eric."

His steady approach up the walkway halts and his face twists with irritation. "Don't call me that."

"Eric?" I ask. "That's your name, isn't it? It's the name your mother gave you."

"I don't have a mother." He clasps his hands behind his back and regains his composure before proceeding up the aisle.

With me in such a gorgeous dress and his slow processional, it's like we're getting married in some bizarre backwards wedding where the bride waits for the groom.

"So a god then? Parentless? Maybe you even hatched from an egg?"

"I had a spiritual rebirth." Caldwell's gaze is set on mine. His intense stare is so very much like Chaplain's, the dark orbs holding the candelabras' flame. "Like many great men of our time. And when I was reborn I took a new name."

I ignore his declarations. "Was it you who took Gideon away? *Eric*?" I grin viciously at his mounting irritation.

Now it's his turn to smile. "I didn't hurt him. In fact, once we reached an agreement, I let him go. He's on his way to your friends now."

"My friends?" I taunt, grabbing the hem of my dress and pulling it up a little. I can't get over how good the fabric feels on my skin, how good everything feels. I want to roll around on the red carpet and stare up at the pretty stained glass above. The influx of power I get from absorbing a partis' gift is better than a dose of ecstasy.

Caldwell's eyes slip down, sliding over my breasts, my thighs, and I laugh.

"So you *are* a man under all of that?" I ask, willing him to come a little closer. I want him within my reach.

"I could have told you that," a voice says. The woman

with the sleek hair pulled into a severe bun steps from behind a column on my right. She's closer to me than she is to Caldwell, who's stopped just out of my arms' length.

Black-smoke extends from her torso, shooting toward me like a viper. I throw up my hands as if to shield myself, and she flies up and back away from me, slamming into a stone column. She deserves it. She and Caldwell threw me around much like this on our last encounter.

Georgia cries out twice. Once when she hits the column and again when she falls to the ground with a crack.

"Oh, I hope that was the sound of her brains spilling all over the stones!"

Caldwell lunges for me, but I'm expecting it. I reach into his chest with my mind and latch onto that fragile organ, thrashing wildly in its bone casing. I squeeze.

Caldwell's eyes go wide and he falls to his knees, mouth coming open in surprise.

"Oh, now we're getting somewhere," I say, in a low tone. I'm practically purring, relishing this moment. "Finally."

Caldwell comes to his hands and knees.

"Oh, can't teleport with your heart in my hands? How interesting."

His eyes widen.

Something strikes me hard on the back of the neck, making the world reel. I stumble forward, on top of Caldwell.

"Oww!" I cry from my hands and knees. I reach back and touch a wet spot on the back of my head. My fingers come away bloody.

On all fours, I crane my neck to see the priest. I'd forgotten all about him and in doing so, I've released him from the cross where he'd been pinned. Now he holds a foot-long statue of Mary like a weapon, raising it up to strike me with it again.

I break his neck without even getting up. He crumples to

the ground. His robes billow out around his body, revealing a length of pale calf before the fabric settles again.

"The dangers of ADD," I grumble as I sit back on my heels and then push myself to standing.

"Now." I turn back to Caldwell, ready to finish what I started. "Where were we?"

Only Caldwell isn't in the center aisle clutching his chest anymore. He's gone.

I run to the other side of the pews, to the place where Georgia fell, but she's gone too. Damn. My opportunity is lost by a jerk wielding a virgin.

Perfect. Just perfect.

CHAPTER TWENTY

Jesse

The house is shaking. The brass bed frame trembles against the wall. An earthquake? I don't know why this is my first thought as I peel my eyes open. Nope. No earthquake or partis come to pull the world down around me. Someone is shaking me.

"Thank god," Ally says, with visible relief. She stops shaking me but leaves one hand on my shoulder. "You were crying for Brinkley. Did you have a bad dream?"

I push myself up on my elbows and stare around the small room crowding in on me. The off color wall paper, the cardboard boxes stacked in one corner. And a desk with several books piled one on top of the other. I search Ally's face for its familiarity. I've never liked waking up in strange places.

"It wasn't a dream," I say, as the room comes into focus around me.

I can still smell the rain on Gabriel's wings and the soft brush of his feathers on my face. I see Brinkley's smile clearly as he stands at the edge of the shore before ducking into the dense trees.

But what I see most clearly is the storm. The large black

clouds rolling toward me over the water, the darkness illumi-nated by sudden violent bursts of lightning, each strike closer than the last. In the distance, sure, but coming. Coming fast. And with it a horrible sense of foreboding.

Brinkley's words are still clear. *I asked too much. Forgive her. Forgive me.*

"Rachel's in trouble." I let go of my last hold on the dream.

"How do you know that?"

"Brinkley told me."

"In Gloria's picture—"

"I don't care if she's cutting someone's head off in Gloria's picture. Brinkley wants me to look out for her." Hadn't Brinkley told Rachel to come help me when he died? To protect me? I always thought that was strange, that he should throw her in front of me so callously. But this idea that I was supposed to protect her in turn, that we were meant to take care of each other—that was the Brinkley I knew. Maybe he didn't have a chance to give me those final orders when he was alive.

"You're right. Innocent until proven guilty." Ally smiles sympathetically.

"What are you doing in here? I thought I locked the door."

"It doesn't work," Ally says. "Sorry. I knocked first, but you didn't answer so I came in. I thought you were having an episode like Maisie."

"What are you talking about? Is she okay?"

"She's fine," Ally says. "She says she felt her mother die."

"What?"

"We don't know what it means," Ally says. "Or at least Gloria isn't telling me anything. She's with Maisie too."

"Do we need to act?" I ask. What the hell did an *episode* mean anyway?

"She's fine," Ally assures me. "I'm more concerned about you. You were dreaming about Rachel?"

"She's not evil."

I know she doesn't believe me. How could she? Not with Nikki filling her head with anti-Rachel sentiment and not in the face of Gloria's ambiguous drawings. But in my heart, I know Rachel is good. I have a thousand memories to prove it.

One night, not long after Brinkley had recruited me and took me to Saint Louis to apprentice under Rachel, I'd woken up screaming.

One minute, I was sleeping peacefully. The next, someone was climbing into bed with me. A hand was on the back of my head, on my arm, and then I was thrashing, screaming.

Rachel had to turn on all the lights and move several feet away from me before I'd calm down.

At long last, chest heaving, I apologized, but I didn't stop squeezing the life out of my pillow.

"What are you sorry for?" Rachel asked.

"For screaming. And I think I slapped you. I'm sorry. I have—nightmares."

"Memories," she corrected. She dared to sit on the end of the bed, keeping a good deal of distance between us. "You have memories. Don't ever degrade your experience."

I could only nod. I'd known her for weeks, maybe a month. I wasn't going to detail my horrible stepfather's *visits*.

"I have memories too," she said at last, her back straightening. "Sometimes they get me at night. Sometimes in broad daylight."

I wanted to ask her then what had happened to her, but she hadn't volunteered the information and I hadn't wanted to share mine. So I let my curiosity lie.

"I guess it'll get easier with time," I said, my breath returning to normal.

"No," Rachel says. She placed her hands on her knees.

"Not really. You'll think you're fine and then one day when you least expect it, all the pain, all the anger will rise up out of nowhere."

I snorted. "This is one hell of a pep talk. Aren't you supposed to make me feel better?"

Light cut across her cheek, her freckles visible even in the dimness. Rachel was the first person I ever met with freckles like me. "It isn't about forgetting what happened. And it sure as hell isn't about convincing yourself that it *didn't* happen."

I understood why she'd forced me to acknowledge my memories were more than mere bad dreams. You can't overcome something if you tell yourself it isn't real. "I don't want to be that person who always plays the victim. Oh woe is me. Something shitty happened. My life was so bad."

Rachel smiled. "That's good. Because you will never be happy if you do."

"But sometimes it's—" *so real* I'd wanted to say. Sometimes the terror is so real that it doesn't feel like the past at all.

"—hard," Rachel said. "It is hard but you're strong Jessup. If anyone can get over it, it's you."

I'd started crying then. Uncontrollably, ridiculously sobbing in a way that is pretty embarrassing to think about now. Rachel had held me.

"It's unfair," she said as she tried to rock me back to sleep.

"Worse things happen to people," I said, wiping at my nose with my sleeve.

"Not what happened," she said. "I mean it seems unfair that because you were strong enough to survive, you get punished for it. Your prize for surviving is the long, hard process of healing."

I hadn't understood what she meant and I think she knew it.

"Surviving is hard. Healing is harder," she said. She tucked me back into the bed and crawled in beside me. "It seems unfair that after all you go through, you're left to clean up the mess. You have to let go of the anger. Then the fear. Then cultivate happiness. And every step is the hardest thing you've ever done."

We'd fallen asleep like that. And on the nights when I woke up screaming and thrashing, Rachel would be there. With a glass of water, to climb in the bed and soothe me back to sleep again.

Forgive her. Forgive me.

"About what you saw in the hallway," Ally begins, pulling me from my thoughts.

"You're still in love with her."

She makes a surprised clucking sound in her throat. "I don't think I was ever in love with Nikki."

"You still like her. Whatever."

Her brow furrows. "I was expressing my concern for you, for Rachel actually, and she was only trying to make me feel better."

"I bet." I flop back against the covers. "Good news. She'll get to do that for the rest of your life."

Ally's mouth falls open. "Excuse me?"

"Come on," I say, more than a little irritated that she is going to make me spell it out for her. Does she think I enjoy thinking about this? "When I'm dead, you know who you'll end up with, and don't pretend like it isn't an agreeable consolation prize."

"When you're dead!" She jumps up from the bed, her jacket falling open. "You think I'm thinking about *when you're dead?*"

"You've thought about it at least once or twice." Now it's my turn to stand up and get indignant. "I'm going to either be murdered or die saving the world, and where does that leave you? In a beach house with two kids!"

Ally's face furrows in confusion.

I'm screaming. I become aware of the volume of my voice only when tears fill her eyes. Shit. Why is it that when she cries I immediately feel like the worst person in the world?

"If you think—" she pauses to draw a ragged breath. "—for even one *second* that I want, that I would rather—" She puts her hands on her hips and squeezes until the knuckles go white.

"Don't cry!" I say, unable to lower my volume much. "At least you're not the one who has to die!"

Ally storms out of the room, slamming the door shut behind her.

Gabriel appears in the corner of the room the second she's gone. He isn't perfectly clear, but he's substantial enough.

"God, what *now*?" I ask.

"You hurt her feelings," he says in a perfectly neutral tone.

My jaw falls open. "Since when do you give a damn about *feelings*?"

"You want to be with her."

"What's your point?"

"Upsetting her runs counter to your desires."

"Okay, I want the cryptic nonsensical angel back," I say. "I don't like the therapist one."

Gabriel flickers and fades as a soft knock comes at the door. Maisie pokes her head in and flinches. "Uh, is this a bad time?"

"I don't think there will be a 'good time' for as long as I live," I say. "What's up?"

Maisie inspects her black nail polish. "Monroe wants to talk to us. He says it's important."

"That sounds nice and ominous."

She snorts. "Wait until you see what he's got set up in his room."

"Is it too late to pretend I'm asleep?"

"Gloria will come up and haul you out of bed," she says. "That's what she did to me."

I linger for a moment longer, staring at the corner where Gabriel last stood. Brinkley's words, Rachel's words, and Ally's words—they all play on a loop in my head while the looming storm builds on the horizon.

CHAPTER TWENTY-ONE
Rachel

I destroy the church, slowly, methodically, and I must admit, I enjoy every minute of it. I start by ripping the ancient tapestries off the wall. I use the remaining flames to set them on fire. I pull down the crosses, the false icons, with my mind and slam them against the floor or a column, often in turn, over and over and over again until the metal bends, the clay breaks. I throw the altar up against the wall and it splits clean in half with a very satisfying *crack*.

I expect Uriel to stop me. Somehow thwart me from desecrating a holy place. Instead, he makes helpful suggestions.

Send the candelabras through the windows.

Set fire to the pulpit.

Break the holy water basin in half and use it to destroy the pews until only firewood is left.

"Isn't this sacrilegious?" I turn from one desecrated row of pews to the other in order to finish the job. I'm making tinder for a giant blaze. If Caldwell doesn't come back for the largest Manhattan bonfire of this century, then I guess he won't be coming back at all.

"No ground is holy where blood has been spilt," Uriel says, but seems uninterested in elaborating. "And very little earth on this planet is clean of bloodshed."

"So maybe you really are ancient aliens." I leap giddily from pile to pile. I use my mind to jump higher and to slow my descent. When I close my eyes, it's like I'm flying. "If you don't give a damn about churches or religions, you must not be angels."

He sneers. "You cannot begin to comprehend what I am."

"Hey." I tap my chest with my index finger. "You chose *me*. Not the other way around."

He says nothing to this.

I find jugs of oil in an alcove behind the pulpit and splash the wood generously. The flame catches, then spreads. It races from one jagged piece of wood to the other. The fire doubles in size faster than I would have thought possible.

I search for Caldwell. I keep expecting him to leap from the flames like a demon come to exact revenge for killing his woman, revenge for burning one of his sacred temples to the ground. But he doesn't come.

"He doesn't want to fight me." I put both hands on my hips. "I got all pretty and powered up and I came to his house and now he won't fight me!"

A wave of disappointment washes over me.

I try screaming his name. I deliberately rip his portrait—a giant oil painting framed in heavy gilded wood—from the wall and toss it into the blaze.

Nothing.

Sweat collects on the back of my neck from the heat. I step back from the building blaze but Caldwell doesn't come.

A sound catches my attention and I whirl, thrusting the intruder up into the air before he reaches me. He dangles about four yards off the ground. His arms are stretched out to either side in a mockery of Christ.

But it isn't Caldwell. It's Gideon.

I let him drop. Then at the last moment, I realize his legs will shatter if I don't slow his fall. I stop him inches above the ground, placing him gently on his feet.

"Darling," he says, breathless. His nostrils are flared as he takes one uncertain step toward me then another. His eyes run up and down my body without shame. "You look ravishing. Have you been shopping?"

"No," I say with a flirtatious grin. "I borrowed this from a friend. Where the hell have you been?"

"In custody."

"Caldwell said he let you go with an agreement."

"I'm to lead him to Maisie and Jesse," he says with a devilish smirk, but it doesn't reach his eyes.

"What's wrong?" I ask, scowling at him. "You don't like my dress."

"I love your dress." His grin widens. He's showing too many teeth. "It's that I'm not sure what you're doing here. We had a plan."

"I've stuck to the plan. Niv is dead and now I want Caldwell but he won't play with me."

"You're adorable when you pout." He wraps his arms around me. He stoops to kiss my cheek, then my neck.

I place my hands on his chest and feel the fretful rhythm of his panicked heart.

"Why is your heart pounding?" I ask.

He snorts. "I was thrown into the air, I'm standing in a burning building, there's a gorgeous woman in a heart-stopping dress. Take your pick, darling."

I start pulling at the top of his pants with both hands.

He laughs low in his throat. "I'm all for reckless danger, my love, but do you really think this is the best moment?"

I look around at the destroyed church, fixating on the lack of Caldwell. "I wish Caldwell were here."

Gideon snorts. "I'll try not to take that personally."

I pull myself out of his arms. "How did you know I was here?"

"They found the boyfriend dead in his apartment." He gives me a once-over. "So I assume you've acquired the girl's power as you wanted?"

"*We* wanted," I correct him, not oblivious to his implication.

"Yes," he's quick to amend. "And then a church, not five blocks away is burning from the inside out. Call it a hunch."

Uriel appears over Gideon's left shoulder, scowling. "He lies. Smite him."

"No," I say to the angel. "I like the boy."

"You do not need him."

"I do not need *you* either," I say to the angel. "Yet here you are."

Uriel's feathers ruffle and his hair seems to darken to a brighter shade of orange-red. They're as vibrant as the flames eating the church alive. I've begun to sweat on my pretty dress and I don't like it.

I stoop and grab Niv's—my—coat off the ground. "I want to leave."

"Are you speaking to me now?" Gideon asks with an arched eyebrow.

"Who else would I be speaking to?" I snap, and march toward the great doors that will take me back to the streets of Manhattan.

Gideon says, "So about our plan—"

"I want to make a small modification."

Gideon's breath hitches. I wonder if he's even noticed what a ridiculously easy read he's become. Is it the new power coursing through my veins? I certainly feel different—more...*more* everything.

"Let's hear the new plan then," Gideon says, aiming for casualness.

"We go to Arizona now. We'll arrive in two days."

"3 or 4," Gideon corrects, matching my stride easily given his height.

I pass through the great doors and descend the stone steps. A small crowd has gathered, a few people on their cell phones reporting the fire to the authorities. I turn back to see black smoke billowing up into the sky. I keep marching in the opposite direction.

"We'll arrive in Arizona in three days, and then I'll kill the girl right away."

Gideon stops walking. I realize the distance is growing between us until I fear he won't follow me. Frankly, I don't want to drive all the way to Arizona by myself. So I turn to face him.

"What now?"

"Killing Maisie was not part of the plan," Gideon takes a slow step toward me, one foot in front of the other. His hands are in his pockets. His brow is deeply creased behind his thick-rimmed eyeglasses. Frowning like this, he looks studious. Like a Columbia graduate student rather than the con man he is. Perhaps that is his way of disarming others. His accent. His sweet smile and intelligent face. He certainly couldn't achieve the same in a gorgeous dress after all.

"Oh don't look at me like that." I place both hands on my hips. "It isn't personal."

He frowns. "What is it then?"

"Practicality. I need more juice. Niv's power was pathetic, but once I absorbed it, I'm—I feel—well, for lack of a better word, unstoppable."

"If you are unstoppable now, why should you need more power? Can't you work with what you have? The plan was a coordinated attack."

"Don't be naïve, Gid—" The end of my words are cut off by a fire truck whipping around a corner into view. Pedestrians scurry as it drives up to the front of the church, mounting the curb and halting before the doors. The firefighters leap out with their equipment and rush inside. "The child is absolutely no use to us. I need her power."

Gideon matches my stride again as we move west toward the sunset.

"And what about Jesse? Do you think she'll *let* you kill the girl?"

My heart skips a beat and my throat tightens, but only for a minute. Then I'm calm again and my purpose is clear. "I'll deal with Jessup."

CHAPTER TWENTY-TWO

Jesse

"Uh, I know we're in the voodoo capital of America and everything, but is all this really necessary?"

I point at the melty votive candles arranged in a circle on the worn wood floor. Strange reddish symbols are scrawled into the bare planks beneath Monroe as he sits cross-legged, smoking one of his hand-rolled cigarettes. Twin streams of smoke rise from his nostrils and cloud the air around him, mixing with the candlelight, adding to the general creepiness of the room.

Maisie coughs and waves her hands in front of her face. "If I wasn't sure that imminent death was in my future, I'd be upset about all this secondhand smoke, dude."

"I'm a little more concerned about the blood." I stare at his ruddy, slick palms. "That's what's all over your hands right?"

I give Gloria a nervous look. It's only the four of us in this room: me, Maisie, Gloria, and Monroe. Ally and Nikki are nowhere to be found. Part of me really, *really* hates that. For all I know, Ally is crying on Nikki's shoulder about what a bitch I am. Nothing I say or do will improve my case on that count. I can't make her unlike Nikki. And I can't unlove Ally.

There's nothing left to do but to lap up all the suckage.

"Chicken blood," Monroe admits, scrapping some of it out from under his fingernails with his teeth. "I want to show you two something real important."

"And why does that involve chicken blood exactly?" I'm looking at Gloria who only nods to Monroe like *pay attention*.

"I'm sure that your angel be showing you things. Important things about what's to come and what's supposed to be happening here. But mine's been showing me too."

"O-kay." I sigh and relinquish the idea that I'm going to get out of this room without playing along first. "So you're going to tell us what these important things are, I take it?"

"No, ma'am," Monroe says with a chuckle.

Maisie yanks her hair up into a messy bun on top of her head and scratches her nose. "But you just said—"

"I'm going to show you." He grins his tobacco-stained grin.

"Are we going to look into a pool of blood and see our futures?" Maisie asks, with an unnerving level of joy in her voice.

"Uh, why are you so excited about buckets of blood?" I ask her.

"I saw it on *Supernatural*," she says. "Dean is so hot. Sam too, but oh my god, *Dean*—"

"When the hell do you have time to watch television?" I don't even have time to take a bath every day.

"It's online." She gives me one of her *duh* stares. "Look it up."

"This is no television program," Monroe says, fighting for our attention. "What I want to show you is real."

I rub my forehead. "The buckets of blood are real?"

"I'm gonna share my dream with you both," he says. "So that you will know what to do when the time comes."

"Here we go with the ominous spooky shit again." I roll my eyes at Maisie who smiles.

"Your life depends on this," Gloria says from behind me. "Take this seriously."

My face flushes and my heart skips a beat. Why is she calling me out?

"So come here and sit in front of me." Monroe waves me forward. "Yes, like that. But Maisie, baby, take off your shoes. We don't want to be interfering with the connection. We got to make good contact the first time."

I look down at my pug socks and worry about getting chicken blood on them. Ally gave me these as a belated Christmas present. Of course, why not destroy them along with everything else in my life. If I think I get to keep any part of this for me, I'm totally lying to myself.

"Why you frownin' so hard?" Monroe asks me.

"She's fighting with Ally," Maisie says.

I scoff. "Mind your own business, twerp!"

"You're the twerp! Don't yell loud enough for the whole house to hear if it's a secret fight!"

"Girls, I need y'all to focus now." His voice rises ever so slightly at the end.

I stick my tongue out at Maisie and then turn my attention to Monroe. "Show me this dream."

"Us," Maisie corrects. "Show *us* the dream. I'm part of this too."

"Yes, Miss Maisie, you sure are." Monroe smiles and pats her knee. "You need two at least for this."

Monroe reaches forward and takes my left hand. Then he takes Maisie's right. He nods at us and I take Maisie's free hand in mine.

"Good good," he says. "Try and clear your head. Some distraction be inevitable, I suppose. But do your best."

I take a deep breath and try to not think about anything. Of course, immediately I see Ally in my head, crying. My mind replays our conversation over and over on a loop. I break up the image with a breath here, an exaggerated sigh here.

At last Monroe squeezes my hand. "That's a good start. Now, I've got to put a little bit of the potion on you."

I open my eyes in time to see Monroe reach a bloody finger toward my eye.

"Whoa." I lean back. "What the hell is that?"

"Chicken blood and herbs." He smears a thumb across my forehead before I can get away.

"Why would you *season* it?" I whine, trying to relax my gag reflex. It's been awhile since I've had to do that. "Who seasons chicken blood?"

The blood is thick, sticky and pretty damn gross. Worse, I can smell it. An acrid stench with a hint of grass and Monroe's tobacco. His thumb is rough and callous and I hope to god he hasn't scratched my skin. That's all I need, some seasoned chicken blood infection in my face.

Maisie swallows and squeezes her eyes shut when it's her turn to receive the bizarre blood blessing. Her nose wrinkles as he swipes his thumb across her forehead. As soon as he takes his hand away, she pantomimes vomiting. Watching her makes my stomach curl.

"Stop that," I beg.

I look over my shoulder at Gloria. "Why aren't you getting blood paint on your face? You're more of a warrior than either of us."

"Mrs. Jackson's done did this. She'll tell you firsthand it works."

Gloria gives a short nod.

The blood starts to itch as it cools on my forehead.

"This is so awesome." Maisie makes a dry heaving motion with her body, cupping her hand over her mouth.

"Seriously, if you do that again, I'm going to puke on you."

"Focus on my voice." Monroe gives my hand a gentle squeeze.

I close my eyes again, trying to do as I'm asked.

Maisie fidgets beside me. "How are you going to do this dream share? I thought your power was the wind thingy."

Monroe squeezes our hands harder. "Shhhh."

At last, we fall quiet. I'm not sure what we are supposed to be listening to exactly. I'm trying not to think about my aching butt on the hard floor or Monroe's blood caked hand in mine.

Then, subtly, I do hear something. The unmistakable sound of waves lapping at a shore.

I open my mouth to ask *what the hell is that* when Monroe gives my hand a gentle squeeze. I swallow my questions. And the sound of the ocean grows louder.

Maisie makes a little sound of surprise beside me and her hand tightens on mine. But she doesn't say anything more as the sounds of the ocean grow louder. A gull cries out, making me jump. Then the heat comes, and with that the feel of sunshine on my bare skin.

I open my eyes expecting to break the spell, to see the dingy little room off the Rue Dauphine.

I see the beach.

The beach is different than the one Gabriel takes me too. Large pebbles and rocks litter this shore, where the ocean meets the land. The smell of salt is strong though, so I know it must be the ocean even as pebbles shift underfoot.

Maisie is standing beside me looking out over the water. She shields her eyes from the sun. "Where are we?"

There's a strange moment when I hear both her voice in

my head and with my ears, back in the room on the Rue Dauphine.

Monroe takes a rolled cigarette from his pocket and puts it between his lips, lighting it in his cupped hand. "Speak with your mind, not your mouth. It'll be easiest that way."

"Is this part of your dream?" The words come out of my dream mouth as if I'd spoken them, but I don't hear the echo of my physical mouth back in the room. So it's like talking to Gabriel. Unfortunately, the ache in my real butt from sitting on the wood floor is still very present.

"This is the meeting place," Monroe blows smoke into the sky. "I think y'all have both been here before, haven't you?"

"Mine is different." I think of the beach house near the shore. The dense jungle that overtakes the beach at a certain point. Here the land goes on and on in all directions. But there is no house. Only a sharp cliff rises behind us. The mossy mountain disappears into the mist high overhead, leaving me without an idea of how tall it really is. It's strange to look back and see the misty mountain only to turn right and see all the sunshine and open sea.

"I see Lake Michigan," Maisie says. "Chicago but with no people."

Her voice begins with the physical echo, but trails into dream speech. Monroe smiles, nodding as if he's pleased with our progress.

"So if we are at 'the meeting place'," I say using air quotes. "Where is this dream we are supposed to see?"

"We've got to go a bit deeper for that." Monroe turns and begins to walk away from us. We follow him down the beach, clamoring over rocks that feel so real. I use my hands to steady myself and the stone is moist with the mist under my palms and my sneakers slide over the surface as if I could really fall and hurt myself on their jagged edges. Dream sneakers, I realize. Courtesy of seasoned chicken blood.

About halfway down the beach I see a group of people. I'm fairly certain that they were not here when I looked up and down the beach before.

But here they stand now. Worse, I recognize them and stiffen.

"Caldwell," I hiss, my ears echoing with my real voice in the little room far away.

"A dream," Monroe says, palms toward me as if to soothe me.

"Mom!" Maisie calls, relief in her voice palpable. She starts running toward the group.

I take off after her. "Wait!"

"They aren't really here." Monroe maintains his patient tone, taking another slow drag on his cigarette. "This is the dream. It always begins this way. I come to the meeting place. I see all of us together, in a circle."

All of us: Me, Caldwell, Georgia, Maisie, Rachel, Liza, Monroe, Cindy, Jason, and a woman I don't recognize. Add a couple of men I don't recognize either. I assume it must be Chaplain and Jake, the only other two partis that I've heard of, but never met, given the fact they both died long before I was on the partis scene.

"Uh, are they ghosts?" I ask. "Is this a ghost beach?"

"What are they doing?" Maisie comes to stand beside me and behind Monroe, gesturing to the pulsating, growing orb in the center of the circle.

I wave my hand in front of Jesse—the other Jesse—but she doesn't seem to react. She's focused on the object in the center of the circle. Everyone is. Only, I'm not entirely convinced that she is really seeing anything at all. Her eyes —*my* eyes—are downcast and unfocused.

"What the hell are they looking at?" I turn to Monroe.

He nods, a low chuckle escaping between his lips. "You've got to step in."

"Say what?"

"The blood will only take us so far. You've got to choose to see it. You must choose to know the truth."

I've got to look as slack jawed and stupid as I feel.

"Go on now." He places a reassuring hand on my back. "Step right on in and you'll see for yourself. You too, Maisie, baby."

Maisie and I exchange worried glances. "When you say step in...?"

"Step into your body. Put one foot where the other is. You'll see what I mean."

Maisie looks as unconvinced as I do.

"If this is some kind of bizarre mind orgy, you'll feel my wrath, Monroe," I warn. Then I take a breath—if what I'm even doing here is called breathing—and I step on myself. I lift one foot and set it down about where the other me's foot is. It's like stepping through a hologram. There's nothing substantial to the other Jesse. I can line my body up with hers.

But as soon as my one foot is lined up with hers, I have a sneaky suspicion that this is going to be more complicated than it seems.

It feels like I've put my foot in a river. A current tugs at my leg, pulling on me.

"I don't know about this," I say to Monroe.

Maisie puts her hands on my back and shoves me forward.

"Hey!" I cry out.

"You first," she calls.

Her voice is swallowed up by the roar in my ears. As soon as I'm fully in the place of hologram Jesse, everything changes.

The beach falls away. Hell, the world falls away. The current surrounds me, pulling me down and down. It feels like a drain, the way I circle around and around, my hair whipping wildly around me. Yet the other eleven partis seem to keep their formation, each of us equidistant from the other. I look up and try to understand what I'm seeing. It's like looking up through the center of a tornado. The cyclone is dark and violent around us. In the center is a brilliant light, flashes of lightning cutting through the torrent. Below, far below from where I'm suspended is...what?

What is that? I try to ask. But my voice doesn't materialize in my head or in the dreamscape.

I'm tiring, Liza says. Her voice shocks me back to my present moment and my bizarre suspension in the cyclone current.

This seems to mean something to everyone else. They reach out and clasp hands. Monroe beside me clasps my hand and Jason on the other side takes the other. I look up from our clasped hands in time to see Liza grow bright white until her entire form is washed away.

The white light spreads, moving into Caldwell and Cindy's hands where they stand holding her. The light leaks from Liza's form into their bodies. The white light that I understand to be what is left of Liza, travels around the full circle until it reaches me. There's a moment of panic just before it touches me that I think to let go, but Monroe's hold on my hand tightens.

The white light is warm, pleasant. But as soon as it settles into my chest, the torrent kicks up, the cyclone growing more violent around me.

Then Minli gives up her power too—and that's when I understand what is happening. They hold on until they can't, then they pass their gift to the others in the group.

The only problem is that the power grows more violent, more turbulent with the lesser number of conduits.

The numbers dwindle down. I watch each partis fade to

bright light that my body absorbs until it is only me and Caldwell, holding hands of all things.

The storm rages and I think it will tear me apart. I think the lightning from above might strike me and burn me to a crisp. I imagine it would be painful. The amount of power rushing through me already feels like lightning under my skin. I don't think I can possibly absorb any more.

Then Caldwell says, "Take it."

No, I think. It was never supposed to be housed by one. It was supposed to be all of us for as long as we could.

"Take it, Jesse."

He begins to glow, lightning filling his eyes, and pouring from his opening mouth. It trails his jaw, neck, and limbs, rushing from his fingers into mine.

I take it, drinking it all down but it's too much. There's too much.

I scream.

I scream and scream, falling back into the black cyclone. I'm falling as I'd done so often in death. The sensation is the same, the immense and impenetrable darkness rising up to envelop me. I try to breath but can't.

I'm dying.

Oh god, no, I'm dying.

"*B*reathe, Jesse," a voice says. It's neither male nor female. And it sounds so far away. "Come on, breathe."

Feeling as though I've broken the surface of an enormous lake, I suck in a great gasping breath. I come up on my elbows, and then roll onto my knees and heave. My hands scrape against the wood. My chest burns as if I've been holding my breath for a long time.

"Thatagirl," Monroe says and slaps my back. "In through your nose."

I open my eyes and the first thing I see are my hands. They're pressed against the wooden floor in the small room inside a tiny house off the Rue Dauphine. I remember the little sidewalk and the rotting screen door. The place comes back to me. I sit back on my knees and find out how shaken I am.

Maisie is sitting against one of the walls, a blanket wrapped around her. She's shaking too, with sweat beading across her forehead and face. Her cheeks are flushed bright red and her eyes dilated. I can still smell the blood, but also ash and the stench of an extinguished candle.

"Why was she in the dream for so long?" Maisie asks. Her teeth chatter around the words.

I reach up and wipe my brow. I'm as sweaty and gross as she is. I feel like I've come out of a feverish delirium, my eyes focusing on the first tangible object I see. Gloria's face.

She pushes a cup toward my face. I take it, but the cup trembles so badly in my hand that Gloria doesn't let go. She holds onto the bottom of the cup.

I take a big gulp of coffee. I know it's coffee from the rich smell, but the taste is off. It's so strong, bitter. "What. The. Fuck?"

"Chicory," Gloria says, holding the cup up to my face until I push it away. "It's better than Dr. Pepper."

"If you say so." I rake my teeth across my tongue. The flesh feels burnt. "Seriously, what the hell just happened?"

"You saw the truth," Monroe says. He's unwrapping the half remaining inch of his cigarette and tapping the unused tobacco out onto his palm.

"O-kay." I pull at my face again, trying to shake off the feverish sickness clinging to me. "What the hell is the truth?"

"We wasn't supposed to be killing each other." He stuffs the last bit of rolling paper in his pocket and slides the sealed container of tobacco back into his front shirt pocket.

Maisie's teeth chatter. "But there's supposed to be an apex. There's only supposed to be one who holds all the power."

"No. It was never meant to be a burden for one soul to bear." Monroe looks absolutely exhausted. Deep puffy bags sit under his dark eyes. He rubs his forehead. "The shield is a gift. If we want to keep this rock spinning, we've got to recharge the shield. How do we recharge?"

"Electricity," Gloria offers. Probably because Maisie's

teeth are chattering too wildly to speak and I feel like my head is split in two.

"Yes, ma'am," Monroe nods, still rubbing his forehead. "They turned on the switch. They be sending the electricity down the wire."

"Who?" I manage.

"The angels. But they need wires. They need batteries to store the juice."

"That's us."

He puts one hand on his knee. "That's us. But the energy transfer will kill us, no avoiding that."

"So then why twelve partis? Why the competition to be the wire?"

"To be the battery, not the wire," Monroe says. "We're all the wires. It's the battery that will power the shield long after the body is gone."

"Why twelve?"

"It be a kindness," Monroe says with sorrow etched deeply in his face. "We were never meant to do this alone."

Before I can process this, Ally bursts into the room. "He's MIA again." Ally's brow furrows when she sees Maisie in a blanket shivering in cold sweat and me wiping my brow. "Are you guys okay? Is that blood all over your face?"

"What the hell was in the chicken blood, Monroe?"

I roll to one side again and dry heave.

"Monroe!" Gloria screams.

Monroe reaches down and grabs the bloody knife off the floor. I look up in time to see the two men collide. Monroe slams into Caldwell, burying the knife to the hilt in Caldwell's neck, in the place where the shoulder meets the collarbone. Caldwell lets out a screeching wail like an animal being gutted alive and stumbles back. Monroe throws his hands up and the torrential wind comes, throwing everyone to the floor except Caldwell who is lifted up and thrown through the wall with the gale force wind. I crawl on my hands and knees toward Maisie. Trying to reach her takes tremendous effort, but then I clasp onto her ankle and yank her into my arms.

Ally's arms wrap around my waist. I want to find Gloria next but the vertigo and nausea keeps washing over me in waves and I feel like I'm on a huge boat out to sea. I don't know what Monroe did with his weird chicken blood shit, but something isn't right.

"Gloria, get over here!" I scream but she stands with her back to the wall, gun raised and waiting. I realize she's covering Monroe. No one in this room believes Caldwell's truly disappeared. Through the hole in the side of the house I see at least four armed guards fully geared. They have their guns up and ready, half pointed at the dense trees behind them, the other half at the space between the lawn and Monroe.

I pull away from Ally and Maisie.

"What are you doing?" Ally demands an answer more than asks a question.

"Keep shielding Maisie," I tell her. "This could be a trick to get Maisie back." It sure feels like he's fucking with us. I've seen Caldwell when he means business. It's all break necks and leave. This cat-mouse game is different.

I power up. I feel the itch of raw energy flow from my chest out to my fingers and toes. It goes to my fingertips crackling electric in the air around me. The hairs on my arms stand up but I don't ignite. I wait. I wait for Caldwell to show his face.

Caldwell appears behind Monroe and Gloria gets two bullets into his chest, then a third a little higher than the first round. But adjusting her aim isn't enough.

He's ripped the knife from his throat. Great spurts of blood hit the floor like a geyser but he acts like he couldn't care less. He stabs Monroe in the chest and Monroe cries out.

His eyes go wide and he cries out again as Caldwell twists the handle.

Gloria gets off a fourth shot and it rips through Caldwell's right ear. He lets go of Monroe and has the good sense to cover his head before Gloria can blow Caldwell's brains out. I would fire bomb his ass, but I don't have a clear shot. Jeremiah's soldiers in the yard must feel the same way. They adjust their positions but can't get a direct line to Caldwell without catching Monroe in the crossfire.

When Caldwell turns around I see his glassy, unfocused eyes. He looks right through me, one hand on his bleeding ear and the other over his cut throat. He's lost too much blood. He's going to pass out and die. As if he decides I'm right, he falls and Gloria's gun goes off.

He never hits the floor. His body simply disappears on the way down. Gloria's bullet goes straight into the floor without having hit its target.

Monroe drops to his knees, clutching his throat and grimacing.

He makes a half-hearted gesture for me to come closer. His eyes slide to Maisie and he waves her forward too.

"Hurry now," he croaks but his voice is strange, probably because of the wound. "I ain't got long."

I crawl across the room, still trying to fight the wave of nausea. Maisie pulls away from Ally as soon as I drop the shield and we reach him at the same time. Maisie is the first to grab his hand.

"No," I say and knock her hand away. "You're going to take his power. Let him die and when he wakes up he'll be fine."

"There's no time for that," Monroe says. "I've got to show you now."

Monroe grabs my hand and Maisie's. It's too much like

the dreamscape with our doppelgangers in all their Kumbaya glory.

"This is how it's supposed to be," Monroe says. "Y'all see what I'm saying. Hold on to me now."

I'm trying to yank my hand away. "Live." I want to scream but he won't let go of me. His old hand is impossibly strong on mine.

Monroe gasps and his hand convulses in mine.

Warmth shoots up my arm, racing toward my heart. My chest is filled with fire and the fire doesn't stop there. It crawls up the back of my throat, burning my nose before settling into my brain. It's like a swarm of fire ants have crawled through my ears and have started liquefying my gray matter.

I want to let go, clutch my skull and scream, but I can't. I can't move my body, or breathe, or call out for help. I'm frozen, locked into the pain of Monroe's death.

I do manage to open my eyes but I don't see Monroe on his knees in the destroyed room. No soldiers with guns. No shocked Ally or Gloria watching helplessly. I open my eyes and see Monroe in the dreamscape. He's glowing white, bright as a star, but I can still see his face. His beautiful smile, so full of relief.

"This is what we were always meant to be," he says and I see the wings. His wings with feathers the color of a dove's stretch out on either side of him. Then the light overtakes him and he's gone.

The room comes back into focus and someone is crying.

Maisie. She's sobbing into her hands, her face covered by her palms. I don't move or say anything.

"Jesse?" Ally kneels down in front of me. The men with guns have climbed through the hole in the wall and are standing in the room awkwardly. Everyone is waiting for something to happen.

Ally reaches up and wipes a thumb under my nose. It comes away bright red with my blood. "Jess? Say something."

Maisie is still crying. "Why would he just die?"

She pulls her knees into her chest and wraps her arms around them, hiding her face. Her sobs grow louder.

"He wanted to die." Gloria holsters her gun and places a hand on Maisie's head. Her voice is hard and steady, but her eyes give her away. Tears pool in the corner of her eyes as she stares at Monroe's lifeless body in the center of the room. It isn't imploding like the others had. No blue fire incineration. His body only lies there.

"Why is he still here? Why didn't he catch fire like the others?" I ask.

Ally looks up and starts talking to someone in black body armor. "Can you—"

"Of course," Nikki says. "Kirch, Franklin. Help me with this."

"Monroe." I seize her armored calf. "His name was Monroe."

She doesn't even fight me on it. "Of course. Please help me with Monroe."

"No, wait," Maisie says. "Wait, wait!"

She crawls toward Monroe's body. She places her hands on his chest and bends over into his face. She's touching his bloody shirt but doesn't seem to notice her hands are staining red.

Gloria grabs her and pulls her off the body.

"Let me try!" Maisie wails. "Let me try!"

"No," Gloria says gently. "It's not what he wanted."

Maisie shrugs her off and lunges but Gloria has to seize her again before she can blow up his nose like she did to Winston a few months ago. Three little puffs and then he might stir, might come back to life. Would it work? We won't find out because Gloria is holding Maisie above the body while the others prepare to take him away.

The body.

Because that's all that's left of Monroe.

"Did you absorb his power or was another partis called?" Ally asks, such a callous question. She's searching Maisie and me for any signs. "You were both touching him at his time of death but neither of you seem to be 'rebooting'?" Ally uses air quotes around the word 'rebooting'. She doesn't like that term, but I agree there isn't a more accurate one.

"They absorbed it," Gloria says. "That is what Monroe wanted you to understand. You can share power. You do not need to kill each other for it. You can give it freely."

I imagine what that might look like: Me, Maisie, and Rachel in a circle, all alive and well. All casting a shield that protects the world. It's not ideal. It's not my 'get the girl and live happily ever after daydream', but having my friends alive, my sister alive, and the woman I love safe is a decent second place prize.

"I do feel a little—funny," Maisie admits.

"I do too." Though it's hard to explain exactly what's changed.

"Cast a shield," Gloria instructs.

"I don't know how that would—"

"Cast a shield and see if you have more power," she insists. "The only way you'd have more power is because he gave it to you. Try."

I cast my shield.

"Shit," Nikki says.

Ally and I are both speechless. The shield is huge. The entire room is coated in a violet glow. It covers the eight of us easily: me, Gloria, Maisie, Nikki, Ally, even Monroe and the two soldier helpers who'd come at Nikki's command to move the body.

"I can feel it." Maisie's eyes grow as wide as half dollars. "I can *feel* your shield."

I try to make the shield bigger and it grows, expanding without effort. Not only is it so much bigger, but it moves with finesse. It passes over objects without knocking anything back. And the purple glow is intense, so much brighter than it ever had been in the past.

I drop the shield, beginning to feel a little tired, with a touch of headache forming behind my eyes.

Maisie bounces with excitement. "I could feel your power. Can you feel me?"

The answer is no. "I guess we won't know until you do the back-to-life thing," I tell her.

Ally helps me to my feet. In the back of my mind, some-where far away, I remember our fight. But now with Monroe's power coursing through me, I can't seem to stay mad. A little sad, maybe, but I can't hold on to my anger.

"If we can get Rachel on board—" Maisie says.

"If she *wants* to share the power," Ally adds, sounding hopeful. "Then perhaps you won't become unstable when you assimilate Caldwell and Georgia's gifts."

I meet her eyes. "Is that why you stopped me from murdering him in the church?"

I envision this again for the second time in as many days: Caldwell and I locked arm in arm, bodies blazing. I would have killed him then if Ally hadn't stopped me.

Her face falls. "I'm afraid that if you—either of you—kill him, it will tear you apart. He has so many powers already. Even absorbing one makes a person unstable. Absorbing so many at once—"

"But we can share now," Maisie says, so hopeful.

"But if Rachel and Caldwell and Georgia won't let you share, it may come to violence," Ally says.

Anger and fear washes over me. *No one is hurting my mom. They won't dare. I'll tear them apart—*

Wait, what?

I turn to Maisie and see all of these emotions playing out on her face.

It's Maisie who cares. Apparently Monroe's hookup is more than a power share. Oh god, I hope the kid isn't getting all my convoluted feels for Ally too.

"Gloria—" Ally looks away as Nikki and the others take hold of Monroe's body. I too let my eyes slide to an indeterminate spot on the floor. "When I was searching for information on the partis, I discovered that Monroe attempted suicide at least twice. Why?"

"His boy was killed," Gloria says without inflection. But she also won't look any of us in the eyes.

He's my heart, that boy. Monroe had said once. But he'd only ever talked about the boy in present tense. I'd assumed he was somewhere safe, like my little brother Daniel. Alive and well and far far away from all this madness.

That's what I get for assuming.

"He wanted his death to mean something in the end," Gloria says. "And now it does."

Maisie and I exchange a glance. She feels guilty. Or I do. I can't tell. Maybe we are sharing guilt over Monroe's bittersweet goodbye.

"But if Rachel is already unstable—"

"It doesn't matter. She's our friend." The anger rises. But it isn't as sharp as before. It's tinged with doubt now. And fear. I shoot Maisie a sharp look.

"I'm sorry!" she says. "But she's crazy!"

"She's our friend," I say, trying to flood her little sensor with all the trust and love I have for Rachel. I think it actually works. Her shoulders relax. "She will help us. I'm sure of it. Especially now that there's another way."

CHAPTER TWENTY-FOUR

Rachel

I can't describe how excited I am to reach Arizona. Everything in me is begging for the next fight.

"Can't you make it go any faster?" I ask, a headache building behind my eyes. It feels like tiny creatures are going to push the top of my head right off.

"I don't have a gadget for controlling traffic, darling." Gideon glances at me from the driver's seat of a brand new Mercedes. It was the first luxury car we could find. At the edge of the lot, we walked right up to the door and climbed in. This was after I unlocked it from the outside, of course. The push button starter required no key at all.

"Drive on the shoulder?"

"What shoulder?" he asks. "There are concrete barriers on both sides."

I look at the long line of red tail lights stretching before me.

You are subject to no one, Uriel says in my ear. He isn't visible. There's no place for him to materialize in this two-seater.

A fresh wave of anger washes over me, flushing my cheeks

with warmth. An idea comes to me and I look at Gideon and grin.

"I am subject to no one," I say aloud.

He gives me a crooked smile. Not entirely pleasure, but also a hint of fear.

I wag my eyebrows. "Hold on pretty boy."

I focus on the cars ahead of me. I concentrate until I can feel that part of my arm, the extension of my power, wrap over the metal bodies. I enclose one after another with my power. Then I lift. The cars go straight up into the air.

Gideon makes a choked sound of surprise. "*No.*"

"Drive," I tell him as the first few cars reveal their underbellies, a map of axles and fuel lines. A few tires spin desperately but find no ground to cling to. "Drive!"

Gideon swears and throws the car into gear. The Mercedes accelerates beautifully, a flawless advance. I look up at the undercarriages as we speed beneath one car, then five and ten. Gideon has to slow once when I don't lift the car as quickly as he's accelerating.

I turn in my seat in time to see the first cars falling back to the highway. They slam against the pavement. Windows burst out. Tires explode on impact.

I'm laughing so hard my sides hurt.

Gideon scowls at me from the driver seat. "You could injure someone."

"Spoil sport," I pout. "Don't ruin all the fun."

His worried features twist in on themselves, until it isn't fear or irritation in that dark brow now. His lips crook up in a smile.

"Admit it." I reach over the gear shift and give his thigh a squeeze. "You're having fun."

He puts one hand on mine, stopping me from going higher to yank open his belt. "We have 3000 pounds dangling overhead."

"You do like it. Danger. Chaos." *And it's why I like you.*

He's grinning now. A genuine smile. Gideon may tell himself that he has morals, but I know what he loves most. A semi begins to lift off the ground and Gideon slows the Mercedes.

"Faster," I say.

He doesn't.

"Hit the gas!"

He obeys and the Mercedes accelerates. I count eighteen wheels before I see the underside of the cabin.

"I'm amazing!"

Gideon laughs. "That you are. There isn't another creature like you on the planet."

I warm at his words. My desire to pull over and fuck the boy wars with my desire to get to Arizona and kill someone. Life is full of tough decisions.

The traffic jam breaks ahead and gives way to slow moving cars. But I don't stop. I shove the cars off the road, clearing a direct lane for Gideon and I.

"How fast can this Mercedes go?"

"About 245 km/h."

"Show me." I press my head back against the seat just before he punches the gas. I focus all my attention on the cars ahead of me, shoving them from our path.

Gideon breaks out into gleeful laughter. "This is so much better than Grand Theft Auto."

I'm laughing too even though a shadow passes over my mind.

Uriel?

Silence.

Something is wrong. I don't know what, but something is happening.

I hear Jesse and Maisie. Voices chatter softly in the back

of my mind. I can't hear the words clearly, but I recognize the tone and pitch. And then the emotions come.

Panic. Anger. Fear.

I try to hold on to it, amplify it, and get a better sense of what is happening, but I can't. A headache explodes behind my eyes and I clasp my hands over my face. I see Jesse and Maisie standing in a circle with others, holding hands and chanting They are in the center of a vortex, wind whipping around them ruthlessly.

Monroe steps forward and places both his hands on the side of my face.

White hot fire shoots from his fingertips into my skull. I try to stagger back from the old man, but he won't let go. And I'm thousands of miles away from Louisiana on a turn-pike in New Jersey. He shouldn't have any power over me here.

Monroe's hold on me tightens. "Remember who your heart is."

"Fuck!" Gideon screams.

I pull my eyes open in time to see a car swerve in front of the Mercedes. I try to move it, but my power is thick and sluggish in my veins.

I only manage to move the baby blue Volkswagen beetle to the left enough that we scrape along its side, door to door. Sparks rain onto the windshield and Gideon. As soon as we are clear of the big blue Ford truck on the right of us, we coast right off into the ditch. Thank goodness the turnpike has grown shoulders. If we'd done this one mile back, there would've been nowhere for us to go but straight into a concrete barrier.

"Christ, Rachel!" Gideon yells. His voice is cold and sharp. "What the bloody hell?"

"Monroe," I say, squeezing the side of my head. "He's doing something to the powerlines."

Gideon's eyes slide up to the sky. His tone is kinder when he speaks again. "What power lines?"

"No," I groan. I tap my temples. "The ones in here."

He stares at me, lips parted. He doesn't say anything else. At last he reaches out and puts a hand on my shoulder. "Are you okay?"

No. It feels like someone has been reading my diary. Someone has gone somewhere they shouldn't. I don't like it one bit.

"Get back on the road." I pry open my eyes and see trees. "We need to catch up to them."

Something flashes across Gideon's face. Fear? Apprehension? I can't get a good read because of my pounding head. I curl up into the seat and press against my temples harder, hoping to relieve some of the pressure there.

"The road is clearing up ahead." He shifts gears and gives me a strained smile from the driver's seat. "It looks like we won't need your immense talents at the moment."

"Good." Because I need to save my strength.

"Authorities say the Mercedes was stolen from a car lot just south of the city, near the interstate. We have positively identified the woman as Rachel Wright, asylum escapee and one of the five terrorists responsible for the kidnapping of Maisie Caldwell, daughter of esteemed church leader Timothy Caldwell. Anyone with any information is encouraged to call 1-888—"

"He's probably still dead from the blood loss," Maisie says around a mouthful of Reese's Pieces. She tosses one to Winston who catches it in the air. "It takes like eight hours, right?"

"The database says six. Its entry was updated this afternoon." Ally turns to me. "Can you imagine it? There are people out there, carrying on, having replacements, completely unaware of all of this."

I watch Winston catch another candy in his mouth. "Lucky dogs."

I curl up deeper into the cushions and hug my knees against my chest. I feel sick. It's like my stomach acid is flooding up the back of my throat.

Winston licks my hand and I give him half-hearted thanks. "What a loyal little buddy." I'm trying not to register the number flashing on the television at the bottom of the news program. What would I say if I called?

Hey, yeah, so that crazy bitch throwing cars all over the interstate is my friend. She's sort of insane with these super-powers, so you should shut down the roads and stay the hell out of her way. By the way we're not terrorists. Stop calling us that.

That'd go over well.

Ally sees my face and uses the remote to change the channel. "Let's watch something else."

Maisie crumples up the candy wrapper and tosses it across the room into a wastebasket. "I'm still hungry. Can we go get some Chinese? No, let's get more of that fried chicken! That stuff was amazeballs."

I rub my forehead. "I'm not sure we can leave."

All three of us look toward the hallway. Nikki and Gloria are in the next room exchanging angry, hushed whispers.

Maisie huffs. "I'll starve to death before they agree on anything. Then I'll wake up and be even hungrier."

Ally turns up the volume on the television.

A female announcer leans forward on her elbows, speaking directly to the camera while footage appears in the box by her head. "We've begun to see irregular flight patterns for birds. More whales than ever before are washing up on shores. Our very own correspondent Cameron Groove reports."

The screen changes. The woman in the warm, dry studio is replaced by a man in a bright yellow wind jacket braced against the torrent tearing at his hair and face. He clutches the microphone against his chest while holding his hood in place with the other hand.

"Cameron here on the highland coast. As you can see behind me, three orcas have washed ashore."

"How sad!" Maisie exclaims. She crushes Winston against her chest. Immediately, he starts rooting around in the folds of her sweater for dropped candies.

"It's the latest in reported beachings. Scientists suggest that ocean conditions and navigational errors are causing these animals to—"

"Can we turn this off?" I ask.

Ally flips the channel. "Maybe something educational?"

"The NOAA reports a very active solar storm brewing on the Sun's surface as we speak. Dr. Okasai is here with us to explain what a solar storm is and how it affects Earth."

"That's correct, Mrs. Hatchet. One storm alone could irreparably damage our ecosystems or extinguish all life on Earth. Thankfully, we have a shield that protects us from this threat. The strong electromagnetic field surrounding the planet prevents radiation, solar winds, and other space debris from entering our atmosphere. Without the shield, life on Earth may not be possible. In recent years, we've seen changes in our shield and given its importance, you can understand why scientists are concerned about the possible consequences of these developments."

"Jesus Christ!" I throw myself back against the pillows. "This planet is falling apart. Why bother saving it?"

Maisie gasps. "Because this is where Winnie Pug lives. And the orcas."

I give Ally a look. "If you don't turn this off, I'm going to explode the TV."

"But I want to watch it," Maisie begs, smushing Winston's wrinkly face against hers. "I'm trying to learn stuff. This is the only education I'm going to get!"

Nikki steps into the room with her hands on her hips and scowls down at me. Ally reaches out and places one hand on my leg while looking up at Nikki. It's a small comfort. Sasquatch looks at the hand, then tugs on her ponytail, tightening it.

"Jackson refuses to let us accompany you."

Ally doesn't say anything. She knows the plan as well as I do, and Nikki and Jeremiah have no part in it. It's us and Caldwell for this final rodeo. More people means interference. And what good are they anyway? When Caldwell showed up, they stood there waiting for a clean shot that never came and now Monroe is dead.

You didn't do anything either a little hateful voice says in my head. *What did you do to save him?*

"You're going to get in your trucks and drive away because you know better than to cross Gloria," I say. It's more of a wishful statement than any kind of command.

"Then you're going to follow us anyway," Ally says still holding Nikki's gaze.

Nikki's face softens, going all doe-eyed. She kneels down so that she can look Ally straight in the eye. "I won't be far."

"Oh god. This isn't a soap opera." I push myself up off the couch. "Get off your knees, Lancelot."

I storm out of the room only to be stopped by Gloria on the landing before I can run up the stairs and lock myself away again. I'm itching to talk to Gabriel. I want his help to decipher Brinkley's message. *Remember* he said.

The problem is my memory isn't so great. But Gabriel helped me with that once before. When I returned to my old house for my mother's funeral, Gabriel made me remember everything I'd forgotten about my past. I'd remembered Ally. Some of the worst parts of Eddie's abuse. My mother and little brother Daniel. It hadn't been pleasant, but I'd remembered. And I want Gabriel to help me remember again.

Gloria stops me on the first step.

"I need to talk to you." A rush of protests come to mind,

but Gloria never asks me for anything. So the pure novelty of the request is enough to surprise me.

"Now?"

"Now." She pushes open the screen door and holds it open.

Damn. Asking for Gabriel's help will have to wait.

Before she closes the door behind us she turns to Ally. "We'll be back in a little while. Stay near the house."

"Okay." Ally looks as surprised by Gloria's request as I am.

"Bring me some chicken!" Maisie shouts. "And a biscuit!"

I wait on the little stoop for Gloria to pull the door closed behind her and descend the steps. She heads down the garden path without looking back to see if I'm following her. I meet up with her as she passes through the wrought iron gate and steps out onto the Rue Dauphine.

"Where are we going?" I ask.

"I want to take a walk," she says, offering no more explanation.

"O-kay," I say, keeping up with her. This part of the French Quarter is relatively deserted. We hurry down the clean streets and vacant balconies. I keep waiting for her to give me a clue what this is about, but she just keeps hurrying along.

At the next intersection, she hooks right onto Toulouse, marching past the green shutters of a hotel, toward two large flags waving in the wind. Like Chicago, this place has a constant breeze that blows in off the water. Unlike Chicago or New York for that matter, this place is pretty warm for January. And I'm not complaining about that one bit.

I settle into the rhythm of our walk and appreciate the breeze on my face. The wind is a welcome change to the stuffiness of Monroe's house. Somehow, it went from cozy to stuffy the moment he died. Funny how a dead body can totally change your mood.

"I'm sorry about your friend," I say. "He seemed like a good guy."

"He was a drunk and a fool," Gloria says, without changing her pace.

I gulp down a fit of laughter. "Uh, I'm sorry about that too...?"

Her face softens as she adjusts her sketchbook under her arm, repinning it between her ribs and left arm. "He was a good man."

"How did his kid die?" I brace myself for some horrible story. Caldwell strung him up and skinned him, trying to get Monroe to comply, to fight and forfeit his power. Or something worse than I can imagine. With Caldwell, any level of depravity was possible.

"It wasn't anyone's fault. It was accidental, but he's dead all the same."

"Do you want to die?" I ask.

She stops walking.

"I just meant that you've lost a lot of people too."

"Yes." Her voice is deep with sorrow. "I think death will be very peaceful."

Before I can add some platitudes about how much she has to live for, she speaks again.

"But I have work to do."

And as if to illustrate this fact, her pace doubles.

My legs start to ache as she hooks a left on Chartres Street. The sound of jazzy trumpets erupts, but the spunky tune isn't enough to cheer me. By the next block a cramp settles into my right ribcage. "Oh my god, where are we going? Are we getting our 10,000 steps for the day? Walking for a cancer cure?"

"I want to show you something." She nods toward some unseen destination up ahead. "Come on."

"Can you show me the light post right here? No really. Let's sit down and admire its, uh, craftsmanship." I wheeze.

"You're out of shape."

"Don't body shame me, G! All bodies are beautiful!"

She picks up her pace. For fuck's sake.

"If I'd known we were going to powerwalk today, I wouldn't have had that fourth pancake at breakfast. You have to tell me these things ahead of time."

Chartres ends at St. Peter, opening up the palatial Jackson Square. The jazz band is in full swing here, with onlookers clapping and dancing along to the tune. Two toddlers in light jackets spin drunken circles on the stone walk as if that is the best way to enjoy this kind of music.

I make eye contact with a girl at a card table and read her little sign aloud. "Tarot Reading. Looking for love, money, or truth? It's right here."

She grins and I see a flash of fangs. As we pass, I also realize her eyes are like a snake's, slits from top to bottom. "Cool contacts," I mumble, hoping both are fake as hell. After all, there's already enough monsters in the world.

I dodge the twirly kids and catch Gloria on the steps of the Jackson cathedral. She maneuvers around the gawking tourists easily and slips into the dim atrium.

I place one hand on her arm, holding on so that I don't lose her in the push of the crowd. She doesn't shrug me off so I take that as permission to hold onto her, even though I'm pretty sure Gloria doesn't like to be touched.

The church is barely lit inside with the exception of small, red candles ignited by patrons seeking blessings. A person can drop their money into the offering box, take a candle, light it, and make a prayer.

Save your money, I want to say. If he loved you, he sure as hell wouldn't pick my ass to save you.

Actually, why don't you hand that cash straight on over to *moi*? I'm the best chance you've got.

Jackson slips into an empty pew and slides over enough so there's room to sit beside her.

"Oh god, we aren't going to pray for our sins, are we?" My heart hammers. "Because we don't have enough time in the world for me to get through that list."

"This is a safe place to talk."

I look around the cathedral at the gaggles of tourists. "Uh, if you say so."

She flips open her sketchbook and finds a page. "When we arrive in Arizona, I'll probably need you to blow through this wall."

She shows me the old military compound with its bright white barrier. It's like a fortress sans moat.

"I can do that."

"Then I will get the power turned on."

"Yeah, don't want to wander around a creepy deserted torture camp in the dark," I say with a gulp.

"The device we intend to trap Georgia in will also require power."

"Right. So blast the wall. Get the lights on and then wait for them to come. Do you think they'll show up early?"

"We would be in danger of that if Monroe had failed to kill him."

"That was on purpose?"

Gloria nods. "If we'd managed to kill him, the plan was to split the power three ways between you, Monroe, and Maisie. But the minimum objective was achieved nonetheless. Monroe bought us safe passage to Arizona. Caldwell will wake up before we arrive, but he will have a hard time tracking us in motion. He's been trying to use A.M.P.s to follow our movements, but they aren't as good as Micah."

I feel like I should apologize again. After all, she had to kill her own brother in order to protect us from Caldwell.

"Now we must focus on making the best decisions," she says.

"I make good decisions," I say, defensively. "Okay, maybe I shouldn't have bought that sixty-dollar blender from the infomercial, but that was *one* time. Well, okay, yes, I guess there was also the hundred-dollar Puppy Plush Palace, but Winston loved that thing!" Before I burned the whole house down that is.

"Here." Gloria looks up from the sketchbook, glancing around her to make sure everyone else is far enough away.

I scoot a little closer so I can look at the picture. It's so dim in here that the detail isn't great. Yet even in the low light, a couple of things stick out.

First of all, the dead bodies. Caldwell. Ally. Gideon.

Ally.

Ally.

"Don't panic." Gloria's voice is perfectly even.

I blink at her, sucking in a sharp breath.

"Don't," she says with slightly more inflection. "There are people in here."

I'm not panicking. I want whoever is making that horrible noise to shut up. Oh wait, that's me. The low guttural moan that actually sounds a lot like panic grows louder.

"Say something."

"She's dead!" I shout. Immediately, several people *shhhh* me. My head snaps up to see an obese woman in socks and sandals pressing one finger over her lips. Gloria's fingers dig into my arm.

"She's dead," I hiss through clenched teeth.

"So is Caldwell," Gloria says.

"Fuck Caldwell, *Ally* is dead."

"I *know*," she says, the first sign of impatience showing in her face and tone.

"What do you mean you *know*, Gloria. What the hell does that mean?"

"Keep your voice down," she whispers. "I don't want to be kicked out. This is one of the few places in the whole city where I can show my drawings and they won't end up on satellites or someone's MyPage."

I bite my tongue so hard I see stars. It swells instantly, which shuts me up more than anything. Pain in the mouth has a way of deflating my rage unlike anything else. It's totally different than stubbing a toe. Stub a toe and I want to murder someone.

"The way I see it," Gloria goes on, emboldened by my self-imposed silence. "We manage to kill Caldwell in the desert as planned. That's what we want."

"I want Ally alive." I want it way more than I want Caldwell dead. In fact, I would probably let Caldwell go be a douche to someone else if it meant that Ally and I could live in peace for the rest of our lives. But I know I'm not that lucky and Ally would never turn a blind eye to injustice.

"Here is the alternative," Gloria says. She flips to the next page and the body count is much higher. In this picture, Gloria is dead. Maisie is dead. Georgia is dead. Gideon is dead. Rachel is dead. Their bodies strewn like litter across the desert floor. Basically everyone but Ally is dead.

"We don't actually fight him in the desert, do we?" I say, a glimmer of hope welling up in my chest. "We're in the facility. So maybe this is wrong. You've been wrong before."

Gloria gives me a hateful look. "If you focus only on saving Ally, we all die and Caldwell gets away. That's the bottom line. I want you to know that before we go in."

"What kind of ultimatum is that?"

"You are free to do what you want," Gloria says.

"It's not like I want you to die," I say, guilt hardening in my stomach.

"I don't care if I live or die," she says in a perfectly even tone. I have to believe her. "It's about the mission. If Caldwell gets away, we do not fulfill the mission. And I haven't chased this man for ten years only to let him go."

She closes the sketchbook and looks up at the angel statue in front of us.

I search for an idea. Anything. *Anything* that will keep Ally alive and take out Georgia and Caldwell as planned. But my mind blanks. Instead of brilliant useful ideas, all I feel is blind panic. The image of Ally dead flashes over and over and over again.

"I have an alternative idea," Gloria says.

"I'm listening."

"We use Maisie as bait, have her draw Georgia into the room so we can get her in the device and have the upper hand. It will be better if Maisie is with Ally, in the shield, and we are exposed."

"They may not come," I say.

"They will if the prize is appealing enough."

I frown.

"If I wound you, you'll seem like easy prey. Caldwell will target you."

I blink at her. "You want to incapacitate *me*, your fire-bombing cannon girl, the moment before the most important fight?"

"Yes."

I'm trying to piece together her ideas. Lie down and play dead. Caldwell comes. We all die. And then what? Maisie brings us back to life. "I don't know. The last time you tried to out-plan the bad guys, Lane and Ally were stabbed to death in a basement. Brinkley and I didn't fare too well either."

Brinkley.

Brinkley and the weird dream—vision—whatever the hell it is, comes back to me.

"And I think Brinkley wants us to save Rachel more than kill Caldwell," I say. Gloria pivots in the pew so she can see my face. She frowns and then arches her eyebrows, encouraging me to spill it.

I tell her about the beach house. I tell her about Brinkley's visit and his message. She smiles once or twice—when I mention the leather jacket and the beer cans. But by the time I finish the story she isn't smiling anymore.

"You don't know it's him," Gloria says.

"It was him," I insist. "I don't know how, but it was him. It—it...it *felt* like him, if that makes sense. It even smelled like him. That cologne—"

"Drakkar Noir," she says without hesitation.

"O-*kay*." I grin. "Don't know how you know that, but sure. Anyway, it was him. He wants us to help her, not kill her."

I realize what I'm saying. How did this happen? How did I go from believing Rachel would never betray me to accepting she's a homicidal maniac?

"Rachel's actions are influencing this outcome as much as yours. That's why the vision is unclear."

"Can I see it again?" I ask, nodding toward the sketchbook.

Gloria opens it up to the page. *If you only focus on Ally, we all die.* That's what she'd said. Yet, when I see her body, Ally is all I can think about.

Could I really let us all die and rely on Maisie to bring us back? What if Maisie is taken before she can? Or is killed? It seems too messy, reckless, and unclear. But keeping Maisie away from Georgia does seem like an inherently better plan. The more I realize what a struggle this is for Maisie, the more I think she should be far away from Georgia during the fight, lest her instincts to protect her mother take over.

In the picture, Ally is lying there so peacefully. Her face perfectly serene and smooth. She could be sleeping. In this version of some possible future, did Caldwell kill her? But how? Her neck isn't twisted. There's no gaping wound from a bullet or assault. No blood even. The only other time I've seen a body just fall dead was because of Georgia. When she uses her death ribbons, the serpentine black smoke makes her victims fall dead without an apparent mark on them.

But I'll be damned if I let Georgia kill Ally. I'll have to be sure *I'm* the one that strikes first.

CHAPTER TWENTY-SIX

Rachel

"What the fuck is this?" I pull myself up tall from where I slump in the passenger seat. We've been in Illinois for a long time and all I've seen is a whole lot of nothing. Empty fields lay barren as far as the eye can see. The monotony is occasionally broken up by a tree here or there, but overall, it's dead, flat land. Jessup was born somewhere out here and it's truly hard to imagine given how urbanized she seems now with her mismatched sneakers and black hoodies and Starbucks coffee.

"There's a roadblock," Gideon says, downshifting. "So much for taking back roads to stay out of sight."

Officers swarm the pavement. Several stand with their boot heels in the gravel shoulder and backs to wide open fields. More are in the road, leaning against the few cars that have clotted at this particular section of blacktop. Three state trooper vehicles block the way with a wooden barricade covering the gap between. If the officer approves a car, then the barricade is lifted and the driver is allowed to pass through to the other side.

"If they aren't looking for us, then they should let us pass." I'm trying to count how many officers there are.

Uriel, I think, hoping to prick the angel's ears. *Do you see something I don't?*

Everything, a haughty voice retorts.

Can I kill them all?

You'll likely die, he says.

"What are the chances they aren't looking for us?" Gideon asks with a derisive sneer, unaware of the internal conversation. "Oh god, why are you smiling like that?"

I giggle. "This will be fun."

"Rach—be reasonable," Gideon says. "You can't squeeze all their hearts or throw their cars without taking at least one bullet to the head and then where will we be? Dare I even mention how vulnerable *I* am?"

"Don't whine, Gideon." I bend down and rub the soft fur on my leopard print heels. "It's not sexy."

The car in front of us inches forward to take its turn as the one in front of it creeps toward the lifted barrier.

"Do as I say, pretty boy, and we will both get out of this alive."

Uriel's laughter rings deep through my ears and I squirm in my seat, at the ready. Gideon must be right, of course. Already, several officers on the side of the road have turned their neutral gazes on us. One points at the large scrape along the side of the Mercedes and I wonder if I should have let Gideon ditch the car in Pennsylvania as he wanted.

A cop with his rifle starts walking toward us as the car in front is given the go ahead to depart.

"Ready," I whisper and Gideon's fingers tense on the gearshift. As the car in front of us is halfway through the barrier, I act. "Go!"

Gideon punches the gas, lurching past two officers. He

barely clips one, sending him tumbling to the pavement. The cops in front raise their rifles, but I was expecting that. I shove them back over their vehicles, their guns shooting worthlessly up into the air. The officer trying to get the barrier back into place gets a nice hard shove too.

I don't stop at the barrier, of course. With my mind, I shove hard against all the cars in front of us. Rubber wheels squeal against the pavement as they slide toward the shoulder. By the time Gideon reaches the barrier, there's a nice big hole for him to fly through.

He's laughing like a school boy.

I turn back to see the officers climbing into their cars.

"Here comes your daily dose of excitement, Cariño."

"Can't. Wait." He shifts and the Mercedes accelerates again, easily overtaking the vehicle that'd passed through the barrier ahead of us.

The troopers gain on us, passing the car that pulled over at the sight of flashing lights.

I turn around in my seat and focus on the car closest to ours.

Uriel, I ask. *Your vision is better than mine. Tell me when they are lined up.*

One trooper moves over to the left trying to pass Gideon but he moves to the center of the road. A car approaches in the opposite lane, but I concentrate on the steering wheel, yanking it hard toward the ditch.

Uriel?

Now.

I don't make the mistake of shoving the cars themselves. To push them back would take a great deal of force. I'd have to override their forward momentum enough to stop them and then use more force to knock them back.

I choose an easier target.

In one swift jerk, I yank up large slabs of concrete stretching behind the Mercedes and the pack of officers gaining on us. It comes up in giant sheets rising up like a great black wave before folding over onto the cars. The underside facing me was clotted with mud and earth, bits of grass sticking to the axle.

The dust cloud is tremendous. When it clears, I see two cop cars have managed to maneuver around this. The car that was closest to us only had its back end lifted. The other must have been near the back of the pack and had more time to escape the danger than his colleagues in the front.

"I'm not sure the taxpayers will appreciate that," Gideon says, but he's smiling. He couldn't care less about taxpayer money.

"Stop the car," I say.

"Love, I don't—"

"Stop the car!" I command and the Mercedes comes to a squealing stop. The front right wheel slides off the road onto the shoulder. Now further from the wreckage of the pile-up and destroyed road, I see three cars still in pursuit. Two from the pack and the one tailing us closely from the start. Five officers in all.

I throw the car door open and hear Gideon groan.

"Stay in the car," I tell him. "You could get shot."

"You aren't bulletproof either," he argues but keeps his head down.

I walk toward the police with my arms up as if in surrender. The man in the closest car lifts his gun and I break his neck. I barely twitch my pinkie and the vertebrae crack like eggs on the side of a frying pan.

A ripple of pleasure rolls through me. Uriel's laughter rumbles from deep in my mind.

"Freeze! On the ground!"

I turn my head to see the three officers approaching in a

triangle formation, guns up and pointed. They look like some strange boy band about to break into song and dance.

I reach out with my mind and grab their hearts. All three and squeeze. Their arms falter in front of them, as they lurch forward, clutching their chests. They drop to their knees. Their guns clatter against the road like plastic toys.

They stop moving.

Rachel! Uriel booms and I jump at the sound of his voice.

A gunshot goes off and a shell strikes me in the chin. It's as if a giant fist has punched me across the jaw. I stumble back as white fire explodes up the side of my face. Hot blood pours down the front of my beautiful dress, making the satin cling to my breasts.

The world is already losing focus as I turn on the fifth officer. No *freeze*. No *hands up*. He sees four officers fall dead and decides not to waste a word on me.

My body weakens from the massive blood loss, and my mind dulls at the edges, either from the pain or blood loss of having my jaw blasted off.

I do see him though and I flex that muscle in my mind bringing him to his knees. I don't know if I kill him quickly or cleanly, but I don't take any more shots to the face.

I sink to my knees and place my palms on the cold pavement.

Gideon's boots pound the pavement as he runs up behind me. He places a hand on my back and tries to gently roll me over. I'm moving in that direction anyway, as my elbows buckle and I collapse completely to the road.

"Holy shit," he says, his eyes wide. "Your face—"

He grimaces, wrinkling his nose and looking away. He doesn't finish the sentence.

What? I want to say. *Aren't I still pretty?*

But I can't use my mouth to make words. I can't even get my throat to swallow the blood I'm choking on until Gideon rolls me onto my side. It probably isn't a coincidence that he points at my fragmented jaw on the pavement.

"Hold on," he tells me.

I want to laugh. Hold on? Hold on to what? What is there to hold on to when the entire world falls away?

CHAPTER TWENTY-SEVEN

Jesse

I'm sitting on the bed in the little bedroom while Gloria loads up the car.

I look at my meager possessions on the bed beside me and try to clear my head. Realizing that everything I own can fit into a backpack isn't helping me gain a positive perspective of my life. My confusion only deepens. Why me? How can I be so totally unlucky? My father dies and it's unlucky. My mother remarries a child molester. Unlucky. I try to kill myself to escape the pain and horror only to find out I'm one of the few people who can't die so easily. Even that makes me unlucky.

And all the shitty things that have happened since: Eve tried to murder me. Liza tried to murder me. Caldwell tried to murder me—is still trying.

I fall back on the bed and press my hands to my face.

All I see is the pencil sketch of Ally dead, lying so peacefully on the desert floor. One softly clasped hand over her breast. It has to be Georgia who does it—kill her without leaving a single mark. I know I have to kill her first, but it isn't that easy.

Maisie doesn't want Georgia to die. I saw that clearly in the bizarre linked power exchange that we shared with Monroe. So I can also expect any attempt I make to kill Georgia and protect Ally will be resisted by Maisie. Hell, Maisie might even try to fight me over it. And since Maisie is my only chance in reviving a dead Ally, I have to hope she stays on my side.

"Why are people so complicated?" I groan and throw myself face down on the bed.

A soft knock comes at the door and it creaks open. Ally peeks inside. "Gloria says we're about ready. Are you packed?"

I groan into the mattress, face down.

"That's a no," she says with a sad smile. "Let me help."

"Don't bother," I say. "I don't need any of this shit anyway."

"Well I for one would appreciate if you packed the toothbrush at least," Ally says and shoved the purple stick into my backpack. "The underwear is optional."

I give her a weak smile.

She squeezes my hand. "Tell me."

"I think you should go with Nikki. Just get away from me."

Her furrow deepens. "We decided sending me away wouldn't keep me safe. We've learned that lesson, haven't we?"

It's true. We have. And we've learned from Gloria's mistakes too—which is why I can't tell Ally she's going to die. What if something changes? What if her new decision seals her fate?

"Please tell me what's going on," Ally begs, squeezing my hand tighter. "You're shutting me out and I don't know why."

"I'm not going to survive this," I say. I look up and search her eyes. "You know that right? I'm going to die."

She looks away first. When she dares to look me in the eyes again, her eyes are tight. "Maybe we'll get lucky."

"I'm not lucky."

Unlucky. That's what's wrong with me. I'm unlucky.

So why in the hell would I think I was lucky enough to get the girl? That'd I'd be lucky enough to get out of this alive?

She smiles. "I'm lucky. I'll be lucky enough for the both of us."

Again I see the image of her dead on the desert floor.

"Maybe you're not lucky either," I say. "You've been stabbed. Assaulted. You ended up dating a big jerk."

Ally snorts. "You're not a big jerk, Jess."

"Are you calling me short?"

She cocks her head, knowing I set her up for that stupid joke. She scoots closer to me. "I was lucky enough to find you after I thought you were dead. I was lucky enough to survive the stabbing and the assault. I get to do this."

She leans in for a kiss. Her soft lips brush mine once, then presses to mine for a second, deeper kiss. I don't stop her.

I clasp one hand on the back of her neck and pull away from the kiss to look into her eyes. Her cheeks are flushed and she's grinning.

"I could kiss you forever," she says, smiling.

"I don't think we'll have forever." My face crumples. Even as I contemplate our impending doom, I realize it's not my death I fear. I don't care about dying. It's about not getting what I want.

I want to be her happily ever after.

I hate the idea of not having her for myself. But would I really want Ally to be alone and sad either? No. I can't wish that on her. She's confessed how depressed and lonely she was after my suicide, unaware that I'd survived, then moved to St. Louis and began working as a death replacement agent. I can't ever wish that on her again. I'd love to dunk Sasquatch's head in a toilet, but I know she'll be good to Ally. Not perfect. She'll never love her the way I love her. But maybe she can at least keep her from feeling so alone.

"A penny for your thoughts." Ally brushes the bangs out of my eyes. "Before Gloria comes up here and drags us out by our ears."

"I was thinking about how much I love you." I pull her into my arms. "I don't think I have a lot of time left with you, but I want you to know that I'll love you forever. I always have, since we were kids, and I always will."

Ally pulls back from me with tears in her eyes. "Don't do anything stupid. Jesse, promise me."

"I don't have a choice."

Her jaw tightens. "What about what I want?"

"What do you want?"

"To be with you. That's the only thing I've ever wanted for as long as I remember."

"You can't be with me if I'm dead," I snort. "Don't be stupid."

"I can be dead too."

"No!" I stand up, knocking her back a little. "We aren't pulling a Thelma and Louise. You're not going to die."

"*You're* not going to die."

We aren't as in control of this as we think, Brinkley had warned. And here Ally and I are fighting about what will happen as if we're calling all the shots.

Gloria shoves the door to the bedroom open. "Now that we have agreed no one will die, would the two of you mind getting in the car?"

Ally shoves all my things into my backpack in one swoop of her hand and zips the top.

"So much for organization." I slip one strap over my shoulder.

We squeeze down the narrow hallway and run into Maisie

and Winston on the landing. Single file we descend the steps and go right out the front door. Gloria doesn't lock it behind her and I'm not sure what good it would have done with a giant hole blasted out one side of the house anyway. Like Monroe cares!

I'm behind Ally, watching her walk toward the Jeep, a black hardtop Wrangler. Gloria has parked on the street outside the iron gate. At the end of the walk, I grab Ally's hand. She looks back at me and gives me a sweet smile. I squeeze her hand tighter and pull myself up to her side and kiss her cheek. Her smile is even bigger.

Good.

As confused and frustrated and downright furious as I am about all this, I don't want to take it out on Ally. I want to enjoy these last few moments I have with her. They feel precious and fleeting.

"I love you," I whisper into her ear. "More than anything."

She turns to kiss me, but her lips never hit their mark. I collapse, pulled down by an explosion of pain in my jaw.

"What's happening?" Ally's shrill question pierces my ears. "Gloria?"

My eyes flutter open and the first thing I see is a giant black tire with white letters etched into its rubber. I blink, trying to clear the pain away and see Gloria under the car. No, Gloria isn't *under* the car. She's on the other side, bent over Maisie, saying her name over and over again, one hand on the kid's cheek, slapping it. Winston howls from the back of the Jeep, like the way he howls if he hears a firetruck's siren.

I feel bits of gravel under my hand as I try to push myself up. But I'm not lying on the Rue Dauphine. I'm in the middle of an interstate hundreds of miles away.

The horrible pain in my jaw. The sight of blood spilling down the front of a dress—Rachel's dress—the way it splatters against the concrete. Gideon's face when he turns me over—turns Rachel over. Then the blackness. The dark suction dragging me down.

I gasp for air.

Ally searches my face, her brown eyes desperately trying to wring some kind of recognition out of me.

"Can you hear me?" she asks as the world comes into focus around her. I can smell the rubber, the oil and gasoline. Ally. The door stands open behind her as she kneels in front of me.

I nod, unsure if my vocal chords will actually work should I try to use them. Ally pulls me to standing by the elbow while I hang onto the car with my other arm. On my feet, I see Maisie through the window, cradling her jaw.

"She got her face blown off." Maisie meets my gaze, her eyes big and wet. "Her fucking face."

"Maisie!" Ally tsks, surprised to hear the kid drop the F-bomb for the first time.

Maisie doesn't even register Ally's shock.

"Did you feel it?" I ask Maisie, noting her wide, frightened eyes. Do I look as shaken?

"I felt you," she said, lips quivering.

I felt you, I repeat in my head. But not Rachel? So Monroe restored the connection between me and Rachel. And me and Maisie, but Rachel and Maisie do not share a connection.

"You looked like you were dying." Ally removes her hand from her heart.

"Rachel died." I give Gloria a hard look. "What the hell did Monroe do?"

"Can you get into the car?" Gloria asks. She opens the door for Maisie.

It had been so clear. So goddamn *vivid*. Not only the pain or the sight of the torn up road. But the cool air, the barren fields stretching in all directions. Even the feel of the satiny fabric rubbing the top of my thighs. The way my feet had begun to ache inside of the leopard print heels. All of it.

Maisie doesn't let go of her jaw as she climbs into the front passenger seat.

"What's going on?" Ally helps me into the back of the car and then crawls in after I slide across the seat.

"Did Monroe explain to you what he was going to do to us?" I ask Gloria.

"What did Monroe do?" Ally asks, her irritation mounting with each question.

"What the hell was in that chicken blood?" I ask, resting my head against the seat. Feeling Rachel die was a hell of a drain on my energy. But why? That was the million-dollar question.

"Chicken blood?" Ally asked. "Is that what was all over your face earlier?"

With everyone in the car and seatbelts on, Gloria turns the Jeep key and we pull away from the little house on Rue Dauphine. A heartbeat later, a big black van pulls off the curb too.

"Are you going to stop Nikki from following you?" Ally asks, turning in her seat to look at the van.

"She has her orders," Gloria says without any sign of irritation. "Let her do as she is told. Less trouble for all of us. I will lose her."

Pedestrians scamper across the street as Gloria swings a left at the next intersection.

"I'm still waiting for the explanation as to why the chicken blood gave me mush brains," I say from the backseat. I swallow down a wave of nausea.

"Should you sit up front?" Ally asks, leaning over me with a worried expression.

"I want to be back here with you."

She presses a cool hand to my forehead and frowns. "You're burning up." Then she leans forward and touches Maisie's head. "So are you. An explanation, please."

Gloria considers the road for a moment longer before

turning out of the French Quarter onto Canal Street. I-10 signs tell her to proceed straight ahead.

"When Caldwell killed Chaplain all those years ago, he severed the connection. Originally, the twelve partis were meant to use their powers in unison. There wasn't supposed to be one apex, but a unified force that protected all of mankind together as long as was necessary."

Maisie and I exchange a weary look. If she's thinking what I'm thinking, then she's picturing us there, in the circle on Monroe's rocky beach, hands clasped until one of us can't go on anymore.

"Partis tends to run between those who have a connection. The affection that you have for one another, the emotional connection, was meant to strengthen this original bond."

"But Caldwell fucked that up for everyone. Of course." The pain in my jaw starts to recede enough that my anger returns.

"To be fair," Gloria says, her eyes meeting mine in the rear view. "That murder was necessary."

No one contradicts her perspective. She was there the night Caldwell killed Chaplain. We weren't.

"His murder of Chaplain changed the flow of power. As Monroe put it, it broke the bond. Monroe believed he could reestablish the bond."

"With his voodoo shit," I grumble.

"Hoodoo, actually," Gloria says. "I was very skeptical, but it worked. It seems that Maisie now has a connection to her mother and you have one with Rachel, Jesse."

"Presumably, Caldwell died from his wound earlier, but Jesse nor Maisie reacted then," Ally says.

Gloria runs a hand across her forehead. "Monroe believed he could do it for those who at least hold affection for one another. That was the primary component of the original connection. It could be so again."

Maisie's shoots up. "So we *can* share the power. We don't have to fight."

"Maisie—" Ally warns, but Gloria beats her to it.

"I am not sure Caldwell will be so easily swayed," she says gently. She spares Maisie a sad look as she turns onto I-10 W.

"But my mom might," Maisie says. "Even if Jesse has to kill Dad, maybe me, mom, Jesse and Rachel can share the powers. Then we can be together and no one has to fight."

Gloria gives me a look in the rearview mirror.

I hope she can read my face. *You started this empathy shit. Don't make me out to be the monster here! You started this 'let's all be friends' shit.* Because it's clear I don't share an emotional connection with Georgia, and Rachel doesn't share one with Maisie. So how the hell we'll bridge that gap, I've no idea.

Ally is staring at her lap in deep concentration. "Maisie, when did you get called?"

Maisie turns around in the seat to look at her. "I was fourteen."

Ally turns to Gloria. "When did Monroe's son die?"

"Yes," Gloria says.

"Yes what?" I ask.

"Monroe's boy was partis," she replies. "And Maisie was called the night he died."

No one says anything for a long time after that. I don't know what's going through anyone else's head while we cruise down the interstate, heading west with the sunset, but I can't help but obsess about chance.

Caldwell is the first one of us that was called.

Presumably Georgia was called before me, also because of her emotional connection to Caldwell. Then when Monroe's boy Kevin died and a new partis was needed, the powers that be chose Maisie, the NRD-positive child of two partis. Prob-ably because her mother loved her so much.

So where the hell did I come in? I wasn't connected to anyone. Was my friendship with Rachel enough to call me into partis-dom?

If not, that leaves me with only one connection. Caldwell himself.

Father or not, I have doubts that by the time my powers started up, Caldwell still held any affection for me at all.

Gabriel, I think, searching for him in the back of my mind. *Gabriel, who called me?*

I chose you, came his faint voice over the roar of the inter-state with its cars whooshing by and the torrent of air assaulting the car. *You are partis because I chose you.*

But who loved me? Who brought me into this?

He doesn't answer. He leaves me alone and questioning as we drive toward the approaching night.

CHAPTER TWENTY-NINE

Rachel

I'm dreaming of Jessup. She's standing in a park with an ice cream cone as big as her face. One scoop cookie dough, one scoop mint chip, and a third cookies and cream. Her favorite combination. No, this isn't a dream. This is a memory.

In the early days, we'd made it a habit. A ritual. For every death replacement, when one or the other was in rigor mortis hell, we would walk down to the ice cream stand south of our apartment and load up. Jesse was stiff and cranky, complaining that they hadn't put enough whip cream on top of her waffle cone, when I decided to lighten the mood.

I shoved the ice cream into her face. Not hard. Just a little push that succeeded in smearing mint chip along the tip of her nose and cheek.

Lucky for me, it's easy to outrun a stiff zombie. So I twirled and danced circles around her while she tried to pay me back.

At first she was mad. And the more she chased me without catching me, the angrier she got. Until something changed and the smile broke out on her face. She tried harder than ever to catch me, while she laughed and laughed. This was the first time I'd seen the kid happy, *really* happy since she became part of our team. Brinkley had stood a few feet away, lapping up his vanilla cone, and I caught him grinning too.

He saw what I saw.

Our girl was healing. She was going to make it.

Remember who your heart is.

Fear seizes my chest.

Fear and pain.

The first sensation I ever encounter upon waking. Not the most pleasant way for a girl to wake up. My body, as durable as it may be, never appreciates the demands made of it.

The memory-dream falls away as I reach up and touch my jaw, half-expecting to touch a cavity or bone. Perhaps my fingers will brush exposed nerve endings and send a fresh jolt of horror through me like a live wire. Instead, I feel the rough gauze wrapped around my whole head. But beneath the gauze it is definitely the shape of my jaw.

Gideon comes to sit beside my bed.

I take in the tacky décor, the lifeless paintings of vague landscapes and know that we must be in some dingy motel. I look down to see I'm wearing cotton pajamas of all things.

"I know what you're thinking," Gideon says, pulling up the chair. "You're wondering if I had my way with you while I had you naked and at my command. You'll be relieved to know I'm not completely depraved."

I'm actually thinking: *Cotton? Really?*

I can't give him a smile or even a laugh. What comes out of my closed mouth is more like a patronizing grunt than recognizable speech.

I reach up to pull off the gauze.

"Ah, ah, ah." Gideon stops my hands with his. "I tried to line up the bone and flesh as best as I could, but it wasn't pretty, love. I would give it a little more time to heal before I remove the gauze, if I were you."

I make a writing motion with my hand.

"Pen and paper?"

I nod.

"Yes, I believe even this motel can accommodate such a request."

He goes to the desk beneath the mirror and grabs the notepad and pen off the tabletop. He hands them to me. I get a whiff of soap and note his wet hair. He showered. Why? Because I bled all over him? What a baby.

It isn't easy writing. Rigor mortis doesn't really lend itself to fine finger movements. But I do my best to scrawl some sloppy letters on the pad.

How long was I out?

"A whole day," Gideon says, leaning forward to read the pad. "Unfortunately, I had to drive us into Oklahoma before stopping. I was afraid we'd get caught by the authorities if we stayed too close to the carnage. So I switched cars and got us across the border before I worked on your face." He grimaces. "Hopefully, it will not scar."

I scrawl another line on the notepad. *Women with scars are hot. Gives us mystery.*

"No doubt," Gideon says and comes forward for a kiss. He's incredibly gentle, offering only the softest brush of lips on my forehead. "I know you must be hungry, but I don't advise trying to chew. Do you want to try drinking a shake? Chocolate is your favorite, I believe. I can go out for some."

No. We need to get back on the road.

"One day won't kill you," Gideon says. "And you need to be 100% when we confront Caldwell."

A broken jaw won't slow me down.

Gideon laughs. "A broken jaw, no. But darling, I picked your jaw off highway 127 and wrapped it in a Taco Bell napkin from a sheriff's glovebox. So this is another case altogether."

I pull my stiff body upright and fall against the headboard. I try to remember the last thoughts I had. Was it important? It was. There was something about—Monroe's voice. *Remember who your heart is.*

I grab the notepad and began furiously scribbling another question. *What happened with Monroe?*

Gideon reads the words. His brow furrows and his eyes tighten at the corners. He tosses the notepad back to me and grabs an orange off the dresser. He begins to peel it, digging his dark fingers into the flesh of the orange.

"Monroe is dead. Jackson says Caldwell killed him," Gideon forces a smile. "Yes, I called because I wanted her to know we were all right, in case she saw your accident and assumed the worst."

My mind returns to the moment I saw Monroe grab ahold of me and that tremendous influx of power washing over me. Who did it come from? Monroe? It was like a great hurricane in the distance. I've never felt anything like it. If I'd known Monroe had been housing that kind of power, I would have killed him right away. Now it's all lost. Another unworthy partis will be called.

But it didn't really feel as though the hurricane had dissipated. Down the line, I felt—something like—

I remember being seven or eight when my parents took me to the beach for the first time. We'd driven from Tucson out to the coast near San Diego, where the Pacific Ocean could actually get warm. My mother—adopted mother— forced me to stand there watching the big beautiful waves crashing on the shore while she applied sunscreen to my shoulders and back. I didn't think I needed it. I'm darker than either of my parents, being Hispanic, not white, but my mother still insisted as if my skin were as pale as hers.

When she finally released me, I tore toward the beach, squealing. All I wanted, all I'd thought about since the moment my father announced the trip, was what the ocean would feel like. Taste like. Look like. I threw myself headfirst into water and wasn't entirely prepared.

The only time I'd been swimming in Tucson was at the city pool and at the Desert Delights water park, which had a wave pool. In my little mind, I thought the ocean was a very *large* wave pool, even though my parents tried to explain the difference between fresh and saltwater.

When I hit the water face first, I sucked in a breath, shocked by how cold it was. This was no shallow city pool. But instead of sucking in air, I sucked in a mouthful of saltwater. It burned my nose and eyes like mad and immediately I tried to stand and get my head above water.

I managed to stand, but I felt the sandy bottom shifting beneath me, sliding out to sea. The great suction caused by an impending wave pulled the floor out from under me and I fell beneath the water again.

I was certain I was going to drown in the ruthless current and had already decided I didn't like the ocean one bit by the time my father's strong arms dipped beneath the waves and liberated me from all the thrashing.

That's what Monroe's—whatever—had been like. All over again, I was standing in the waves, the ocean floor falling away beneath me and a hungry suction pulling at my calves.

Caldwell has his power? I scribble, my jumbled scrawl even worse this time around.

"No," Gideon says and offers no further explanation.

I imagine who might be called next. What unsuspecting soul out there is going about their day—grocery shopping, paying bills, working in their cubicle, only to suddenly feel different. Would they even notice the change? Would they feel it at all? Or maybe only like a temperature shift? A sudden desire to pull on a robe or a sweater.

For me, I knew the moment I woke up from my 212th replacement that the world had changed. Before I even saw Uriel's face, felt him slip his hands inside me and tear me wide open, I heard the buzz of power that hadn't been there hours before I'd replaced Mrs. Whimple, a crazy cat lady running the local animal shelter who had a habit of adopting more pets than she found homes for.

I knew the world had changed then, and I know it's changed now.

What did she say? I scribble.

"She doesn't see any more trouble for us between here and Arizona. That's good news, isn't it?"

I rest my cramping hand and nod instead. The nod isn't much less painful than my joints wracked with rigor mortis.

"How do you feel?" Gideon asks again, oblivious to my desire for silence.

I give him a dismissive wave and roll over onto my side. I don't want to talk, let alone answer stupid questions. How does he think I feel? I had my face blown off and died. Hello?

"He's hiding things from you," Uriel says, materializing suddenly. He looks ridiculous in the motel room. Like a king in a squatter's hovel. It isn't his ornate outfit or flaming hair. It's his rigid back and uplifted chin. Like it's an insult that he is even asked to materialize in a place like this.

I know.

Everything about the bed irritates me. The cheap, scratchy coverlet probably covered in semen from a thousand men. The stale scent of cigarette smoke blooming every time the pillow is fluffed. Rain splatters against the window and the sound of it makes my flesh crawl.

Remember who your heart is.

No. I have no heart. Perhaps I did once, but now I'm a god. And a god has no use for such weakness.

CHAPTER THIRTY

Jesse

I start out of sleep, heart pounding. I pull my cheek off the cold window and sit up straight, trying to stretch out the ache in my lower back. *Danger*, my mind screams. *Danger*. But I don't see the danger. Maisie sleeps in the front seat, Winston curled up and snoring in her lap.

Ally starts awake beside me, rubbing her bleary eyes. "What? What is it?"

Gloria's eyes meet mine in the rear view mirror. She seems to be waiting for me to speak.

"I think I was having a bad dream." I press my hand to my chest. My heart races like a rabbit being chased by a fox. "But I can't remember it now."

Gloria's cell phone buzzes in the cup holder, plastic vibrating against plastic. She snatches it up and answers it without Maisie stirring. Maybe the kid is a heavier sleeper than we thought.

"I'm here," Gloria says. Then a long stretch of silence echoes through the car while she presumably listens to someone. "We will think of something. Is that all?"

Another stretch of silence.

"Understood." Gloria pushes a button on the screen and dumps the cell phone back into the vacant cup holder.

A car passes us on the interstate, barreling on toward its own destination in the dark. The green digital clock in the dashboard reads 2:02 am.

"Is it really so early?" I ask, stretching forward in my seat.

"We gained an hour when we crossed into Mountain Time," Gloria says. "It's one." Gloria looks behind her at the pitch black darkness of the abandoned highway. There isn't a headlight in sight. And the car that passed us is barely a red glow on the distant horizon.

She pulls off on to the shoulder. "I need to stop."

"Want me to drive?" Ally asks, unbuckling her seatbelt.

"I need to draw and would rather not do it in motion."

Ally and I exchange a glance which probably means the same thing. *Something must have happened if she doesn't want us to go any farther.* God, I hope it doesn't mean we have to change the plan. Again.

"I need to stretch my legs. Want to get out with me?" Ally asks and gives my hand a gentle squeeze. Her palm is warm in mine and her smile is so pretty in the dim car that I think I'd have said yes to anything. Will you marry me? Yes. Have a couple of kids? Sure thing. Wear this butt plug?

Okay. Maybe not yes to everything.

Ally opens her car door and steps out onto the shoulder. I slide out behind her and try to shut the door as quietly as I can. After I do, I peer into the front seat to make sure Maisie is still sleeping. She is, fogging the glass with each exhale. Winston lifts his head, sniffs my face through the glass, then seemingly satisfied, nuzzles back into the crook of Maisie's elbow.

Ally pulls me off the shoulder and into the desert. "God, it's so beautiful."

I look up and see more stars than I've ever seen in my life. "Wow."

Her breath puffs around her face. "You'd never know how many there are if you lived in the city your whole life. Have you ever seen so many?"

"Yes," I say. "A long time ago."

When I was six, my dad took me camping. It was only the two of us. He wanted me to see where he grew up, on a little farm in the middle of nowhere with his brother Dyson. Apparently his parents had had a lot of farm land. His brother had died before I was born, and I don't remember the stories about his parents or the weathered house. But I do remember my first night out there in the cold and the way the stars had been so big and bright that I thought I could reach up and grab them like sparkly stones on a beach.

I stared at them, dumbfounded while Eric had made me a s'more and told me ridiculous scary stories that weren't scary at all. If he'd told me the story about how one day he'd die and become a monster that would try to kill me, that would've scared the shit out of me.

I turn to see Ally's eyes wet and shiny in the dark.

"It's breathtaking," she says and grabs my hand, pulling me further away from the car. "One day, when this is all over, we should build a house in the middle of nowhere so we can look up and see the stars like this every night. Wouldn't it be amazing?"

"Only if you're there," I say.

She wraps her arms around me and kisses me then. "Is there anything you want to tell me?"

"No," I say reflexively. But even after a moment of consideration, my answer doesn't change.

"You're having bad dreams," she presses. "Are they about Rachel? It's perfectly normal to be worried about—"

I shut her up with a kiss. Despite the chilly air around us, icing my cheeks and making my breath billow in front of my face, her lips are hot. When I slip my tongue into her mouth and she opens a little wider to let me in, I find her hotter still. I wrap my arms around her and kiss her like I'm trying to suck all the air out of her body. She goes all soft in my arms, and I know I'm the one holding us up.

She giggles. "Wow. *Jess.* I should threaten you with talks more often."

I kiss her ear, then lower on her neck because I know she loves it. She told me more than once how it makes her go all weak in the knees to have her neck kissed. And I can tell by the way she sags heavier in my arms that I'm doing it right.

"Okay, okay," she laughs, pushing herself away. "I won't ask you what you're worried about. I swear. I just want to make sure you're okay."

I snort. "I'll never be okay."

I talk to angels. I hallucinate. I'm unstable and temperamental. I tell Ally that I adore her one second, and then I'm horribly mean to her the next. I'm as likely to kiss her breathless as I am to scream at her. What the hell is wrong with me?

You can't bear the thought of losing her.

Gabriel's voice is like a caress up the back of my spine.

Promise me I won't. I demand. *Promise me I'll never see her die and I swear I'll do whatever shitty world saving thing you want.*

He says nothing.

Promise me.

Would you have me lie?

I hug Ally tighter.

"If this works, it'll be over soon, baby," Ally coos, sensing the shift in my mood. "We only have to be tough for a little longer."

"I'm tired."

"One day at a time. Tomorrow will be different."

"We're not promised tomorrow," I say, trying to remember who I'm quoting.

"Then let's enjoy this." She tugs me to the ground.

I sit, knees splayed open, and she snuggles between them, leaning back against me like I'm a chair. I wrap my arms around her, smelling her hair, kissing her ear. She sighs and goes soft in my arms.

The stars are breathtaking. A black ocean glittering, and thick swirls of stardust. I try to relax but I can't. The night is beautiful. There's a gorgeous girl who loves me in my arms, but I'm wound tight. I can't forget what's coming.

"It was worth it," she says, kissing the arm draped over her.

"What?"

"All of it. All the waiting. All the missing you. It was worth it just to have this one perfect moment."

I squeeze her against me for a long time. Her breath evens out in the crook of my shoulder and I know she's dozing. We haven't been out here for more than twenty or thirty minutes and I've never known Gloria to sketch for less than an hour. So I don't wake her. I feel her chest rise and fall against mine, and I try to appreciate the moment despite the crushing waves of sadness and loneliness washing over me.

It was worth it to have this one perfect moment.

I hope that's true—for her at least. I want her to have some part of me, even if it is a teeny tiny part, when I'm gone.

For me, there will never be enough.

CHAPTER THIRTY-ONE

Rachel

I come awake and Gideon isn't in the hotel room. I sit up, listening for any sounds that might signal he's in the bathroom.

"He's outside talking to Gloria," Uriel says, materializing in his stately manner at my bedside. "He's not saying nice things."

I throw back the covers and go to the door. I crack it open and see that Gideon is in the parking lot, leaning against a red Jetta and talking on his cell phone. He's looking at the hotel and I think for a moment he's seen me. But his eyes slide away as he switches the phone to the other ear. With the gauze still wrapped around my head, I remember that I can't talk to Uriel with my words.

What's he saying?

"That you're unstable and can't be trusted. He's asking if he should even bring you to the compound for your assault against Caldwell. He thinks perhaps the girls will fare better without you."

That's not possible, I say, in my mind at least. Our attack against Caldwell must be coordinated. And Maisie doesn't have an active power. In fact, she's only going to get in the way.

Uriel shrugs. "You do not need any of them. Desert Gideon here and go on your own. You'll make it to the facility ahead of the others and take hold of the place. You will make it *your* stronghold."

I like the sound of that. I shut the door and creep into the bathroom. I lean over the sink and begin to peel the thick, scratchy gauze off of my face. I unravel it again and again and again and notice that each layer is a little pinker than the last, until it's clear I'm seeing blood soaked through the material.

When the last strip falls away, I turn on the light to get a better look at my face.

It's an ugly scar. A crooked line starts from the middle of my chin and juts upward jaggedly toward my ear before disappearing beneath my hairline. It looks like a child scrawled on my face with a sharpie. Gideon's stitches are methodical but lack finesse. Either he has never had to stitch someone up, which I find hard to believe, or he found it difficult to stitch me up.

I imagine him getting sick at the sight of my face. Maybe stopping once or twice to vomit in the toilet before returning to the task with shaking hands. And his hands must've been shaky given how uneven the line across my face is.

I open my mouth wide, wider, until a sharp pain jolts up the side of my face, dissolving to an intense burn.

I open and close my jaw to inspect how bad the damage might be beneath the flesh. It aches with each move. Not unlike the time Chaplain punched me hard across the jaw. The muscles are tense and it clicks as I open and close it. It appears to have grown back into place as least. But the poorly stitched flesh looks red with infection.

"That's going to be hideous," I rasp. I regret my light-hearted jabs about sexy women with mysterious scars. This isn't the right kind of scar for conversation. An eyepatch I can utilize as a conversational piece. But *this?* This is the kind of scar people will politely not notice.

Maybe with time it will grow faint and then I'll draw curiosity from those who get close enough to see it.

Now I really *can't be an actress.*

I can't blame that on Gideon's hands, however. The death of my dreams are solely Chaplain's fault.

"What's a beautiful girl like you doing in a place like this?"

It was dinner time at the Blue Flamingo, a 5-diamond restaurant in one of St. Louis's richest neighborhoods. I'd started my shift three hours ago and was itching for my first break when I was assigned Chaplain's table. I stood there with a silver pitcher in one hand, his water glass in the other.

"I won't be here forever. I'll be in LA by the end of summer, and I'll probably have my big break by the end of next year."

I filled his glass and put the water on the table.

"An actress waiting tables?" Chaplain had laughed. "Imagine that!"

I was furious. I'd made Gretchen finish his order and I took my break. But when my break ended, he was still there.

At the end of the meal, he approached me. "I'm sorry I laughed earlier. But you will too once you hear me out."

I closed my fist around a pen in my apron and arched an eyebrow.

"I'm actually a director. Not for Hollywood, mind you. But I do run a very successful online channel. I was about to offer you a part in my new series I'm starting when you stormed off."

It sounded too good to be true.

"I only laughed because I couldn't believe I'd actually discovered a bona fide actress in a restaurant of all places."

"No offense, but I want to star in movies. Not YouTube."

Chaplain grinned. "I know. But this is a very popular program. And women are discovered on the internet all the time. Won't you at least come by and see my studio?"

Renewed anger consumes me. The soap, sample shampoo bottles, and mirror behind the sink begin to tremble.

I can make all your dreams come true.

It doesn't matter that Hispanic women like me rarely gain recognition in Hollywood. It doesn't matter that even if I did succeed, someone would say it was because I was *raised white*. It's the fact that Chaplain took my dream and used it against me. What he did to me changed the entire course of my life and for that, he didn't deserve to live.

Yet some small part of him is out there, walking around. *Existing*. And that is unacceptable. If any part of him must survive, I will own it.

A crack shoots up the center of the mirror, dividing the glass. I take a breath and the toiletries grow still on the countertop.

"We're going to Arizona now. I'm going to kill Caldwell myself."

"He's leaving," Uriel says. "He will not stray far. He's kept a very close eye on you while you slept."

"How sweet," I murmur. I search the room for something I can change into. Surely Gideon bought me more than these cotton pajamas. He didn't think I'd wear this cupcake shirt into battle against Caldwell, did he?

I find a pile of women's clothing in a plastic shopping bag. None of it is particularly glamourous. But I'll settle for the black jeans and black turtleneck. There's no cash though. No cards.

I can't find the heels.

I look under the bed, in all the drawers. I search every inch of the room but my leopard print heels are nowhere to be found.

I scream and the bathroom mirror explodes into a hundred shards.

I throw open the hotel room door with the intention of searching the car but Gideon is gone, taking the car with him. I have no choice but to walk barefoot from the motel.

Oh well. I'll take what I need, when I need it.

I've never had a problem getting what I wanted before.

CHAPTER THIRTY-TWO

Jesse

My head slams against the glass and I jolt awake, clutching my head. "*Oww.*"

Ally stirs in my lap where she's slept the rest of the night as we passed through the desert toward the Mexican border. "What's happening?"

"Bumps in the road," Maisie says, snickering from the front seat.

"It's not nice to laugh at your sister," I chide her. "That hurt."

"I know." She snorts. "I hit mine, like, two miles back."

"Calm down. She will turn up again." Gloria is speaking through her teeth into the phone. Whoever she's talking to, they're taxing her self-control. Actually, now that I think about it, I know exactly who she's talking to. There's no one else that grates on Gloria's nerves that way.

"Who's she talking to?" Ally asks in my ear, staying cuddled close to my side. Ever since we walked back to the Jeep, she's been super affectionate. I'm not complaining.

"Gideon, I think," I say and throw one arm around her. Maisie nods her head to confirm.

"I did look," Gloria hisses. "I did it the second we hung up. But it's the same. Nothing has changed."

A stretch of silence fills the car, each of us watching the back of Gloria's head like some fascinating television show instead of what it is—the back of her head. Then she hangs up the phone and tosses it into the cup holder without saying goodbye.

"So—" I begin, ready to take a guess at what the hell is going on. "Rachel took off?"

"Yes," Gloria says. "Gideon returned to the room and she was gone. He's worried she's going to draw more attention to herself, especially with her face the way it is."

"What's wrong with her face?" I ask. Then the vivid memory returns from the moment I mind-melded with Rach. A jaw shot clean off. That's what's wrong with her face. Maisie gives me an *oh-my-god-shut-up* look. "Right. Never mind."

"She won't make it to Cochise before we do."

"Is that a bad thing?" I ask. Ally must think so. She's gnawing on her bottom lip.

Gloria meets my eyes in the rearview. "You need to be ready for her."

"Brinkley says that even if she has totally lost her shit, it doesn't matter. She's one of us. We'll take care of her."

We're a team. If we have to, we sacrifice for the team.

That was what Brinkley had said to me the day Rachel went into the hospital. I'd been sitting in the hospital reception area, waiting to hear the news of what had happened. When she'd totally lost her shit the first time and started carving herself up with a kitchen knife and trying to stab me to death, they'd taken her to a hospital first. She'd cut herself pretty badly so they sedated her and cleaned her up.

Then they sent her over to the asylum, pumping her with enough medication that she slept 23 hours a day. But we still visited her for the first few weeks until Brinkley moved me to Nashville.

What's going to happen to her? I'd asked on our last visit before leaving town. I'd asked not only because I was afraid for Rachel. I asked because even then I somehow understood that whatever was going to happen to her was going to happen to me.

We'll take care of her.

Gloria reads the green sign aloud. "Cochise 15 miles."

"That's where we're going right?" Maisie asks, craning her neck to look at the sign as we pass it.

"Yes," Gloria says. "We'll be there in twenty minutes."

"Are you sure it's deserted?" I ask. "You said it was the shebang back in the day. Maybe there's still a secret operation going on there."

"No," Gloria insists. "They shut it down in 2010, on Caldwell's command. He never wanted anyone to set foot inside this place again."

"But that's why we're doing it," Maisie says. Her voice is low and strained. "Because we want to scare him. And it'll scare my mom too." Maisie looks out the window at the passing desert, her voice far away and dreamy. "She told me horrible stories about this place."

A mixture of sadness, horror, and longing washes over me. My stomach sinks. My mind blanks. My limbs, throat, and face tense. God. So many *feelings*. Maisie's grief is unbearable.

I watch Maisie stare out of the window, her thoughts taking her far away from us and what we're going to have to do in order to still be breathing next week. I watch her smooth face and something there unsettles me. I have a horrible feeling that if Georgia gets away from me and kills Ally, there's only one person I'll be blaming for that.

The hotel or motel, whatever the hell the difference is, is a good half mile behind me before I find civilization. A grocery store no bigger than a house sits on a gravel parking lot. One gas pump stands out by the road, and there's an empty car parked beside it. The nozzle is still connected to the side of the beat up pickup, but the gas has stopped pumping, the readout frozen at $43.43.

"Cameras?" I ask Uriel, my eyes falling on the only other car in the lot—a white Camaro near the door.

"One," Uriel says. "Easy enough to disable, if you so please."

"I would."

The gravel parking lot doesn't feel pleasant to my bare feet. Jagged rocks poke my heel and arch. I manage nonetheless. The door dings when I step over the threshold. Cold tile is a welcome relief, even if it's obviously as filthy as the ground outside. A squat woman with two chins and a blue apron looks up from behind the register. She sits down a magazine and her eyes widen.

"You're—" she begins, chins trembling.

I don't wait for her to finish. I flex my mind and her windpipe is crushed shut. She claws her throat and deep red scratches well up on the delicate skin. Then she collapses behind the counter and hits the floor.

I find her as an unmoving blob on the floor behind the counter. I take off her shoes.

They are too wide, but I find a package of socks in the aisle beside the motor oil and boxes of macaroni and cheese. I put on two layers before lacing her ugly shoes onto my feet. Even though they are scuffed and puffy, at least they are black and go well enough with the rest of me.

"Where's the camera?" I ask Uriel who's standing in the first aisle, eyeing the candy bars with a wrinkled nose.

"Over your left shoulder," he says, without looking up. "Is this *food?*"

"Some people think so."

At last I see the camera. I reach up and rip it off the wall without using any muscle. It crashes to the floor, bouncing off the cashier's face.

"Oops, sorry." My hand goes to my mouth reflexively.

The bathroom door opens, the sound of a flushing toilet following someone into the store. I hear the footsteps but don't see anyone until he reaches the end of the aisle. A very short old man wearing a flannel shirt and a star belt buckle appears beside a display of sunflower seeds and air fresheners.

"Where's Marge?" he asks, his mouth falling open in surprise.

"She's dead," I say and squeeze his heart until he hits his knees gasping. Then I drag his body behind the counter out of sight.

"She recognized you." Uriel glances down at the open newspaper the cashier left on the countertop.

I look up from the man's body and follow his gaze.

On the first page, it's our pictures—me, Jesse, Ally, Gloria. *Suspected Terrorists at Large*.

"Ugh! This is a shitty picture of me," I whine, crumpling up the newspaper.

"Would you rather they took your picture *now*?" Uriel asks with a snide sneer.

I catch sight of my reflection in the glass of a lottery ticket dispenser and even in the pale reflection the jagged scar is hideous.

"Good point. Celebrity is celebrity."

I'm wishing a second person would come out of the bathroom, someone else I can kill.

Uriel grins. "Yes, you're getting very good at it. Dispensing with the unworthy."

I arch an eyebrow. "Is that what I'm doing? I thought angels were supposed to condemn murder. And besides, these people aren't anything to me. The only person I care about is in Arizona. And she needs me."

My heart flutters. *Remember who your heart is.*

The only person I care about.

"I never claimed to be an angel. But if I am, Satan was an angel, according to your mythology. Isn't he supposed to be the evilest of us all?"

"Yet more evidence that you're an ancient alien," I chirp, stepping over the cashier's body. "One of these days I'll get you to confess it outright."

He arches his eyebrows. "You will want to destroy the recording device in the back room."

"Okay," I tell him. "And don't think I didn't notice that you changed the subject."

I march into the backroom, past rows of unstocked items and an employee bathroom. In the office, which I have to unlock from the inside, I find what Uriel is talking about. The camera was feeding everything to this recording station, a pile of VCR like devices, one on top of the other and three televisions showcasing the store from different angles.

"The wire here—" Uriel begins.

"Don't care." I yank the whole system out of the wall and throw it up into the ceiling. Then I slam it down on the industrial desk and up again. Then I slam it side to side, bouncing it off one cinder block wall then another, until there's nothing to throw around but a pile of pieces.

"Did that do it?" I ask.

"Yes," Uriel says, stepping back so I can get out of the office.

"Good. We're done here."

The red pickup, though beat-up, is actually in better condition than the white Camaro. Another strike against the Camaro is that it's a stick, and I don't drive stick. So I unhook the nozzle from the red truck and return it to the gas pump.

I admit it isn't luxurious. The truck smells stale and greasy, and the leather steering wheel is slick in my hands. And what the hell is the Putin Bobblehead all about? Couple the hideous vehicle with the fact that I hurt my face and I'm wearing ugly shoes and cotton clothes—I feel like I've reached a low point. At least I'm behind the wheel again. I'm in control.

And none of these setbacks are going to stop me. I'm going to put this truck in drive and get to the base even if I have to drive through Hell to do it.

Chaplain, I'm going to finish what you started.

"How long do you think it'll take us to get to Arizona?" I ask Uriel as I release the parking brake and move the shift into the drive position. He folds his wings against his back in the passenger seat, trying to get comfortable in the cramped space.

"Before sunset on this day," Uriel says.

"Good." My shoulders relax for the first time all day. "I can hardly wait."

CHAPTER THIRTY-FOUR

Jesse

"Oh. My. God." I press my forehead to the glass window. "Could this place be any freaking creepier?"

"At least it's daylight," Ally offers. "I'm sure this place is more menacing at night."

Early morning sun or not, the landscape is barren. There's nothing for miles and miles in any direction. To the east of us sits a cluster of buildings that no one on Earth would call a "town" except the crazy fucker who named it Cochise.

To the west is the large, desolate army base. The place looks like a square fortress of white limestone, stark and obvious in the landscape. The compound is enclosed in a solid wall, the same color as the rest of the buildings it protects. The wall must be at least twenty feet high.

Gloria drives to the west side of the compound and parks the Jeep behind a big boulder about a quarter of a mile from the wall.

"We'll leave the car here," Gloria says.

"What if someone steals it?" Maisie asks, twisting in her seat to look around.

"We are going *into* the compound, right?" I ask. I see

Gloria's drawing again, all the bodies tossed in the sand that could easily be the stretch of land between here and the enclosed army base.

"Yes," Gloria says, stepping out of the Jeep.

"Well this isn't ideal for a quick getaway." Ally frowns and slides out of the Jeep too, leaving me and Maisie to look at each other with weary faces.

Gloria nods in the distance, toward the end of this stretch of wall. "If you stay on this side, no one from the town will see the blast."

"Fine, fine," I say and start marching toward the end of the wall. I've been walking for a full ten minutes, longer than a quarter mile between the car and the closest edge of the wall, and I still haven't reached the end. The compound must be huge inside. Of course, once upon a time it had been a fully operational military base. But that was twenty years ago. I don't think anyone has been here in years, not since Brinkley and Caldwell managed to expose the camps for the hellholes they were and got them shut down. Was Brinkley the last one to come here? Gathering intel on Caldwell from old records in hopes of finding anything that could bring him down?

"You let the monster out," I think aloud to Brinkley. "And here I am trying to stuff him back in."

Finally, once I see the end of the wall in the distance and know I'm about as far from anyone and anything as I can get, I decide to do it. I lean my body against the stone barrier and feel the warm rock through my clothes.

Gabriel appears, a striking figure in the desert landscape. So beautiful in fact with his black suit and brilliant green eyes that my breath hitches at the sight of him. He watches me through dark lashes.

The air around me shimmers, then kicks to life, sparking to flame.

"Let's keep the noise level down," I tell him. "So one big explosion should do it."

The power rolls through me, making me grimace enough that my lips pull back and expose my teeth. My eyes pinch shut against the intensity. I can feel my jaw clench and unclench with each wave of power. All the muscles in my body do the same. I'm on the verge of screaming, when the release comes. The power flares, slamming into the barrier.

The first explosion rips a giant crack through the wall, chunks of rock raining down on me until I quickly erect my barrier to protect me from the larger flying rubble.

So much for one and done.

I reposition my body against the rock and pulse again. Immediately, I fall forward when the rock tumbles out from beneath me. I'm glad my shield stays in place, since I'm sure falling onto a pile of jagged rock, or concrete, or whatever the hell this shit is, would've hurt.

When the dust clears, my shield fades. I collapse onto the rocks. The pain isn't too bad, but a sharp jolt shoots up my knee into my hip. Another jolt shoots from my wrist to my elbow where I catch myself.

Gabriel appears in front of me, his sleek black wings trailing through the sand. His back is to me as he surveys the carnage.

Bodies. All over the place like red solo cups on a frat house lawn.

There must be no less than thirty bodies littering the yard between the barrier and the closest building. They lay where they were slain, in various stages of decomposition. I'm super thankful that it doesn't smell like death. The carrions have done a good job of carting away most of the flesh that would have created such a stench. As if he knew I was talking about him, a crow takes flight, lifting up into the sky, cawing his protest.

The rest of the bodies look... mummified.

"What the hell happened here?" I ask, pulling myself to standing. The rubble shifts beneath me as I slide off the mound onto the soft earth. I bump into Gabriel and find him solid. I'd forgotten he could do that. Never around Rachel or Maisie, of course. But when it's the two of us, his body can feel as real as Ally's.

The back of our hands brush and his feathers twitch. The tie around his neck deepens to a midnight blue.

"He wanted blood from everyone who had harmed him."

"So he *has* been back here." I lean against Gabriel's arm. I keep expecting him to disappear, to vaporize like a shimmery heat on the horizon. But he remains as solid as the rock I blasted through. "Maybe this place won't have the effect on him that we are hoping for."

"He will be unnerved," Gabriel assures me. He stretches back his left wing and encircles me. It darkens out the bright desert sun for a moment, enveloping me in a thick shadow. "I am worried for you."

"Worried?" I snort.

"Worry or concern," he says, looking down at me as he uses his wings to curl me closer to his body. "I believe those are the words your people use to convey this sentiment."

A feather brushes my cheek, giving me chills. "You told me this would work. Are you saying you're not sure if Caldwell—"

"Caldwell does not concern me," Gabriel says. "You concern me."

I push the soft black feathers out of my face before one of them stabs me in the eye. "We talked about cryptic messages, Gabe. If you want me to understand something, you have to articulate the entire idea, remember?"

Gabriel considers my face for a moment. And the longer that he stares at me the more reality thins and I realize I'm looking at another being. Not an angel. No, not an angel but a—

"It will be difficult for you," he says and the desert comes into focus. "You will choose Alice, I believe. But it will be very hard for you."

His wings spring open in a great whoosh and the air kicks up around me. He disappears entirely as Ally and Maisie clamber through the hole created by my blast. His dramatic departure blows sand into my eye. I pinch it closed, blinking furiously.

"Not cool!"

Maisie shrieks and slides on the rubble, dropping the fat pug in her arms. Ally grabs her elbow at the last moment to steady her.

I blink away tears. It takes a moment before I can see both Ally and Maisie clearly.

It will be very hard for you to choose.

"*B*ut you *must* kill her," Uriel says, his vehemence apparent. Wind from the cracked window blows back his fiery locks. It's strange seeing him appear so real. Jesse and I talked about that once. We compared notes trying to decide exactly what these so called angels were. I must admit, my idea of the ancient aliens appearing as a benevolent force never seemed more correct than it does now.

My affinity for Thundercats can't be overlooked. After all, if you were a crazy alien trying to brainwash a girl into doing something insane, wouldn't you appear as her childhood hero? Why else would a so-called angel come to me in this ridiculous get up?

"Something's changed." I stare at the endless highway stretching before me.

I imagine Brinkley holding Jessup by the shoulders the day they checked me into the asylum. I was kicking, screaming, thrashing. But before they sedated me, I heard Brinkley console her: *We're a team. If we have to, we sacrifice for the team.*

"You want Earth to burn."

I give Uriel a sharp look. "Don't be dramatic."

He raises a malicious eyebrow. "What do you want? Truly?"

I look out at the road, Cochise 15 miles.

We're a team. If we have to, we sacrifice for the team.

We were a team. What are we now? What is Jessup to me now?

"Your desires change so rapidly within your own mind, that I do not comprehend them," Uriel goes on. He doesn't bother to look out at the road. He continues to stare at me with his brow furrowed. We could be driving through hell, a trailer park, or a battlefield. He seems equally indifferent to the landscape.

I consider his words for a heartbeat longer until I have my answer. "I want Caldwell dead and that last little piece of Chaplain erased from existence."

"You are not strong enough to destroy him. You will have to kill the others first, if you hope to achieve that."

A memory surfaces from the inky depths of my mind. I was in my new apartment in St. Louis. The setting sun had just touched the river and it was as if it was dissolving into the water, melting into a stream of red, pink, and orange. The uppermost part of the sky was already turning a darker violet. I remember in that moment wondering where they'd put Chaplain's body—I hadn't known at the time as I do now, that the partis simply incinerate to ash when their power is absorbed.

I sat there wanting to see his body, wanting to put an ear to his chest and make sure there was no heartbeat. I still want that.

Brinkley knocked on the door of my apartment, calling out in the gruff voice I miss so terribly much, and I told him to come in.

He didn't come in alone.

Trailing behind him was this scrawny kid. She hunched

over slightly, her arms wrapped tightly around her chest. Part of her hair had been singed off on one side but was regrowing. She looked like she'd just walked out of Hell, literally, ash marks and fire scarred to prove it.

"This is Jesse," Brinkley said, slipping his hands into his pockets. "She's the newest member of our team."

I arched an eyebrow but didn't say anything.

"I'd like her to bunk with you until we can set her up with her own place," Brinkley said. What he didn't say spoke volumes: *I wasn't expecting this anymore than you were, but we're doing this anyway. Throw me a bone here.*

"And I'd like her to shadow you in the Hutch replacement Saturday," he went on. "Show her how it's done."

How it's done. So she had NRD and wanted to be an agent. I gave Jesse another once-over. She didn't look like the kind of overzealous kid who might sign up for this job for the sheer morbidity of it. So she was here because, like me, she was running away from something worse.

"Hi Jesse," I said at last, climbing off the sofa. "You can put your stuff in here." I pointed toward my bedroom.

"I don't have any stuff," she said.

I expected her to burst into tears by the strain in her voice. But her jaw set tight and her chin lifted a little higher. So I'd been right. She was a survivor.

"I'm going to give Jesse some money to get started. I know tomorrow is your only day off, but I was hoping you'd take her shopping, show her around the city. Get her a bus pass and all that."

"I can do it myself," Jesse piped up.

"St. Louis can be a little rough," Brinkley said. He'd always been overprotective. "It'd be nice if Rachel can give you an idea of the better parts of town before you go off on your own."

"Don't worry," I told her, sensing her annoyance. "I'm

not your chaperone. You can do whatever the hell you want. But I hope you'll let me come with you because I *love* shopping."

"I hate shopping."

"Then you definitely should take me along. Unless you want to wear the same pair of underwear *forever*."

That got a smile out of her.

"Cherry Coke float?" I asked. "I've got the Coke and the vanilla."

She hesitated, looking for the catch. "That'd be awesome."

Brinkley gave me an appreciative smile. "I've got to get back to the bureau and process her paperwork. Call me if you need anything."

"Yes, *dad*." Brinkley wasn't fooled by my tone and I was glad he didn't take it personally. I wanted the kid to warm up to me.

When the door closed, Jesse sat on the bar stool and watched me make her float. Two scoops of vanilla and half a can of Cherry Coke. I slid it across the counter with a teaspoon.

She frowned at it. "This is a tiny spoon! Don't you have anything bigger?"

"Desserts are best enjoyed with small spoons. Trust me." I nodded at the float when her brow creased. "Try it."

She did and nodded. "You're right."

"And it'll last longer," I added, before moving right into better topics. "You can have the bed tonight. You look like you need a good night's sleep. Besides, I sleep like the dead no matter where I pass out. So the couch will be fine with me."

"I can't take your bed," she said.

"You can and you will," I said. "The only problem here is you didn't laugh at my joke 'sleep like the dead'...get it?"

She gave me a pitiful smile. "You need better jokes."

"See if I make you another float!" I said and tried to steal her glass.

She slid away from me. "No, no. I'm sorry. This is so good."

I gave her a once-over. "What do you usually wear?"

She frowned at herself. "Jeans. Hoodies."

I frowned. "I don't know who sells those."

"I like comfortable clothes."

"Hmmm. We'll go for urban chic then. I know some boutiques downtown that might have some stuff you like."

"I don't want to spend too much money." She looked at her hands self-consciously before abandoning the little spoon altogether. She lifted the glass and gulped down the remainder of the float.

"The FBRD is footing the bill. Consider it a sign-on bonus. And you have to start all over, so we can't be frugal here. Is there anything you need tonight?"

Jesse shrugged. "I don't have a toothbrush."

"Let's go out for dinner and we'll pick one up at the drugstore on the way back. There's a Walgreens by this little Mexican restaurant I love. They have this amazing goat cheese dip." I pretended to drool on myself. "We'll stop there and get you the essentials. Deodorant. Toothbrush. A hair brush. Makeup, whatever you want. They have all that."

"I don't wear makeup," she said.

I placed one hand on my heart. "Well, I guess we will keep you anyway."

She looked at the empty float glass and then back up at me again.

"Want another?" I asked, trying to read the expression on her face. Longing? Shyness? I wasn't sure.

"No, I'm full. Thanks." Then her expression darkened even more. "I'll pay you back. Just figure up what all this costs. Add your rent and utilities and—"

"Let me stop you there," I said, squeezing her arm. She flinched and I dropped my hand. Abuse then. I knew that reaction as well as anyone. The way the body could react to sudden unwanted touching.

"I don't want to owe you anything," Jesse said and now I was sure she really would cry.

"You won't. I'm not doing any of this because I want you to owe me something."

"But the money—"

"Fuck the money," I said.

Her eyes went wide and the she let out a startled laugh.

"This is your *job*. You're getting paid. The bureau will reimburse me for any expense I report. They have to cover your expenses because this can be a shitty job, and you deserve to be paid well. Not everyone can do it."

She didn't look entirely convinced. "Brinkley said only 2% of the population has NRD. And only a small percentage of those people are willing to be death replacements."

"Death replacement agents," I corrected and put her glass and spoon in the sink. "Yes. So you're very valuable. Got it? The least they can do is buy you some clean underwear."

This won me another surprised laugh. "And they'll pay you back?"

"Oh sure. It's in the contract. Did Brinkley show you the contract?" I asked.

She bit her lip. "I had to sign it."

I frown. "How old are you?"

"Seventeen. I'll be eighteen in August."

So *young*. Granted, I didn't have much on her, but she wasn't even old enough to *be* a death-replacement agent. She'd be shadowing me until August at least.

"So what do you want to do before dinner?" I asked her. I pulled the ice cream from the freezer again and started to make my own float. Seeing her devour hers had awakened in me a hunger I didn't know I had.

She shrugged. "I wish I could call someone."

"A friend?" I asked, my curiosity piqued as I licked ice cream off the spoon.

"Yeah," she said. Another self-conscious smile spread over her face. "I want to tell my best friend I'm not dead. She'll freak out."

I open another can of Cherry Coke and nod toward the cell phone on the table. "Help yourself."

The kid hopped off the stool and snatched up the phone resting on a turquoise placemat. She flipped it open, punched some numbers and waited. The longer she waited, the more nervous she looked, gnawing on her lip first, then her thumb. Finally, her brow shot up. "Mrs. Gallagher? Is Ally home?"

Jesse's face hardened.

"It's me, Jesse." She frowned and hung up without saying goodbye.

She stared at the phone on the table for a minute longer before she seemed to realize I was still in the room, watching her.

"I'm tired," she said. "I think I'll take a shower and then a nap, if you don't care."

I nodded toward my bedroom. "There's clean towels in the closet opposite the toilet. Just don't pick a red one. That's the color I'm using."

She disappeared from the room leaving me to eat my float alone.

I would catch Jesse making phone calls to that number at all hours, day and night. But she would never say anything. Though once or twice she did leave a message. I thought she would go on like that forever and ever until about two days after Jesse's first death replacement.

She picked up her phone—in celebration of her first

replacement, Brinkley had gotten her own cell phone—and started to dial a number. Half way through the dialing she stopped.

"I—" Her voice trailed away.

"What's wrong?" I asked, when she didn't finish.

"I can't remember her number."

Since she'd been sneaking around with mine up until this point, trying over and over again to contact this Ally but never getting through—either her bitch of a mother would shoot her down right from hello, or she'd delete the answering machine messages Jesse left—whatever the case, contact had not been made, but I had the number.

I punched it into her phone for her. Thinking maybe she wanted to try from the new phone, throw the bitch off her trail. Caller ID was still a thing back then.

But Jesse wouldn't press send on her phone.

"What's wrong now?" I asked.

"I can't remember her name."

"Ally," I said, hoping to knock a memory loose for her.

"Ally," she repeated.

"Ally. Smart. Really good at track. Was going to be valedictorian or some shit. Go to college. Then law school and join her brother's law firm." I was pretty sure this Alice girl was the subject of some homoerotic wet dreams, but that hardly seemed like the thing to bring up *now*.

"I can't—I can't remember her face. Oh my god, what the —" the first wave of panic washed over her. Her face seized up and her fingers blanched as she squeezed her phone.

"Hey, hey," I said, pulling the phone out of her hand. "It's okay. It's normal. Death replacing tends to burn through a few memories. Be grateful. I'm sure there's some shit you wanted to forget."

I for one had forgotten some of what Chaplain had done, but it wasn't enough. Sometimes I'd wake up in the dead of night feeling like I'd just been stabbed in the chest or had my throat slit, drenched in sweat and heart pounding, without the ability to vividly recall what I'd just been dreaming.

"I forgot?" she asked, as if she wasn't entirely sure she believed me. "Brinkley said I'd forget."

"Yeah and you've been calling her for months. It's probably time you gave up on this so-called friend."

She sat her phone down in agreement but her face didn't relax.

I never saw Jesse call Ally again. By the time she'd completed her sixth replacement, she never even talked about the girl and I never brought her up. I knew it would confuse her. Hurt her. And I couldn't bear to take her peace away.

By then, I more than loved the kid.

Remember who your heart is.

Love is a luxury and immortality isn't free. Sometimes you have to pay a price to keep it.

Even if that price is your dearest friend.

Gloria has to break the door down, but she manages it after a few tries. Maisie keeps her eyes on Winston, her gaze sliding to take in a corpse only once or twice. She bends to pick up the pug, cooing encouraging words I think are mostly for her. After all, he lifts his nose and sniffs the air like "what's that strange smell?" but otherwise seems absolutely uninterested in the bodies strewn about.

With one more hard shove of Gloria's shoulder, the door gives. It's awfully dark inside, so no one is quick to walk in first. When we look around, as reluctant to move as we feel, Gloria frowns at us. "This is only the utility shed. I'll restore power and then we will breach the main building. It is very unlikely we will find a body inside."

No one moves.

Gloria presses the door open farther with the flat of her hand and pulls out a large flashlight. She clicks it on and the beam springs to life. "Wait here."

The three of us nod enthusiastically, and Winston too because Maisie shakes him so hard.

Gloria disappears into the shadowed hallway and the door starts to shut after her. I grab it at the last moment and Gloria calls out, her voice already from somewhere far down the hall. "The hinge is broken. No need to prop it open."

I let go of the door and feel foolish. "God, why does this place make me so jumpy?"

The heat grows. So super cold at night. Really hot during the day. Got it. Cancel my subscription to the Arizona real estate catalogue then. I pull at my collar.

"Uh, because it's super creepy!" Maisie says, rubbing Winston's exposed belly. She gestures around us at the exposed corpses, stripped of their flesh like carrion. "The place has some bad juju or karma or whatever you want to call it. Horrible things happened here."

I give Maisie a look. "What did your mom say?"

"She told me what they did to her here." Maisie's voice tightens.

After Caldwell took me hostage for the first time with the intention of murdering me slowly, he'd done his mind trick on me, where he broadcasts memories or false images directly into a person's mind. And with that little mind trick, he showed me what it was like in this camp. He projected the sharp image of Georgia having her arm amputated above the elbow, without anesthesia, and for no real reason except the scientists and military wanted to see what her amazing NRD positive body could do.

"Why would she describe that stuff to you?" I ask, angry at Georgia. The idea that Georgia was just as horrible of mother as my own frustrates the hell out of me. What could be gained by telling your kid that stuff?

"She wanted to be sure that I understood bad things can happen to me."

"Tough lesson," Ally murmurs giving me the side eye. "If he brings Georgia—"

"He'll bring her," Maisie insists, peering into the dim hall for Gloria.

"—then we can expect her to be just as affected by this place, if not more so than Caldwell. That's good right?"

"Yeah," I say, turning the plan over in my mind, searching its seams for flaws. "We want them confused and not thinking straight."

"The battleground is as important as the battle," a voice says and we all scream.

Gloria pushes the door open and scowls at us. "You know my voice."

Our mouths snap shut.

"Did you get the power to come on?" I ask.

"Only in two of the buildings," she says.

"Um, then let's stick to those," Maisie says immediately.

"Ditto," Ally and I say in unison.

"As fun as it might sound to you, running around in the dark with Georgia and Caldwell—"

"—and Rachel," Ally interjects.

I shoot her a glare. "—I'd rather not."

"It's fine," Gloria says, stepping out into the light. "One of the buildings I was able to turn on is where they held Georgia. It will suffice for our objective."

Again I see the horrible memory of Georgia's torture in my mind and the way Caldwell's face twisted with rage at the account.

"Let's hope so," Ally says as the four of us, plus pug, follow Gloria to a building up ahead. I lag near the back with Maisie.

"So, I'm sure you've noticed that since Monroe did his weird Voodoo thing—" I whisper.

"Hoodoo," Maisie corrects. "Voodoo is a religion. Hoodoo is a practice."

A headache intensifies behind my eyes. "Whatever, look, I can feel all your emotions."

"And I can feel yours," Maisie says.

That's upsetting, but not entirely surprising. Of course she can. Why shouldn't it be a two-way street?

"Okay, so I know that you don't want us to hurt your mom, but are you going to try to stop me from blowing them up or—"

Maisie's face crumples. For a minute, she looks like she'll sob uncontrollably. But then her face hardens. She adjusts Winston in her arms. But she doesn't meet my eyes. She talks to the desert floor.

"We have to save the world."

"Or so they keep telling me," I grumble.

The tears collect in the corners of her eyes, sparkling in the high sun overhead. Her sadness spikes, rolling through me until I feel like I'm going to cry. Or scream. Or both.

"Fuck, Maze, it's not like I *want* to murder your mom," I say.

"I know." Her voice hitches and the sadness wins, pushing the anger aside. "God, I know. I'm not taking it personally. I don't think I can *watch*."

"No one is asking you to." Horrified, I stop walking. "I don't want you to see that."

If I'd seen Eric Sullivan die when I was a kid, that would have totally screwed me up. If I'd seen my mother die in her car wreck, even with all the anger I harbored toward her, I still think that would've been really hard. I would never ask Maisie, this sweet big-hearted kid to endure that.

"I'll make sure that Ally keeps you far away from all that," I say. Because that's where I want her, with Ally in case the worst happens.

"I have to do something," Maisie says. "I have to contribute."

"You'll contribute," I assure her. "You have three objectives. Very important objectives."

I'm careful not to talk in a patronizing voice. I want her to know I'm serious.

"Keep Ally alive. Keep Winston alive. Don't get captured."

"Keep Ally alive. Keep Winston alive. Don't get captured," she repeats. "Is that in order of importance?"

A hitch of melancholy rings through our connection.

"No," I say. "I care just as much about you not getting hurt as I do Winston and Ally."

It feels like a lie. I don't want Maisie to get hurt, of course not. Come on, I'm not a sadist. And I don't want her to end up with her parents again. But I also feel like I'm using her for her awesome ability.

"I promise to try to talk your mom into sharing the power with us. That's the best I can do, Maze."

A swirl of emotions plays over Maisie's face, until her features soften into recognizable relief.

"You're feeling everything I am, aren't you?"

Maisie gives me a crooked smile. "I think so. I'll try not to freak out when the fighting starts."

The realization hits me. "Oh, shit." This whole time I've been worried that Maisie might interfere with what I have to do. I completely overlooked the fact that through our freaky little connection, I might be as freaked out by the idea of assaulting Georgia as if Maisie had tried to do it herself. "*Shit.*"

"I'll try," Maisie insists. "I promise."

I make a mental note to try and attack Georgia out of Maisie's line of sight.

Gabriel's words are coming back to haunt me. *You'll find it very difficult.*

What must be true for me and Maisie must also be true

for me and Rachel. Assuming she does try to kill us, will my desire to live overpower her desire to kill me? Vice versa? And what if she wants to kill Maisie for her power? What then?

"Have you felt any emotions from Rachel?" I ask her. "Apart from the whole blown off jaw thing."

Maisie shook her head. "No. Why?"

"I'm not sure," I admit. Maisie has put that fear in my head. That maybe this awesome plan we have might not be as thorough as we thought. After all, we never planned on Monroe's weird blood magic. The original plan was everyone had one goal. One plan. And we would work together to achieve that objective. But it looks like that's changed. I still want Caldwell dead, but Maisie wants Georgia alive. And Rachel? Who knows what the hell she wants.

Revenge, Gabriel whispers in my ear. *She seeks revenge.*

Against who?

We follow Gloria's lead. She has never actually admitted to us whether or not she'd been to this military camp, either during its incarnation as a detainment center or after. But she had "viewed" this place enough times that I'm sure it is as familiar to her as her own home back in Nashville.

And the way she moves around the place proves this more than anything. She knows which doors lead to which rooms. When we come to a nondescript intersection of two identical hallways, she doesn't even hesitate before saying, "This way."

But despite her self-assured way of stomping through this place, it's still creepy as hell. I'm the last in our bizarre conga line, and I can't help but look back over my shoulder again and again, expecting to see someone or some*thing* creep up on me. This place has a horrible vibe. If one of the dead soldiers were to rise up suddenly and come after our brains like old school zombies, I wouldn't be all that surprised.

We cut another corner and Maisie, who's been right on Gloria's heels, gasps. I bump into Ally's back with an *oomph*.

I peer around their bodies and see a boot. Well, not only a boot. The boot covers a foot, protruding from the corner of the hallway ahead. It isn't only the legs of a body stretching across the hallway that makes Maisie shriek. It is the fact that it's only *one* boot covering *one* foot.

It mostly certainly begs the question of where the hell the other leg is.

Gloria frowns at Maisie. "Wait here."

She marches toward the leg in her usual soldier's gait and stops before the boot. She looks down at it the way one might survey a problem, examining how best to solve it. Oh we're out of milk? Hmmm. I shall pick some up!

Gloria kneels, grabs the boot and throws it further down the hallway.

Maisie gasps again. I, on the other hand, suppress the intense desire to giggle. For a heartbeat anyway. Until Gloria's expression stiffens. Her eyes fix on something down the hallway and she takes a step back before pivoting on her heels and marching back toward us.

"This way," she says, leading us away.

"I thought we had to go that way?" Ally asks.

"No," Gloria says and then as if she realizes how sharp her voice is, she says it again, more softly. "There's another way."

"Fine by me," Maisie snorts. "I don't want to see what's worse than a torn off leg."

The next hallway must've been used for living quarters. The rooms are stark white and tiny, with barely enough room for a twin-sized bed. No toilet, no sink. Nowhere to sit except for the bed. But sometimes the rooms have a chair in them, as if a visitor might stop by for a chat at any time. Some beds were still rumpled, giving the haunting impression that someone has just woken up and perhaps is wandering around this place. Other beds are perfectly made. Also haunting. After all, it's terrifying to think that one of these rooms could have been mine if I'd been born twenty or thirty years earlier.

We turn a corner.

This place is proving to be a hell of a maze. What we hoped would give us a psychological edge might actually work against us, I think. After all, Caldwell and Georgia know their way around this hellhole better than we do.

Gloria stops power marching and turns toward a room at the end of the hall.

It's a medical room. There's no label of course that says "We did medical stuff in here." Or "Infirmary" or even one of those red equal crosses. But there's a gurney with straps and a metal table with—tools.

Maisie turns away and Ally wraps her arms around her. Gloria doesn't seem to notice. She pulls open the door and steps inside. I step into the room with her, leaving Ally and Maisie alone in the hallway. That way if the door locks from the outside they can let us out.

Gloria looks at the bed, inclined to a sitting position. The metal table at its side holds a tray with freaky looking instruments. One is a giant hook. Another has what looks like a file on one side and a needle on the other. There's a handsaw that I've seen at mortuaries, presumably for cutting open the skulls and looking into the brain. My stomach turns at the thought of someone cutting open *my* skull and poking my gray matter.

"This is where they kept her." Gloria smooths the sheet with one hand.

"How could you possibly know that?" I ask. Because Gloria can only draw the present and future, not the past. There's no way she'd be able to view the entire history of this place from the moment they broke ground and built it until Caldwell came back to exact his revenge.

Gloria pulls the sketchbook out from under her arm and

opens it. I expect her to flip it to a particular page, but instead, she flips it to the back and grabs a wad of sketches. These pages are folded in half and a different color paper than the rest of the sketchbook. She opens them up and I can tell by the torn fringe they were from a different kind of notebook all together.

"When Sullivan disappeared, Brinkley asked me to look into him, to see if we could track him and make sure Maisie was okay." Gloria fingers the drawings, holding them up so I can't really see the images. She thumbs through until she finds the one she wants. She pulls it free from the others. "One of the first sketches I drew."

She flattens the drawing on the metal table beside the torture instruments as if they were as innocuous as a party tray with little cheese cubes and crackers. In the drawing, Georgia is hanging off this gurney—maybe not this exact gurney—but an identical one in an identical room with identical little instruments beside her. Except those instruments in the drawing are bloody and freshly used.

Georgia is halfway in Caldwell's arms as he supports her, his face a twisted confusion of relief and fury. She looks barely conscious, her eyelids half closed. And she's covered in blood.

"Jesus Christ," I say. And try to take the picture from her for closer examination, but she won't let go.

"Watch it."

Her eyes cut to the door and Ally and Maisie standing in the hallway. Then I realize her back is blocking their view of the image.

"Fine, fine," I say and stop trying to pull the drawing from her grip. "But that is fucked up."

"He managed to walk out of here with her before we took Maisie's case, jumping like he does," she goes on, keeping her voice low. "But when they were told to close their doors, they refused to comply. Furthermore, to punish Sullivan for his exposure, they took Georgia back."

"They kidnapped her *after* he'd already rescued Maisie?"

Gloria nods.

"Where the hell was Maisie when he came and tore this place apart?" Because Maisie couldn't have been more than six or seven and you don't take six or seven year olds to a massacre.

Gloria's eyes slide away from mine.

I gasp. "You?"

"Keep your voice down," Gloria hisses, her nostrils flaring. "She doesn't remember."

"How do you know?"

"I've tested her. I tried to spark memories. Nothing."

"So, what, he dropped her off at your house and you had a Disney princess marathon until he'd slain all the baddies?"

"He knew I cared and he knew there wasn't anywhere I could go that he wouldn't find us. I knew it too." A deep sadness consumes her face. Her lips pout, her eyes droop and for the first time that I can recall, Gloria looks like an old woman. Wrinkled. Tired. "Brinkley never knew."

This shocks me. I thought Brinkley and Gloria had no secrets. Reading the journal put that idea into my head and made me reevaluate every conversation, every exchange between the two of them. I don't know how I didn't see their bond earlier. It would've been obvious to a dude with only one eye.

I want to give her a hug because she looks so fucking sad, but I get a distinct vibe of *don't you dare*. I settle for a question. "Why are you telling me all this?"

"You have your favorite. And I have mine."

Gloria cuts her eyes to the hallway and I follow her gaze. Ally and Maisie chatter away until turning to look down the hallway with wide eyes.

"We have to do what's best for her. She's a child."

I frown. "I know that. Why does everyone act like I'm the crazy murderer?"

"Protect her," Gloria says in a low voice. She squeezes my hand like she's going to break it. "Don't let anything happen to her. Not now that we've finally got her back."

My chest aches. I don't know what to do in the face of Gloria's feelings. It's shocking that she has them at all. I mean, of course she has feelings! She's always so tough. It never occurred to me that I'm not the only one terrified of dying from a broken heart.

"I'll do my best, G. I swear."

Gloria lets go of my hand and her smooth, unreadable warrior face returns.

Ally bursts in, throwing the door wide. "Someone's here."

CHAPTER THIRTY-SEVEN

Rachel

I coast the truck through the ghost town. According to the internet, fifty people live in Cochise. I see no one. Where the hell they sleep, eat, buy groceries, or work, I've no idea. There isn't a store, post office, school, factory, or hospital. A few dilapidated buildings worn down by sand stand apart from one another like cacti, but nothing looks habitable.

But I do see the military base.

The white compound gleams like an Arabian palace in the distance. I half expect to see men on camels gallop past the truck, or women in full body garb carrying baskets on their head.

It's strange being out here in the desert. By the end of the day, I'll have my revenge in the same place where I began. It's like coming full circle.

I often begged my mother to tell me the story of how they became my parents.

My father had been part of the militia who patrolled the border. He usually patrolled every night with a couple of his friends, trying to catch illegal immigrants and their paid "coyotes" crossing the border. One night he was out alone. His two border patrol buddies were sick or busy that night. I'm not sure which because my mother's story would always change a little with each telling. Her point: that night he was alone.

As he drove through the desert, windows down to enjoy the summer breeze, he caught sight of something in the distance. At first he thought it was a desert fox with a critter in its mouth, perhaps a large hare by the awkward way it moved. But as he got closer he saw a child.

He slowed the Jeep and got out. My mother said it was like I knew him. I came right over to him and opened my arms to be picked up. My father liked to tell me that he loved me from that moment, but I know it was really my mother that persuaded him to keep me.

He put me in the front seat, buckled me in and drove around the area searching for my family. My father couldn't believe that a child would be dropped off in the desert alone. He was certain that someone had seen his approaching lights and had run. But after several hours, he gave up. He couldn't find anyone.

Then he did something he'd never done. Instead of driving me to the police station, where they took all the other immigrants they found, he drove me home to my mother. Two years and a great deal of money and paperwork later, I became Rachel Wright, named after my mother's mother.

In another version of the story, when my father put me in the car, he had a candy bar in the cup holder that he'd taken a bite out of and as soon as I saw it, I pumped my little fists desperately. He laughed as I gnawed the chocolate log the way a starving dog might gnaw on a bone.

And you've been eating us out of house and home ever since.

I don't remember any of this. I remember only what I've been told.

Then the final version of my origin story came, but not from my parents.

Bud, my father's drunken friend, told me this version: My parents *were* the coyotes. They took outrageous sums of money from desperate Mexicans hoping for a new life far away from the gangs, drugs, and violence back home. And my mother, my birth mother, was a young woman who paid a fortune to come over with her little *hija*. But she was betrayed by the kindly couple who vowed to help her. She was left to die in the desert. And her *hija* was raised by the coyote smugglers that betrayed her.

Bud was a guy with a penchant for slobbery Rottweilers, Coors beer and double barrel shotguns. Not to mention a love of talking about *dirty wetback spics*. So I didn't believe him outright. When I confronted my parents, my father denied it after an awkward pause, his face red with anger. My mother burst into tears.

The day before I heard this version of the story, my friend Cara, a perky blond with dreams of being the next Katie Couric, invited me to move to St. Louis. She needed someone who could pay half the rent.

St. Louis was the opposite direction of L.A. and my actress dreams, but it was somewhere to go far away from my parents and their lies. I went to St. Louis for five years, working and saving for my relocation to Hollywood. I'd just bought my plane ticket and was set to fly in three weeks when Chaplain came along—and changed everything.

I wonder what my parents think of me now. They must have seen my face on the news. How did they take it? Would they believe I'm not a terrorist who kidnaps children?

Or would they assume I'd turned out like my parents after all?

Their opinions are nothing, Uriel says. *They are unworthy.*

I blink away tears and focus on the base ahead.

The only bad thing about this compound being out in the middle of nowhere is the fact I can't creep up on it. If anyone is watching, they'll see me coming from a mile away.

"Do not waste time," Uriel instructs. "Wasting time lessens your chance of success. Kill each partis the moment you see them. Then I will return to you and assist you in the ascension."

"Yeah, yeah," I say, my eyes desperately scanning the landscape for a car or any evidence that they're already here. "I can't wait to see the mothership."

I slow the truck the closer I get to the base, until I'm creeping along the wall. I'm moving slower than I would be if I were walking. I circle once around the base, but I don't see any cars.

Am I the first one here?

No.

There is a big gaping hole in the side of the base's exterior wall.

A mound of white stone was blasted away, rubble strewn all over the desert floor. Some pieces were blown out onto the sand.

Jesse could have done that. Or anyone with explosives. Or has it been that way for years? The destruction just sitting out here, forgotten, a relic of Caldwell's past?

The sun sinks lower and I catch the glint of the truck's hood reflecting the sun. I pull forward, slinking past the hole created by the blast. As I pull around the boulder, a car comes into view.

I park beside it, trying to see if anyone is inside. Its windows are down, revealing twin empty seats. It's some kind of black muscle car. I recognize the type but can't recall the make or model. I don't think it would belong to Caldwell. We all know how he will arrive. It seems too small to be Gloria's. I try to imagine it bringing Ally, Jesse, Maisie, Gloria *and* the pug all the way out here from Louisiana. If there's enough room in the back seat it's possible, but it wouldn't be comfortable.

Maybe Gloria decided speed over comfort was best? Especially in a getaway car.

I put the red pickup into reverse and look over my shoulder to make sure I don't hit anything.

Caldwell appears, grinning like a psychopath. If I put a chainsaw in his hands right now, it wouldn't look one bit out of place.

Without thinking, I slam on the gas pedal. The truck's tires spin, kicking up sand and obscuring my view. Then the cab lurches backward. At the last minute, I realize I'm going to hit the outer barrier and slam on the brakes.

The truck slides into the wall. I'm knocked forward. I scream as my breasts bang against the wheel and I'm breathless. My neck doesn't feel too awesome either. And I've got nothing to show for it. There was no satisfying *bump* of running over Caldwell's body before hitting the wall. Caldwell reappears in front of the truck, grinning like a fox.

"You fucker," I murmur and throw the car into drive. "Having a blast, are we?"

I mash the gas pedal again and the tires spin until they catch. Caldwell is laughing, growing bigger and bigger until I'm absolutely certain he's going to let me hit him. I reach out with my power and seize him with my mind. I hold him in place the best I can. *I'd like to see you jump now, fucker.*

His eyes go wide. His teeth pull back in a snarl and I howl with glee.

"Got you! Got *you*!" I sing.

He staggers as if ripping himself from my mental grip and disappears as the truck blasts through the space where he stood a moment before and speeds out into the open desert.

I stop the truck and turn around in my seat wildly, trying to get a clear look at where he'd gone.

But despite all my neck craning I don't see him.

"Damn!" I ram my fist against the steering wheel. The horn blares.

"You need more power," Uriel says. "Kill the girls first."

I moan and throw open the driver side door. I hop down onto the sand, lamenting the sweat collecting under my arms and behind my knees. I try to pull the fabric away from my skin and allow air to pass through the cotton.

I wait, half-expecting Caldwell or his bitch to materialize beside me and try to kill me outright. He doesn't come.

"You love to fuck with me, don't you?" I ask the open desert.

Something catches my eye and I squint at the distance, bringing my hand up to shield my eyes from the sun.

Trails of dust rise up to the sky. They swirl and collide with one another, forming a single giant plume that's hard to distinguish individually. But at least three cars traverse the desert, coming this way. They've got to be heading to the base. It's not like they're out here for the Dairy Queen.

But it can't be Caldwell and Georgia. And Gideon wouldn't travel with an entourage.

So who the hell is coming to crash our party?

I'm about to find out.

CHAPTER THIRTY-EIGHT

Jesse

I look to the left and the right but see no one.

"What do you mean there's someone here?" I hiss, my heart hammering in my throat. We haven't had nearly enough time to explore the facility or set the trap that would snare Caldwell. We were supposed to have at least a couple of hours before anyone showed up.

"They crashed into the wall," Maisie says. She's holding Winston a little too tight, his big eyes bulging.

"He can't breathe," I point out and her grip loosens.

"A car hit the wall and a horn blared," Ally agrees. "Then we heard footsteps inside the building."

"*This* building?" Gloria and I say in unison.

I'm still trying to pick my jaw up off the floor and get my heart out of my throat when Gloria springs into action. "Come on."

We hurry after her.

Sliding around corners, we skid to a halt in front of a control room. Or at least that's what it looks like with all of the knobs and dials and screens.

Gloria dives under the desk, leaving the three of us to

huddle in fear. I peek out into the hallway, looking left and right again for any sign of the enemy. The enemy because I'm not sure who the hell is out there. Caldwell wouldn't drive into a wall would he? That doesn't sound like his MO. But then again, he could be trying for surprise?

"Are you okay down there?" Ally asks as the sounds of destruction are interspersed with swear words.

"The connection isn't—yes. Here we go." The screens hum to life, the buzz of electricity audible in the small space. But it's all snow.

"Maybe the cameras aren't functional anymore," Ally suggests.

A small sound catches my ear and I turn just in time to see a hand clasp over my mouth.

I ignite without thinking. Maisie, and Ally jump back and so does the hand that covered my mouth.

"Bloody hell, it's *me*," Gideon says, shaking blue fire off his hand.

"Gee-*zus*," I moan. "I almost shat myself."

"Keep your voice down," he hisses. "There was a bloody reason why I didn't want any of you screaming. We aren't alone."

He looks up from his wounded hand and glares at me.

"I'm not sorry," I say. "You shouldn't sneak up on people with superpowers. It was a stupid thing to do."

"Super stupid," Maisie adds.

"Fix it," Gloria commands, shoving us all back against the wall so Gideon can fit into the control room.

He wraps his hand in a black cloth from his pocket and shuts the door behind him. "Lock that."

"Did you drive into the barrier?" Ally asks.

"That was Rachel," Gideon says, ducking beneath the work table. "But Caldwell is also here, scouting."

"Scouting?"

"I suspect he wants the lay of the land before he brings Georgia," Gloria says.

Gideon climbs out from under the desk and starts pounding commands into the keyboard. "Ah, no. I guess not. How about—ah no. Hmm. Well, maybe—"

"Caldwell *and* Rachel are here?" I give Gloria a weary look. Who the hell are we going to deal with first? Would it have been too much to ask for one problem at a time? Of course it would.

"And we've another problem as well," Gideon says, his lips flattening to a thin line. The cameras flare to life, the snow fizzling away.

We're gifted with an encompassing view of the building. Every hallway, every room, everything is perfectly illuminated for us in black and white. It's omniscience.

In one screen, three car loads of men pile out with guns.

"More company." Gideon presses his finger to this monitor as if he could stamp out the men with a jab of his finger. "Damn."

"Idiot. You led them here," I say. "Who are they?"

"They belong to Caldwell." Gideon runs a hand over his head. "They passed Rachel over hoping she would lead them back to you. He wanted me here as well. Now I know why. I'm an idiot for not realizing it before."

"I told you to come," Gloria says.

Gideon exhales. "I'm a liability rather than an ally."

"How?" Maisie asks.

"Caldwell will puppet him if he can," Gloria says, she's rummaging through her bag. "We're immune."

"I don't have NRD. He could just as easily use me against any of you," Ally adds.

"He hasn't before," I say. "I feel like if he could use you against us, he would have done it by now."

Because the heart is pure. It is incorruptible, Gabriel whispers in my ear. I turn, expecting to see him in the room, but it's only us. Weird.

And this means what? I ask with my mind.

You have the benefit of being both a heart and a partis.

"There is a first time for everything," Gloria warns.

I blink at her trying to refocus my attention on the room. It's hard with Gabriel pulling on me.

"Jackson," Gideon says, turning to Gloria. "Perhaps you shouldn't give me anything dangerous, nonetheless."

She considers this warning. Then says, "Has he been in your head?"

"Yes," he freely admits. "When he had me in New York, he poked around in there liberally. He wanted to know all about Brinkley, what I knew about the girls, and my connections and capabilities. I believe he considered killing me outright."

"But he didn't," Gloria says, her eyes narrowing.

Gideon arches an eyebrow. "He said, 'waste not, want not'. It doesn't change the fact that he must know about the chamber and our plan. We've lost the element of surprise."

"We will have to make up a new plan."

"There's no time!" Ally cries.

"We'll wing it," I say, trying to stay positive. And let's be honest here, most of the time I'm winging it. "We can do this."

Ally rubs her forehead. "Jess, we worked on this plan for months. We—"

"Think about every death replacement we've ever done," I remind her. "We never knew how the person would die. There was no way to prepare for it. We only knew that it was coming. We made decisions as we had to make them—one at a time."

Her lips press into a thin line but at least she's stopped arguing.

"We know he will be here and we know we want to kill him, and that he will die," I say. I look to Gloria for confirmation.

"I saw him dead," Gloria says and at last Ally's shoulders relax.

"We can do this," I tell her. And I look to the others. I hope I sound inspirational and motivational and not like a desperate maniac. "We'll make it up as we go. And we *will* win."

Because you're not getting even one more day of my life, Caldwell.

"First problem," Gideon says, his accent particularly strong. "How do we keep him from using me to kill you?"

"You recognize the feeling don't you?" Gloria asks.

"Why yes, I do. Intense pressure behind the eyes. Bees buzzing in my head."

She nods. "You're no good to us disarmed. If you feel the pressure, the buzzing, you'll have a few seconds before he seizes complete control. Use that time to disarm, and if you can't or he won't let you, then try to warn us."

Gideon gives her a weary look. "Don't you think it's better to tie me to the chair now?"

"We need you," she says without looking at him.

Gideon's face softens at her compliment. "I'm happy to be of service, Captain Jackson." And even I hear the unspoken words. *One last time.*

Gloria's eyes are focused on the monitors. Caldwell's goons slide down hallways in full tactical gear, guns up, hunting us. Rachel walks from room to room, peering in to see where we are hiding. And Caldwell, he's the most difficult to track. He flits from one screen to another. Hopping from hallway to hallway on his own version of a hunt.

"We're out of time," Gloria says, ejecting and reinserting the magazine of her gun. "Time to wing it."

CHAPTER THIRTY-NINE
Rachel

This place is a maze. I cut another corner and find a hallway identical to the last. Same white tiles. Same walls: half white cinder blocks, half glass windows.

I duck into four outbuildings before I find one with electricity. I have both eyes open for Caldwell, but he doesn't show his face. Of course, I have the distinct impression Caldwell is playing with me.

The idea that he doesn't take me seriously ruffles my feathers. I am *not* weak. I have more power than his little brat and more control than Jessup. Sure, her power is flashier, but she hasn't had her power for nearly as long as I have.

Kill the brat and you'll be even stronger, Uriel says in my mind. *Kill the brat and Georgia may even confront you head on. You would be at an advantage, fighting her while she is emotional.* I think of the last time I saw Georgia. I shoved her up into the ceiling before dropping her and crushing her leg. It had been easy enough. And now I am so much stronger.

"Good idea," I coo to Uriel. "I'll kill the girl, *then* her mother. That will leave only me, Jessup and Caldwell. She'll help me take him down and then—*badda boom*. It's over." His laughter echoes through my mind. If he can't materialize it means Jesse or Maisie are close. Or Georgia and Caldwell.

I look back over my shoulder as a strange feeling of being watched washes over me. There's no one in sight. I turn back and there's Caldwell. Without thinking, I shove him hard with my mind and he flies backward. I suck in a breath, waiting to see his body slam against the concrete wall, but he disappears midair.

"Damn." I break into a run. I don't want to be in the exact same place should he rematerialize.

As soon as I cut around the corner, there he is. He wraps both his hands around my throat and lifts me off the ground. He slams my body into the wall, winding me. Stars dance in my vision as my back muscles seize in pain. Then he lifts me off my feet again so that I can see right over his head to the hallway stretching beyond him.

In the flickering light, his woman saunters toward me. Her gaze afire with hate. I reach out and squeeze his heart. He drops me.

I hit the ground hard and my vision wavers. A sharp pain shoots up my hip and into my chest. A man grunts, then the sound of screeching metal jerks my head up in time to see Gideon swing a pipe. Caldwell takes a step back and Gideon collapses over my body, covering me.

I'm pinned beneath him looking at the ceiling tiles above. Fire bursts over us, flames shooting in Caldwell's direction.

"Stay down," Gideon says into my ear.

The flames shoot again in the same controlled wave and someone hoots and hollers. I lay beneath Gideon, feeling the weight of his body on mine. He smells like sweat and cinnamon gum. It's hard to draw a breath beneath the full weight of him.

The flames disappear, revealing the ceiling tiles again. Only then does Gideon get off of me, offering me a hand.

I sit up, seeing Jesse and Maisie about ten feet away.

"Woo!" Maisie says, laughing and jumping up and down. "It worked. We are so cool!"

"How is that even possible?" I search Jessup's face but find it blank and guarded.

Because she is your enemy, Uriel reminds me.

Maisie bounces on her toes. "Because we've got the channel thingy and now Jesse and I are totally awesome and if I just concentrate it goes exactly where we want it to!"

"You were very slow at first," Jessup gripes.

"My mom was right there!" Maisie frowns. "I thought you said we wanted to scare them off not hurt them."

"So you have control because of some newfound connection?" Finally taking Gideon's hand, I pull myself up to standing. I recall the strange sensation that had consumed me at Monroe's death. Monroe grabbing ahold of me in my mind and demanding that I remember who my heart is.

No.

I feel apprehension. Reserve. Weary reluctance. All of these emotions play across Jessup's face.

"So you can control your fire now because of your connection to Maisie?" I ask again.

"Yes!" Maisie says, giggling. "It's awesome."

"Maisie," Jessup warns. And her face hardens even more. Is she reading me as hard as I'm reading her?

"Good to know." Before the last word is even fully out of my mouth, I shove Gideon hard down one end of the hallway and push Jesse hard down the other. Both fly through the air away from me. The purple shimmer of Jesse's shield flares to life before I hear her crash to the ground, so I know I have even less time.

Maisie stands stunned in the middle of the hallway. Her eyes are round as half-dollars.

"Come here," I command, but I have no intention of waiting for her to comply. One yank and she's pulled toward me down the hallway, kicking and screaming all the way.

CHAPTER FORTY

Jesse

I hate flying. And by flying I mean sailing through the air into nothing, and then pinballing off the walls like a marble in an arcade game. I skid to a stop against a wall.

I pull myself into a sitting position and find that I'm hip deep in a pile of limbs.

Limbs.

I suck in a breath as I pull myself off a severed leg here, a detached arm there. The blood dried a long time ago.

I'm up and running before I can even be fully sure I'm okay. My legs are moving and the only pair of legs I'm dealing with are my own—so that's certainly an improvement. Breath is coming in and out of my nose. I haven't vomited on myself. Nor have I given over to the blind panic that tells me Caldwell is going to tear me limb from limb too, the second he has the chance. And then all that's going to be left of me will be a little pile like the one I just crawled out of.

My sneakers squeak on the tile as I try to recover the ground I lost. Rachel stands dramatically beneath an overhead light shining down on her black bob. It's fallen forward, covering the unblemished side of her face. I knew she had a scar, but seeing it was different. It's shiny in the harsh light. As she grins, it stretches into a ragged sneer.

Rachel yanks Maisie off her feet and her sneer cracks open. Maisie cries out and clutches her chest. I shoot fire at her legs. Rachel drops Maisie and sidesteps the flames.

"Cover your head!" I shout at her and fire bomb Rachel again. I'm trying to keep the fire off of Maisie, but I'd rather singe the kid's hair than let Rachel hurt her worse. The worst —at least I hope—that'd give her is a flesh wound. Rachel intends to do more.

Rachel ducks into the adjacent hallway for protection.

I keep my shield up until I'm in front of Maisie, then I drop it long enough to grab ahold of the kid. In that momentary lapse, Rachel throws herself at me. Her body slams against the shield the moment I erect it again and the purple light wavers, shimmering under her assault.

She screams like a wild animal, her face contorted in a rage I didn't even know she was capable of.

"Rachel!" I scream. "Get ahold of yourself!"

Rachel falls back off my shield and places her hands on her hips. "Give me the girl, Jessup."

"Uh, *no*!" The shield remains fixed around us, but Maisie isn't getting up. I speak to her without taking my eyes off Rachel. "Are you okay?"

"I think I broke my ankle," Maisie whispers. "It hurts so bad."

"Try to stand on it."

"Give me the girl!" Rachel screams again. Ceiling tiles are ripped from overhead and strewn about the hallway, several ricocheting off my shield.

"No," I say. "Come on. Pull yourself together."

Rachel screams and the glass from two rooms explodes.

"Throw all the tantrums you want, but I'm not going to

let you murder someone. She's my sister. And you don't want to hurt her. It's the power talking. You're juiced up. It's like an addiction. You'll get over it, like last time."

Rachel sneers, her laughter cold. With the scar along the side of her face, still red, it makes her look all the more broken. Unhinged. "Oh Jessup. How stupid can you be?"

Well let's see. I let a dead guy who used to be my handler convince me I should reason with a homicidal maniac, bring her back from the dark side with a little pep talk—so I think that makes me pretty stupid. I take a breath and try to figure out how to enter this conversation.

"You're a good person," I say. It sounds so stupid.

"Good doesn't matter! Do you think the angels picked us because we're *good?* Do you think they give a fuck about that? It's about what needs to be done. When are you going to figure out there is no going back?" she snaps. "There is no happily ever after. You're not going to save anyone from dying. You're not going to protect the world. You're going to die like the rest of us. Stop pretending like there's another way. Give her to me."

"No," I say and I realize I'm shaking. She shoves against my shield and it ripples, acknowledging her force, but it doesn't give. Her face screws up with more anger and frustration. Debris, shards of plaster and concrete, broken glass start to whirl around me. It's Gloria's vision come to life.

She intends to kill you, Gloria said. Now that I'm here it certainly looks like it. I feel stupid for arguing on Rachel's behalf now. Gloria and Ally might be hiding in the control room now, watching all this, thinking *told you so, you dumb ass.*

I don't know if killing the girl in New York actually made her stronger, or if she is drawing on our power the way Maisie and I did. Is the connection still there? Can Rachel feel me the way I can feel her? And if so, why aren't I juiced up and crazy too?

I protect you, Gabriel whispers through my mind. If Gabriel is still here, then Rachel must have access to Uriel too. What has he told her?

"Forget what Uriel says." Anger hardens my voice. "We don't have to kill each other to be the apex. We were never supposed to kill each other. Caldwell fucked that up when he killed Chaplain."

Rachel screams like I've just ripped off part of her face. "Chaplain deserved to die!"

She throws herself against my shield and I step back reflexively, forgetting for a moment she can't hit me. Maisie's fingers bite into my arm, and I realize she's pulled herself to standing. Rachel thrashes against the shield. Her face is a vicious mask of hate as she wails on the purple field protecting us.

"Enough!" I yell. Anger and fear wash over me. I can't just stand here and let her wail on my shield until she exhausts herself. Who knows how long that'll be?

My fire erupts forward, projected from my body in the same controlled way I managed earlier with Maisie's help. It hits Rachel, knocking her back. She smacks the ground howling. She sails backwards, rolling feet over head before sprawling motionless in the center of the aisle.

"Goddamn it." I break away from Maisie and run toward Rachel, collapsing to my knees beside her body.

I roll her over and see she's conscious, but dazed. The front of her clothes are blackened, revealing raw flesh beneath. She bares her teeth at me hissing like an animal. The wounds look bad, but she'll heal. If I can just shake her out of this, the way we did before. Maybe put her back in the asylum. She needs time. She can heal if I can buy her time.

"Damn it," I say. The tears are hot in my eyes. "You're a moron. There's no reason for this. Me, you, *and* Maisie can be the apex. Together."

She sucks in a ragged breath. "He has to die, Jessup. He *has* to."

Rachel's gaze slides away from mine and I have to turn and take my eyes off of her long enough to see Ally standing in the hallway, kneeling beside Maisie.

Rachel frowns. Her scowl deepens and she reaches a hand toward me. I take it, but she squirms in my grip. She places a hand over my chest and her fingers curl into claws. There's a horrible instance where I think she's going to try to claw my heart out of my chest.

Her scowl softens into laughter. Hideous, abrupt and crazy. "Of course. Of *fucking* course."

"We're friends," I remind her, because who knows what the hell Uriel has made her believe. "I would never hurt you. And I don't believe you'd hurt me."

She reaches up and cups my cheek. Her lips part and an expression that any idiot would mistake for tenderness sits in her big eyes and soft lips. Until of course, her lips pull into a sneer and her hand hardens on my face.

"You have too much faith in me, Jessup."

CHAPTER FORTY-ONE

Rachel

I try to seize Jessup's heart again, but it doesn't work for a third time.

Why? I ask Uriel. *Why?*

No answer.

My will falters. Jessup's cheek is warm and soft in my hand. She still looks so young. So sweet. *Uriel?*

"No, no, Gideon's okay," Ally says, consoling Maisie. "He's only unconscious."

I reach out for Ally. I reach out with my power and crush her heart in my grip.

Alice gasps, placing one hand on her chest. Her eyes go wide with surprise. When her eyes meet mine, her mouth parts in surprise.

"No!" Jesse's fists ball up at her side. "Rachel, stop!"

She ignites in flames. Blue fire erupts around us and I squeeze my eyes shut. Pain rips through me and I roll away from her fire. The cinder block feels cool on my hand. I try to breathe.

My mind conjures a memory. When I was called to be a

partis. I was consumed with power. I was clumsy with it and landed myself in an asylum.

But the consequences of my actions weren't real for me until weeks later when Jesse stood in the doorway of my ward room, searching my eyes for answers I didn't have. That had hurt more than losing my freedom, my job, and my friends. The fear on her face. The disappointment.

It's the same look she gives me now as she watches me slump against the wall.

Once upon a time she looked up to me. She made me feel like someone worthy of admiration. Mentoring her had begun to heal a part of me that Chaplain had destroyed. With every death, every secret, every affection, every laugh, we healed. And when I got out of the asylum, I'd wanted to be that person for her again.

But by the time Brinkley had died, she didn't need me anymore.

Caldwell takes this moment to appear.

And Jesse whirls on him, and her heartbreaking disappointment transforms into another emotion entirely. Anger.

Gloria fires two bullets into Caldwell's chest. He disappears, but Gloria is ready for this and throws an elbow behind her, connecting with Caldwell's jaw the moment he reappears.

Forget the girl, Uriel says. He diverts my attention from Ally. Her heart is weakened by my attack, but it didn't kill her. My contact was too brief.

When they are weak, exhausted from the fight, take the power for yourself.

Uriel's plan rings true. Who cares about Ally? She's weak and human.

I need to remain focused on one thing: taking the power for myself. Caldwell's power. Georgia's power. Maisie's power —even Jesse's. There's no reason why I shouldn't. After all, if

Jesse doesn't need me anymore, doesn't admire or respect me anymore—

So be it.

She will fear me instead.

CHAPTER FORTY-TWO

Jesse

I can't decide if I'm supposed to stare at Rachel or Caldwell. With two sharks in the water, I can't afford to take my eyes off either one. But Rachel looks wounded, or at the very least, winded.

Make it up as we go, I'd argued. And here we are. What do I need to do first? First—

We need Caldwell to stay in one place. And maybe I can keep Rachel busy at the same time. After all, *the enemy of my enemy…*

"Do your job!" I scream at her. "Hold him."

Rachel hisses at me, her face more akin to a feral cat than human.

Caldwell staggers then stumbles to the side. He cradles his jaw. But he doesn't jump. His eyes cut to Rachel and his hate is apparent. He roars.

"Maisie!" I scream. It's the only warning I can manage. I reach out and tap our emotional connection. She sucks a breath and shudders beside Ally who sits slumped, clutching her chest.

I feel more power wane, slipping away from me.

No, no, no. Don't lose focus now. Ally is okay. Or she'll be okay. Focus, Jesse. So close—

Do not forget I am here, Gabriel reminds me, a breeze through my mind. But his voice gives me strength nonetheless.

"Do *your* job!" Rachel wails.

I reach out and grab at Maisie's power again, rolling it up in my own.

"Gloria!" I shout and she ducks, barely being missed by the flare of power that explodes across the hall.

Caldwell screams as the fire licks up his body.

"I can't—" Rachel says, dropping to one knee. Thick sweat beads on her brow.

I run across the corridor and seize Caldwell before he can jump. The moment I grab hold of him, I ignite again.

He thrashes in my arms, but I don't let go. I close my eyes and hold on tighter. He disappears, taking me with him. The unmistakable shift of worlds happens around us, but I don't let go. Gloria and the blinding white hallway disappear, only to appear again in the light of the blue flames.

Please, Gabriel. Give me the strength to hold on. I want him dead. I want this to be over.

White hot fire slides between my ribs and I scream out. I let go for an instant before tightening my hold.

Caldwell's lips press against my ear. "I've waited so long for this."

He twists his hand and the sharp pain intensifies. I feel like he has grabbed one of my ribs and is wrenching it from my body. A battle between the pain and the itching sensation of my healing gift merge into a single unbearable burn.

He twists again and I'm screaming.

I'm dying. I know I must be dying. But my flames keep burning and I still have hold of him.

You want to burn? Let's burn. I said this to him once before, but hadn't been able to deliver on my promise that time. But now—now nothing could make me let go.

My whole body shakes. I keep trying to breathe but it feels like I'm drowning. I can't get enough air and black sparks dance in my eyes. But still I hold onto him and I burn.

When I refuse to let go, refuse to stop burning him, he begins the mental assault. He shows me beautiful image after beautiful image. Me as a baby, and the feelings of euphoria and wonder as he took me into his arms for the first time.

Me as a toddler, opening and closing my chubby fists. Wanting to be picked up.

Then on a tricycle on our street. Me in a lavender dress collecting plastic eggs in a basket. Me skipping to school with a rainbow backpack and a frog painted on my cheek.

The way he would twirl me in his arms when he picked me up. The feel of my little arms around his neck.

He wants to rob me of my anger. My hate. My fuel.

Stop, I beg him. Because his love is more wretched than his disdain.

Gabriel, please. I can't hold on. I can't hold on any longer.

My flames sputter and Caldwell's blackened face comes into focus through a thin sheen of blue fire.

Please let this be over.

The whoosh of black wings cuts through the roar of flames. A great blast of air cools my cheek and the soft scent of rain envelops me. The burning in my ribs stops. The pain leaves my body. It's a miracle.

I am your strength, Gabriel says. And it must be true. All of the pain is gone.

All I feel is peace.

Caldwell has stopped thrashing. We've reached a calm in the eye of the storm. One last image assails me, loud and clear:

Eric Sullivan hides in the shadow of a tree outside my

house, watching me through my bedroom window. This must be a couple of years after his death. In my room, I'm stretched out on my belly, flipping through my school books and sucking on a ring pop, and singing the jingle from a gum commercial.

He watches me for a long time, or at least in the memory it feels like a long time, as he tries to convince himself to let me go.

I realize we have stopped moving. The white room is bright around me.

I never let you go, Caldwell whispers. *I* couldn't *let you go.*

"Let go," Gloria begs. "Jesse, it's okay. You can let go."

I'm crying.

I squeeze my eyes shut and the memories are still there. I wipe my face with the heels of my hands. I finger the wound at my side and it comes away warm and sticky with blood.

"What the fuck did he stab me with?" I shudder. I feel the holes seal themselves thanks to Jason's healing gift, but the pain won't go away. Whatever relief Gabriel was able to provide was temporary at best. I'm left with the last seed Caldwell planted: his regrets.

He's given me so many scars. What's a few more?

"This." Gloria picks a knife off the floor. It's slick with my blood all the way up to the end of the handle. Clearly, he buried it to the hilt.

"Hey!" Maisie screams. "Hey stop!" And I whirl expecting the worst. Georgia. Caldwell's goons.

I didn't expect to see Rachel leaning over Caldwell's body.

"No! Wait!" I scream. I lunge forward but Rachel waves her hand and I'm thrown against the wall. Gloria is also caught in the blast and lands a few feet away from me. Her gun clatters to the floor.

No, no, no. Rachel can't absorb Caldwell powers. We can't

let her. Her mind will be beyond repair if she does. Not to mention what she'll do to me and Maisie next.

I pull myself up to my hands and knees and scream at her. "Stop!"

Ally reaches her first. Ally was closer to Caldwell's body and she dared take her head-on. I can only stare in horror, scrambling toward them, as Ally kicks Rachel in the face. Rachel slides back away from Caldwell's body, giving Ally the moment she needs to put herself between Caldwell and Rachel. Rachel touches her broken nose, blood gushing down her face.

"You bitch!" she says in a thick, blood-coated voice.

Ally clutches her chest again.

"No!" I scream. "Rachel don't hurt her! Please!"

I'm running and it's like the hallway is a funhouse stretching longer and longer, preventing me from reaching them. Ally's face pinches, and her breath goes shallow. A choked sound escapes her mouth. Then that's it. Her eyes glaze and she slumps to the floor, lying side-by-side with Caldwell. Just as dead as he is.

Jessup's face blanches. Her eyes slide from Caldwell to Ally, but she remains frozen in the middle of the hallway. Gunfire erupts nearby, but she doesn't even move. Her eyes glazed, fixed on the bodies but not seeing them. I've seen this before in the asylum. Some patients would slip into catatonia for months. They wouldn't move, eat, or speak.

This is a hell of a time to go all stupid, Jessup.

A bullet shatters a window and I duck, shielding my head. Jessup still doesn't move. She's in shock. Either because her father is dead, because Ally is dead, or because both deaths happened in such quick succession of one another. Is she going to cry about it? This is hardly the time. Caldwell's men will be on us in minutes.

I pull myself up. Gloria and Gideon both stir toward consciousness.

If I'm going to take Caldwell's powers *now* is the time. But it will kill me. So where can I go where they won't follow?

Before I can think of an answer, two hands grab me and yank me off of my feet. My skin burns at the touch and I wail.

"You killed him!" Georgia screams. Mascara trails down her face in two dark streams. "You killed him you bitch!"

I wrench myself from her grip the same moment that I shove her away from me. She trips over Caldwell's body and hits her head against the back of the wall. For a heartbeat she's dazed, her eyes swimming in their sockets. Then her focus sharpens and the black ribbons unfurl from her back.

Another bullet zings down the hall and pierces her shoulder.

She cries out and blood blooms through her clothes. The gunfire intensifies as if a small army is just around the corner. Georgia and I are forced into a truce in order to duck for cover or risk having our brains blown out.

Georgia barks orders. "Help me carry him! Maisie!"

"No!" the girl says. Gideon's eyes fly open and he pulls his weapon, pointing the barrel at Georgia.

Maisie wails. "No!" She shoves the barrel down and it goes off, putting a bullet in Caldwell's lifeless body. "That's my mom!"

The gunfire keeps spilling into this hallway, but there's no bodies. If the soldiers themselves appeared, I could throw them or stop their hearts. But my powers don't work on flying bullets.

"Your shield!" I shout to Jessup, as if my voice is going to lift her out of her shock. "Erect your shield, idiot, or we're going to be shot!"

"You won't have to worry about that pretty little face of yours," Georgia sneers. Pretty little face? She dares to taunt me about my scar, the bitch.

I reach out with my mind and seize her heart. Her eyes go wide. Her ribbons arch up, ready to strike.

"No," Maisie wails. But I see Gideon pulling her away from us and the immediate battle.

CHAPTER FORTY-FOUR

Jesse

*C*aldwell is dead. Ally is dead. And now my best friend is my enemy.

I can't move. I can't breathe.

Rachel killed Ally. Oh my god, Rachel killed Ally.

How could you do this to me?

A strange pantomime of emotion consumes me. I feel everything until it crescendos into nothing. A void grows in my mind.

A bullet whizzes past my face, cutting my cheek. Then there's hot blood. Then the burn of its healing.

Gabriel tries to pull me to the surface of the dark pond I'm drowning in.

If you do not shield yourself, you will be shot in the head.

Nothing.

I don't care about myself. I never did any of this for me.

He tries again.

If you don't shield Alice, her head could be shot and then Maisie cannot revive her.

This brings the world into sharp focus.

Maisie can revive her.

Another stray bullet ricochets off the cinder block wall and straight through the remaining glass window. Another hits my shield the moment after I erect it.

Four soldiers in full combat gear duck into our hallway, glancing at us only once before aiming their guns. The soldier on the left is struck and he goes down, his faceplate busted open from the gunshot.

A man in a suit appears and tries to shoot a second soldier before another soldier whirls and strikes him in the face with the butt of her gun. He crumples and the gunfire stops. I watch them as if what is happening beyond the shield is the most important thing. I should be killing Rachel. Or I could at least kill Georgia, though she sits just beyond the shield. A purple shimmer separating her from Caldwell's body.

I can't even look at Ally's body.

Forgive her. Forgive me, Brinkley said.

My heart kicks in my chest. What if Brinkley never expected me to save Rachel? What if he knew Ally would die and the whole *forgive her* bit was about not blaming her for what she did to Ally?

Never. I can never forgive her.

With three of the soldiers dead and the gunfire ceased, the last soldier tears off her helmet to reveal stark blond hair and a thick orange streak beneath.

"Sasquatch." I drop the shield and for once in my life, I'm happy to see her.

Nikki isn't looking at me. Her eyes are fixed on Ally.

"You killed her," Nikki says. Her face blanches.

"Rachel—" I begin but I choke on the name.

"You killed her!" Nikki lifts her gun and shoves the barrel against my temple.

CHAPTER FORTY-FIVE

Rachel

The moment Jesse's shield erects, knocking Georgia back, I descend on Caldwell. I search my pockets for the small weapon that I used to kill Niv, but it's gone. On the floor several feet away, there's a knife that Caldwell used to stab Jessup. I scurry toward it on hands and knees and snatch it up, leaving bloody fingerprints along the linoleum.

I rush back to the body. If I kill Caldwell, maybe I can use his teleportation to jump the moment the blue fire erupts. At least that way, I can be dead somewhere else, far from here. By the time Gloria sketches my location, I'll be alive and well. Maybe even ready for a second assault.

My whole body quivers with anticipation. The knife trembles in my fist. I'm so excited I could howl.

I grin at Caldwell's body. The face is placid. Not a wrinkle to worry his brow or tighten his mouth. He looks so peaceful.

I remember Brinkley's journal entry for how they defeated Chaplain—by stabbing him through the eye.

Yes.

That's exactly what he deserves.

I slam the knife down, aiming for the left eye when a dark hand seizes mine. The knife stops inches above his eye.

Gideon holds my wrist there. "No."

"Let go of me!"

"No, love," he says, his voice softening. "That's enough."

Anger seizes me. I ram the knife into Gideon's chest and he doesn't even look surprised. He grimaces, but that's it. No revulsion. No look of betrayal. Only sadness. I try to shove him away from me. But because he won't let go, we slide together across the floor.

"Cariño," he says, using my own nickname against me. He crushes me against him so tightly that I can't move. "You're better than this. Brinkley knew you were better than this."

Brinkley.

Brinkley's rugged and beautiful face.

The moment he leaned over Chaplain's bed and undid the restraints choking me. The moment he slipped off his jacket and wrapped me up in it, giving me decency for the first time in months. I'd sobbed in his arms for what seemed like forever. His gruff voice reassuring me that I was safe now.

He's dead, Brinkley had said. *He's dead and he's never going to hurt you again.*

I'm looking at Gideon's face, but it's Brinkley's voice I hear.

"We're a team. We are all you have."

Part of me wants to kill Caldwell, wants my revenge on Chaplain—but here's Brinkley, telling me Chaplain is gone, telling me he'll never hurt me again.

And what would I do? If I have all the powers, if everyone is dead—

I would only be alone. In darkness.

No Gideon. No Jesse. No one.

I don't want to be alone.

I let go of Gideon's body and it slumps to the floor.

"What have I done?"

"Are you going to cry about it?" Georgia sneers. "Ruin that pretty little face?"

She taunts me but her eyes are fixed on Jesse. The moment the shield fails, Georgia is going to strike her, kill her, and absorb her power.

I can't bring Gideon back. I can't bring Brinkley back. But there is *something* I can do.

Jesse's purple shield fails.

In that instance, I leap to my feet and place myself between her and the darkness.

CHAPTER FORTY-SIX

Jesse

Rachel collapses the moment Georgia's black ribbons strike her. Dead. And a heartbeat later, Georgia's body erupts in blue flame. I stand dumb, frozen as Rachel's body is incinerated to ash. Every last recognizable feature of my best friend gone.

I crumple to my knees.

Only Maisie is alive in a sea of bodies. Gideon. Ally. Rachel. Georgia. Caldwell. They're all dead. The kid wipes tears off her face with the heels of her hands.

Nikki presses the muzzle of her gun to my head again.

"I didn't kill Ally."

"You may not have done it yourself, but your arrogance, your reckless regard for her life got her killed."

I can't even argue. Ally is dead. Rachel is dead. Brinkley is dead. And who can be blamed for that except me?

"It's not her fault!" Maisie squeals, still cradling her hurt ankle.

"Calm down," Gloria says, using her negotiator voice. "Take a breath, Tamsin."

"I can bring her back!" Maisie says, desperation straining her words.

Nikki's barrel slides along my skull.

I want her to do it. Part of me wants her to blow my brains out all over the linoleum. Only the smallest voice inside me begs for the alternative. *Revive Ally. And take her far, far away from all this.*

"Maisie is partis," Gloria adds in the same steady tone. "She can save Alice."

Nikki doesn't lower the gun. "You *will* bring her back."

"No, I thought I'd leave her dead forever," I snap. That part of me that welcomes death, that's *begging* for it, wants to provoke her. "Prop her up around the house and dress her according to the holiday. Reindeer antlers at Christmas, turkey feathers at Thanksgiving."

"You're such a smart ass."

"Wait until you hear my plan for Easter." I'm spitting the words at her. "She'll look like a freaking Playboy bunny!"

Nikki lowers her weapon.

"It's over, Jesse," Gloria says, turning that frighteningly calm voice on me. Then to Maisie, "Go ahead. Wake them up."

Maisie leans over Ally's body, hiding her face from my view. It looks like they are kissing. A hot-cold wave slides down my spine and all the gooseflesh on my arms rise. Then I feel Ally spark to life and all the air is pulled from my chest.

Maisie sits back and sucks in a deep breath.

Is that what it's like for her? To use her power? It feels like suffocation. Like jumping into an icy lake and the shock of frigid water enveloping my body.

My suspicions are confirmed when I feel the same sensation again as she revives Gideon.

Maisie sits back and puts a hand to her forehead.

"Are you okay?" Gloria asks, rushing to her.

"I feel a little woozy." She rubs her forehead. "I've never done...two in a row before."

Ally is breathing. Seeing her chest rise and fall in a steady rhythm changes everything. It's like I've broken the surface of an immense ocean. My chest loosens. My mind clears.

"We need to take care of them before they wake up," Gloria says.

For a heartbeat, I think she's talking about Gideon and Ally. Yes, absolutely. Let's make them comfortable. Have we got any soup, or warm blankets? Comfy pillows?

Then I realize she means Georgia and Caldwell. We need to destroy their brains before either can reboot.

"No!" Maisie wails.

"We have to," I say. Strength returns to my voice. I still can't look directly at the ashy smears, all that's left of Rachel. But she's everywhere now. She's floating through the air before my eyes. She's settling against my skin. She's under my nails.

I was wrong. When I saw Gloria's drawing, I thought it was Georgia who killed Ally, leaving her so peaceful as if in sleep. It was my own friend. Rachel was right. How could I be so stupid?

"Hey, are you okay?" Nikki asks.

I'm crying. "I'm...overwhelmed." I sound so angry.

Because...Rachel is dead? Caldwell is dead? Georgia is dead?

Or is it because I know the time has come?

I have to absorb all their powers—and then what?

I am here, Gabriel's voice flits through my head and the usual scent of rain washes over me. *Do not be afraid.*

But I am afraid. Afraid I'll become a monster like them. Afraid I'll become someone Ally doesn't even recognize.

I kneel down beside Georgia.

"No," Maisie begs again. "It's my mom!"

"Put their bodies somewhere safe." I barely recognize my own voice. No one moves. I turn and look into Nikki's eyes. "Please. You have to put her somewhere safe."

"The control room," Gloria says without missing a beat.

"No, no, no!" Maisie squeals. She's near hysterical. She clutches her mother tighter as if we are trying to wrench her away.

We leave her, focused on moving Gideon and Ally away from the scene. It's a smart, but sobering move. We're doing this because we have no idea what's going to happen. Maybe the power will move smoothly from them to us. Maybe Maisie and I will take all their combined powers—eight, if I'm counting right—as easy as one takes a stroll around the block.

Or maybe this will go horribly, *horribly* wrong.

I am here. Invisible feathers brush my cheeks. *Do not be afraid.*

Then Gideon and Ally are tucked away and it's only the four of us and two bodies—I don't count Rachel's ashes.

My heart aches.

I remember the first time I met her. Rachel, this elegant creature draped over a fuchsia sofa reading some entertainment magazine. The way she arched her eyebrow coquettishly at Brinkley when he strode in. How comfortable she seemed in her own skin.

She was beautiful. She was confident.

And she fed me ice cream.

Look where we are now.

"Brinkley would understand," Gloria says, squeezing my arm hard. I'm forced to look away from the ashes and blink back tears.

"Let's get this over with," I say, dropping onto my knees beside Maisie.

"No," she screams. If my mere whimpering is a 3 on the

crying scale, Maisie is sobbing furiously at a solid 9.5. "Jesse, she's my mom."

I try to pull her away from Georgia's body.

"She's my *mom*!" Snot coats her face and she chokes on her own spit. "Please. *Please*, don't do this. She's all I have."

"She's not all you have." Gloria kneels and puts a hand on Maisie's back.

Nikki watches all this in silence, her brow deeply creased.

Maisie's eyes search mine. "She'll work with us. She'll share the power. I *know* she will. Please, Jesse, please. Please. *Please*." Every please is more hysterical than the last.

It's killing me.

"We will start with Caldwell." It's the only compromise I see and because I can't bear to hear her say *please* even one more time.

Maisie can share Caldwell's four powers with me. And if I'm not totally batshit crazy when that is over, then maybe I can take on all four of Georgia's powers on my own. I can't force Maisie to have a hand in her mother's death. I already have doubts she's going to be able to help me with all of Caldwell's juice, given her hysteria.

I can only hope that Georgia's power doesn't make me crazy enough that I'd hurt Maisie.

"Okay." Maisie sniffs and wipes her face on her sleeve. "Okay. Dad first."

She shuffles over to Caldwell's body without protest.

I place a knee on either side of Caldwell's head. Maisie places on hand on my knee and the other on Caldwell's chest. I am about to ignite when Gloria grabs my wrist.

"Are you sure this won't hurt her?" Gloria whispers.

The fact that the all-seeing eye has even asked me such a question stuns me. "How the hell am I supposed to know?"

"I didn't see this," she says. Concern creases her face.

"That could be a good thing," I say. "Our 'winging it' turned out okay."

Still Gloria's face is furrowed with apprehension, but she lets go of my wrist. Her worried expression fixed on Maisie. "Hurry."

My hand ignites and I lower it toward Caldwell's face.

For better or worse, I think, hoping Gabriel hasn't abandoned me. This would be the worst time.

Caldwell's face glows blue.

I suck in a breath and thrust my hand into his body.

Only my hand doesn't move.

It freezes mid-air, suspended like a bizarre ethereal torch above Caldwell's face. His eyebrows, singed by my fire, start to curl on the ends, and the distinct stench of burnt hair assails me.

Georgia sits up.

She pulls herself to standing and not one of us can stop her. Out of the corner of my eye, I see Gloria quivering, her gun only half raised. As she strains to lift it, her whole body shakes. Out of the other corner of my eye, Nikki isn't doing any better.

On her feet, Georgia yanks Caldwell's body away from me. His corpse slides across the floor toward her. Then Maisie is yanked down the hall too.

I'm paralyzed.

"No!" Maisie screams. "Mom, *no*."

She lunges at her mother and tugs on her arm.

Her hold on us wavers and everything happens at once. Nikki starts shooting at Georgia, driving her back. I lunge for Nikki and knock down her gun.

"That's my sister you're shooting at!"

"I have excellent aim!"

"She's sixteen!" I have no idea why I think this is a logical argument.

Georgia knocks us both back against the wall. For the second time today, I'm sailing through the air. I erect my shield and it buffers my fall. Then I'm up and running.

Gloria is sawing at Caldwell's head with his own knife. Blood pools over her lap and pours out over the white linoleum. The crimson stream mixes with the black ash.

"No!" Georgia screams. She knocks Gloria back and she sails down the hall. She hits the cinder block wall, her skull cracking against the stone with a sickening sound.

I cast my shield bigger. I can't cover Maisie or Caldwell, but I do manage to protect Gloria and Nikki from any more attacks.

Georgia pushes against my shield but it doesn't give. Her telekinesis is definitely stronger than Rachel's. It's probably because Georgia now has four powers instead of Rachel's two. That's all I need. A vengeful woman twice as strong and crazy as Rachel out to kill my ass.

Georgia lifts Caldwell's body and the head rolls to the side precariously. Gloria almost succeeded in decapitating it. Too bad she didn't. We needed only a part of him in order to absorb his power.

Georgia's black ribbons descend on us. They cloud everything, casting deep shadows. It's as if night has fallen on the hallway. Nikki raises her gun.

"Drop your shield."

"That's death," I tell her. "If I drop the shield we're all dead."

"She's getting away!"

I know. But what the hell can I do about it? I hear Maisie's screams, her pleading as it echoes down the hallways. It grows more and more distant with each passing moment.

Until the light returns and the black death smoke is gone.

Maisie, Caldwell, and Georgia are gone.

"I'm going to need you to stay with them!" I rush to Gloria's side.

"You're going after them?" Nikki asks, keeping pace with me.

"Georgia is fucked while Caldwell's dead. She can only escape on foot—"

"—or car," Nikki interjects.

I groan. "I didn't mean literally on foot. Why are you such a bitch?"

"Go on," Nikki says, her face softening. "I'm sure you had a point."

I press my fingers to Gloria's throat. Her heart is beating loud and clear. Thank god. "One of two things is going to happen. Georgia is going to absorb Caldwell's power or she's going to try to resurrect him. I don't think she'll kill him, which means she's going to try to put his head back on his body and hope he heals."

"He can't possibly wake up from that."

"Wrong." I lean her forward to inspect the wound on the back of her head. "We didn't damage his brain. I've had my neck vertebrae disintegrated by a shotgun blast and I was almost completely decapitated myself. I've probably got two days tops before he wakes up or she's forced to absorb his power. One or the other is going to happen. So I have to catch them now."

Fresh blood coats the back of Gloria's skull. That can't be good. I keep my hands on her chest but I don't feel the pull of death—nothing that calls for me to replace her.

Gabriel?

She will live.

I ease Gloria back into her original position as gently as possible. "Can you get people here to help her? She needs medical attention."

"Of course."

I rush to the control room and find Gideon and Ally laying side by side on the floor, with Winston sleeping in the crook of Ally's arms. I'm wasting time, but I had to see that she was okay. I kiss his nose just as Sasquatch skids to a stop at my heels.

They're okay, I tell myself. *They're all going to be fine. We don't have Caldwell and they have Maisie, but we're all still alive.*

Not all of us, a hateful voice retorts.

You must hurry, Gabriel whispers. His voice is strong now. He's closer without the other partis to interfere with our connection.

I touch Ally's face, feeling her warm breath on my hand. "I have to trust you not to be a *total* jerk, Sasquatch. You want the happily ever after?"

Her lips part, but I wasn't looking for an actual answer.

"Prove it. Save Gloria. Keep Ally safe. And it'd be nice if you took care of my dog too."

I can hear Gideon's crisp British voice in my head, *and who am I? The pool boy?*

I smile and kneel beside Ally. I kiss her once on the mouth. Her warm breath on my face is such a huge relief that I kiss her a second and third time.

"You'll see me again," I whisper into her ear. I look up and meet Gabriel's eyes.

He nods. *At least once more.*

CHAPTER FORTY-SEVEN

Jesse

Somehow I manage to escape the maze of the building and step out into the brilliant desert sun. Fresh bodies of Nikki's men—or should I say Jeremiah's soldiers—lay littered alongside the corpses that Caldwell made so long ago.

An engine sputters to life somewhere beyond the wall.

"Damn." I climb over chunks of rock and through the opening I blasted earlier. It feels like a million years ago. A million years since we went inside the building and everyone I loved was murdered. I jump off of a large boulder onto the other side.

My hands and feet connect with hot sand.

"Here," Gabriel says to my right. I run toward him and he disappears, reappearing a few feet further away. "This way."

I follow him and find a black car tucked behind some rocks out of sight. I jump inside, roll down the windows to let out some heat that collected inside and turn the key kindly left in the ignition. I smash on the gas, and sand spews out the back. I sit up a little higher in my seat and tear across the desert.

"Which way?" I beg Gabriel. "Which way did they go?"

I see him in the sky. His big beautiful wings flap around him like a misshapen, grotesquely large crow, raining black feathers down onto me and the black Mustang with each thrust. It's like I'm driving through some macabre snow storm.

There, he says and I tear my eyes from the sky to the horizon stretching ahead. The red pickup kicks dust into the air, a thick cloud surrounding the vehicle not unlike a force field.

My car gains on them and I know it's only a matter of minutes before I catch up. I can only hope that I have the strength to finish Georgia in front of Maisie. It looks like I won't have any other choice.

I feel Gloria's hand crushing mine. Her earlier desperate plea on Maisie's behalf. *Protect her.*

My car gets so close to the truck that I can see Maisie, turned in her seat, watching my approach. Her eyes are wide and pleading as the truck bounces and lurches through the desert.

Protect her.

"I'll get her back," I whisper and I'll kill Georgia, although my sister might not want anything to do with me by the end of this.

The end.

Caldwell is dead, but it's not over.

Why did I ever believe it would be that easy?

Did you enjoy this book? You can make a BIG difference.

I don't have the same power as big New York publishers who can buy full spread ads in magazines and you won't see my covers on the side of a bus anytime soon, but what I *do* have are wonderful readers like you.

And honest reviews from readers garner more attention for my books and help my career more than anything else I could possibly do—and I can't get a review without **you!**

So if you would be so kind, I'd be very grateful if you would post a review. It only takes a minute or so of your time and yet you can't imagine how much it helps me.

It can be as short as you like and yes, I cherish every. single. one.

So please go to your preferred retailer and leave a review for this book today.

Eternally grateful,

Kory

Get Your Three Free Stories Today

Thank you so much for reading *Worth Dying For*. I hope you're enjoying Jesse's story. If you'd like more, I have a free, exclusive Jesse Sullivan story for you. See Ally survive her first death replacement gig, during her first week as Jesse's assistant. You'll also see how the lovable Winston came to be Jesse's loyal companion.

You can only read this story for free by signing up for my newsletter. If you would like this story, you can get your copy by visiting **www.korymshrum.com/jessenewsletteroffer**

I will also send you free stories from the other series that I write. If you've signed up for my newsletter already, no need to sign up again. You should have already received this story from me. Check your email! Can't find it? ➜ Email me at **kory@korymshrum.com** and I'll take care of it.

As to the newsletter itself, I send out 2-3 a month and host a monthly giveaway exclusive to my subscribers. The prizes are usually signed books or other freebies that I think you'll enjoy. I also share information about my current projects, and personal anecdotes.

If you want these free stories and access to the giveaways, you can sign up for the newsletter at ➜ **www.korymshrum.com/jessenewsletteroffer**

If this is not your cup of tea (I love tea), you can follow me on Facebook at **www.facebook.com/korymshrum** in order to be notified of my new releases.

You have just finished *Worth Dying For*, the fifth novel in the Dying for a Living series. Keep reading for a special preview of *Dying Breath*, the sixth novel in the Dying for a Living series.

Maisie

The truck slides to the right, hooking around a huge boulder. Sand sprays in a swooping arc around us; half of it is spit through my open window into my face and eyes.

"Slow down!" I cough and fumble for anything to grab ahold of. My tears clear the sand from my eyes as I grope the air. I snatch the seatbelt dangling over my right shoulder. I miss the snap twice before I hear the reassuring *click*. The belt hugs me against the warm seat.

Mom doesn't slow down. She hits another medium-sized rock in the desert and the truck pops up and skids.

"You're going to kill us!"

"We have to lose her." Mom's fierce blue eyes cut to the rear view mirror. Blood smears across her right cheek and I can't help but stare at it, fixated on the way it fills the creases around her mouth when she speaks. If she flicks out her tongue, she's going to taste it. Maybe she already does.

I look at my own hands and fingers. Blood everywhere. It pools on the seat, soaking the side of my jeans.

My father's dead body slouches between us. Most of him rests against Mom. But the head, barely attached, wobbles, threatening to tumble over into my lap at any moment. It's freaky and gross and looking down at my blood-soaked legs and grubby hands isn't helping.

I'm going to puke.

"Shit." Mom is still focused on the rear view mirror, watching the road behind us more than the vast desert ahead.

I turn toward the open window between our seats. I look out over the empty truck bed and see the black Mustang gaining on us.

Jesse is coming.

Of course my sister is coming.

But not for me.

She wants Dad's head. She wants to blow him up and make sure the crazy bastard never wakes up again. But Mom wants the exact opposite. And here's me stuck in the middle. The blood reaches my skin. It's sticky against the back of my knees and the gross, crawly sensation only makes me nauseated.

I pinch my eyes shut, but this makes it so much worse. Mom's jerky driving intensifies the dizziness. I open my eyes and find a fixed point in the desert. A white building in the distance, pinched between a beautiful blue sky and chalky orange sand.

I focus on this building and draw in deep breaths, but stop.

Dad's body is starting to smell.

It's the heat. The hot air coming through the truck's open windows. His body is putrefying faster in the sweltering sun.

"I have to stop her." Mom calls up her power. I can feel it. Through our psychic connection or whatever you want to call it, I feel her power before I see it. Phantom snakes, twin coils of black smoke start to unfurl from Mom's abdomen. If she even grazes Jesse with the smoke, then Jesse is dead.

No. An impulse to protect my sister overwhelms me, blocking out the nausea and the overbearing heat. *Do something. Say something.*

"You don't have a good shot. You'll end up killing me." I'm not really pleading for my life and Mom knows it. "She'll just use her shield to block you."

With a frustrated hiss, Mom retracts her power.

So she *is* still trying to keep me alive. I know it's really messed up to be surprised by that. No one believes that their own Mom wants to kill them. And I guess Mom doesn't want to kill me with her own hands.

If Dad decides it's time to rip my head off, I don't think she'll stop him. And I know that should make me mad and I'm kind of pissed about it. But she's also my mom. I love her. And she's in danger too.

So what am I supposed to do about it?

"You have to wake him up," Mom barks, hooking a sharp right. The truck slides as it corrects itself. The white building disappears and now there's only blue sky. Nothing to focus on.

Vomit burns in the back of my throat. I swallow. "No."

"Damn it, Maisie." Mom grits her teeth. "We need his help to fight her. Wake him up."

"We don't have to fight," I say. "I told you that but you won't listen. We can share the power. We were always supposed to share it!"

I think of Monroe. I think of his awesome infectious

laugh and his sweet eyes. He had puppy dog eyes, like Winnie Pug. More importantly than being the kindest man I've ever met, Monroe told us—me and Jesse—the truth. The truth about our powers and how we are supposed to use them. They were never meant to be used against one another. They were supposed to be used together. But Dad made a mistake and it broke the connection and everyone else has been making the same stupid mistake ever since.

But we still have time to fix it. We can make it better.

How can I make Mom understand that? They've been fighting forever. I don't know what to say that will make her put down her proverbial weapons.

"She's a liar." Mom's face softens with pity. "Whatever Jesse told you was a lie."

"She wasn't the one who told me. And it's not a lie."

The Mustang hits the back of the truck and we lurch forward.

"Do you think she's going to let him live?" Her eyes cut to Dad's body. "She's going to kill him."

"If he ever wakes up, do you think he's going to let *you* live? Or me? He's a monster."

"Maisie!" My mother screams. She reaches across Dad and slaps me hard across the face. She looks as shocked as I am. She's never hit me before. Not once. Not ever. "What did she do to you?"

"What's he done to you?" I snap back. My face stings and I want to cup my cheek, but I don't dare. I want her to see the mark she's left on my face. "Since when are you the crazy abusive one?"

Her hands wring the steering wheel.

"Leave him," I beg her.

"He's your father."

And a monster. But I don't say it for a second time. "Me,

you, and Jesse don't have to fight. If we fight, it's your own fault."

"You know better." Mom scowls at me. "You know she'll kill me. It's why you woke me up."

Why I woke her up—

My argument dissipates. The fight replays in my head. Mom killed Rachel. They erupted in blue fire and then mom collapsed dead on the hallway's floor. I bent over and blew into her nose, waking her up in that special way I can because —because—she's right. Because I knew Gideon, Gloria, and Jesse would overpower me. They would kill her and make me watch.

I couldn't let that happen.

My mom isn't perfect. I know that. I know she might even be a bad person by most people's standards.

But she's my mom. And she's always loved me. Protected me—or at least she did until I became partis with powers and that changed everything. Dad stopped ignoring me, stopped looking at me like I was a bug on the floor. He started to look at me the way he looked at Jesse.

My silence makes Mom think she's won.

"It's either me or her, Maisie," she pushes. "Whose side are you on?"

My fist tightens around the seatbelt. *Whose side am I on?*

The longer I don't answer, the more Mom's face pinches in betrayal. "This isn't you. She did this to you. She turned you against your own mother."

"No, I—"

"We have to kill her. We have to protect your father and kill her."

"What about us?" My temper explodes. "What about protecting *us*?"

"He won't," Mom says, but I know that voice. It's the *he*

will never hurt you while I'm alive voice. But my mom won't always be alive. She was dead an hour ago.

I cross my arms over my chest. "I won't wake him up and I'm not going to help you hurt Jesse either."

"I'm your mother!"

The Mustang pulls around the side of the truck. The driver's side window rolls down and there's my sister all wide-eyed and freaked out.

She casts her shield. It covers me and part of the truck.

She looks as surprised as I am that this works. She screams. "Jump!"

Jump? Out of a moving truck?

"Jump! I'll catch you," she screams again, over the sound of sand and wind and roaring engines while her dark hair whips around her head.

She wants me.

She wants me more than she wants Dad's dead body.

Because she loves you a voice whispers through my mind. A voice I haven't heard in a long, long time.

It's all the courage I need.

I throw my door open and reach for the release on my seatbelt.

"No!" Mom cuts the wheel hard to the right, slamming the side of the truck into Jesse's Mustang. My door is ripped away by an invisible, angry hand. Sparks spray into the cab as metal scrapes metal. Stray shards sting my cheeks. I cover my face, hoping my arms and legs stay inside the cab enough not to be ripped off.

I open my eyes and Jesse is still there, keeping up with us. The side of her Mustang looks like it was stepped on by a huge boot. Through the open window, she's still shouting.

"I've got you! Jump!"

"Fuck off!" My mother screams. With one flick of her

hand, the Mustang's two front wheels are lifted off the sand and thrown back into the air.

"No!" I scream, but this doesn't do anything to stop the Mustang from flying through the air and then dropping back to Earth like a bomb.

The black car rolls head over tail before slamming into the side of a boulder.

Oh my god, no!

The car explodes on impact, the black muscle car disappearing in a plume of fire and smoke.

"Oh god, no. No, no, *no.*"

I blink back tears, hanging out the open side of the truck. My mother's fierce fingers bite into the flesh of my upper arm, trying to yank me back into the truck. But I can't look away from the burning wreckage.

I'm desperate for any sign, *any* that Jesse survived.

I don't get one. All I see is fire and the mushroom cloud darkening the blue sky.

My sister's funeral pyre. All that's left of her, a swirling, black blaze.

Did you enjoy this excerpt from *Dying Breath*? You can find and purchase the book at your favorite retailer or learn more at www.korymshrum.com.

Any one of my close friends can vouch for my dark and twisted imagination. It's been a source of amusement for years. And if you've made it this far, you probably have a sense for how I prefer to handle difficult truths (sarcasm). But this once, I cannot take credit for inventing the horrific circumstances that Rachel, Nivedha, or the others suffered at the hands of Chaplain, and it's no time to be sarcastic.

What happened to Rachel in the cold basement of a house in St. Louis was not nearly as fictitious a circumstance as you may believe. Nor can I impress upon you the real and immediate danger of the issue.

Many of you have heard the term human trafficking. In fact, the word has been thrown around so much recently, that it is becoming one of those terms the eye can slide right over. Yet, I'm going to ask you to sit up and pay attention, at least for the next thirty seconds. And in those thirty seconds or so, I'm going to separate the fiction from the facts.

- **Fact**: Over thirty million people are living in slavery today. That's almost three times the number of slaves taken from Africa before the civil war (12.5 million). Over 80% of them are women and girls. And children.

- **Fiction**: This only happens in impoverished, so-called "third-world" nations.
- **Fact**: It's happening right here in America. If you live in Los Angeles, San Francisco, Atlanta, or another airport hub, it's happening in your backyard.
- **Fiction**: There's nothing you can do about it.

You can educate yourself. I suggest the amazing TedTalk by Jimmy Carter for starters. It's only 16-minutes and we both know that you spend more time than that watching cat or Facebook memes in a given sitting.

And if you're feeling *really* ambitious, I challenge you to fall down an internet spiral and learn all you can about this serious problem until you ask yourself "What can I do?"

How can you use your unique skills and abilities to fight the Chaplains of the world?

Yet again, if you have no idea where to start, I've got a fancy list of twenty things you can do here:

https://www.state.gov/j/tip/id/help/

This isn't an issue you can just throw money at. A great deal of it is wrapped up in the decisions you make every day.

So educate yourself. Make educated decisions.

Use your power to speak up for the voiceless.

ACKNOWLEDGMENTS

We've done it again! I am both expectant and surprised when a book is finished. On one hand, I think "of course the book is done! I worked so hard!" and on the other I marvel that somehow I've managed to do it. But not alone. Never alone.

Thanks to the fans first and foremost. If it wasn't for your enthusiasm for Jesse, Ally and crew, I'm not sure I would have the fortitude to continue with their story. You hold me accountable in all the right ways, and there's nothing like a piece of fan mail to bolster my spirits when the writing gets tough. So thank you for reading the book, liking the book, telling me you like the book, and showing your enthusiasm for the next one. All of this is more important to me than you know.

Some fans of particular importance (though in no particular order) are Leslie Church, Elizabeth Poole, Sharon Stogner, Louise Villeneuve, Kriss Morton, Tiffany Halliday, Rebecca Poole, Colleen McGuire, Andrea Cook, Joe Thomas, A.B. Shepherd, Bill King, Marcia Roeder, Mike Billington, Rachel Menzies, Ashley Ferguson, Wendy Nelson, Katie Robbins, and CC Ryburn. You're always excited about the latest installment and are usually the first ones to spread the word and post reviews. Thank you for that.

Victoria Solomon, your "list" of what you wanted for Gabriel and Rachel were immensely helpful. I hope I have fulfilled all your requests to your satisfaction. If not, there are two more books coming...so give me another chance?

Special nod to my critique group, The Four Horsemen of the Bookocalypse: Angela Roquet, Monica La Porta, and Katie Pendleton. You're awesome midwives. Thanks for steering Jesse and I in the right direction.

John K. Addis did it again! How he keeps turning out these lovely covers despite my inept and convoluted requests, I have no idea. He must be magic. Pure magic. Maybe that's why his daughter calls him Princess Unicorn.

Last but not least, my love Kimberly Anne. I'm going to marry you so hard in October. Prepare yourself.

Kory M. Shrum is author of the bestselling *Shadows in the Water* and *Dying for a Living* series, as well as several other novels. She has loved books and words all her life. She reads almost every genre you can think of, but when she writes, she writes science fiction, fantasy, and thrillers, or often something that's all of the above.

In 2020, she launched a true crime podcast "Who Killed My Mother?" sharing the true story of her mother's tragic death. You can listen for free on YouTube or your favorite podcast app.

When not writing or producing her show, she can usually be found under thick blankets with snacks. The kettle is almost always on. When she's not eating, reading, writing, or indulging in her true calling as a stay-at-home dog mom, she loves to plan her next adventure. (Travel.)

She lives in Michigan with her equally bookish wife, Kim, and their rescue pug, Charley.

She'd love to hear from you!
www.korymshrum.com

ALSO BY KORY M. SHRUM

Dying for a Living series

Dying for a Living

Dying by the Hour

Dying for Her: A Companion Novel

Dying Light

Worth Dying For

Dying Breath

Dying Day

Shadows in the Water: Lou Thorne Thrillers

Shadows in the Water

Under the Bones

Danse Macabre

Carnival

Devil's Luck

Design Your Destiny Castle Cove series

Welcome to Castle Cove

Night Tide

The City: the 2603 novels

The City Below

The City Within

Learn more about Kory's work at: www.korymshrum.com